Take Me Home

Dream Catchers Series - Book 4

A Novel by Sandy Lo

www.sandylo.com

This book is a work of fiction. Names, characters, places, and incidents are the product of the author's imagination or are used fictitiously. Any resemblance to actual events, locales, or personas, living or dead, is coincidental.

Copyright © 2013 by Sandy Lo.
All rights reserved. No part of this book may be reproduced in any form or by any electronic or mechanical means, including information storage and retrieval systems, without permission in writing from the author, except by a reviewer who may quote brief passages in a review.

Cover art by Sandy Lo.

Published by Amazon
For more information, visit www.sandylo.com.
Printed in the United States of America
Second Edition: February 2023
ISBN: 9798376286685

PROLOGUE

I don't know how I got here. I don't know why this happened to me. I can't breathe, or eat, or sleep. Hell, I am not sure if I even feel anymore. Empty. That's all I am. I never thought I would end up alone at thirty-six. Well, I guess I'm not alone entirely. There is my three-week old son that I don't know what to do with.

He looks at me through sleepy eyes. He is probably thinking I'm pathetic, and wondering why his Daddy visits for a couple of hours a day before high-tailing it out of our penthouse overlooking Central Park to see his girlfriend on Madison Avenue.

So, I may be going through some serious postpartum depression, but who could blame me? My depression is valid—newborn baby or not. Aside from my son who isn't much company at this stage, I am definitely alone. My marriage is officially ending and I have shut the world out.

I never had many real friends anyway. I'm what most people would call an "ice queen". I have prided myself in my career as a successful entertainment manager and didn't stop to make friends along the way. Aside from Haley, I guess. I didn't know whose side she was going to take in the divorce, though. Haley is Jordan Walsh's wife. Jordan is Danny DeSano, my estranged husband's, best friend. Oh, did I mention Jordan and Danny are in a band together? Or how I manage that band? Yup, I'm alone, most certainly.

Maybe now, while the band—my band—since I feel I deserve some credit for making them the multi-platinum act they have been for the past eighteen years... Anyway, I was saying... maybe while the band goes on tour in a few months and I'm alone with myself and the baby—who only eats, sleeps and poops at this point, I should reflect back on my life and figure out how I ended up Cami Woods, the lonely loser with a broken heart.

CHAPTER ONE

I grew up in Bedford Stuyvesant, Brooklyn. I didn't live in a fancy apartment like I own now. My mom and I were poor and I mean *really* poor. I began kicking in for food as soon as I was old enough to make lemonade. Mom put me to work in any way she could. Paper routes, babysitting, lemonade stands in the summer, and hot chocolate stands in the winter.

I was good at selling, too. I had that fast-talking New York attitude for a little girl. I was adorable to boot. Mom did her fair share. She worked two jobs, sometimes going weeks without a day off.

Mom was an Italian immigrant. She had left a poor neighborhood in Sicily for a better life. She hoped to marry an American, but instead fell in love with my father—a half-Filipino, half-Irish man from Manila, whom I never met. Don't ask me how I ended up with a simple last name like Woods coming from two foreign parents.

I saw all of two pictures of my dad and he was gorgeous. Mom always told me I looked just like him.

"Camilla," she would hold my face in her hands. "Bellisima, just like your papa."

I would smile proudly. I had my father's olive skin tone, his big, almond shaped eyes and dark hair. I had my mother's light blue eyes, though, which popped against my tan skin.

I knew I was uniquely pretty. I wasn't short on people telling me that. Older women in Bed Sty would pinch my cheeks and tell me I was going to be a heartbreaker. As a pre-teen, grown men would stare at me. Mom would curse them out in Sicilian.

"Disgraziato!" she'd yell with a hand up as if she would slap them.

The men would practically run away. I loved Mama. She was the toughest woman I ever met. She was lonely, though. After my father abandoned her when I was just a baby, she focused on providing for me. Outside of me and work, she didn't have much. She was always so tired. She worked jobs where she was on her feet for long hours.

By the time I was fourteen, Mama was sick at least once a month. In order to help more with the bills, I started home-schooling. I graduated high school at sixteen and went to a business school in Manhattan to get my Associate's degree.

A month after my seventeenth birthday, Mama passed away due to complications from pneumonia and bronchitis. Her immune system was weakened over the years from asthma and diabetes. She was in her forties. I remember feeling numb. I couldn't stay in Brooklyn. Without Mama, my life in Bed Sty was nothing. I didn't have many friends since I was home-schooled for so long and the kids in my schools weren't exactly on the right path. Girls hated me because of the way I looked and boys looked at me like they wanted to attack me.

With whatever money Mama had saved, I used it to find a rundown apartment in downtown Manhattan. I got a job as a waitress in a diner nearby. I also interned for Mega Music Management while I finished school. I had a knack for selling things and knew how to negotiate. I figured management and marketing was right for me. I didn't want to hate my job, though. I didn't want to be a manager of some big retailer or in a restaurant. I wanted to be part of something bigger. Music was my therapy growing up and I knew that. I just wasn't quite sure how or when I'd find my place in the industry.

After I finished school, I had to make some case for myself to Mega Music Management to allow me to continue a nonpaid internship, though I had hoped they would actually hire me. I mostly did tedious tasks and wished they would give me more responsibility. I predominantly worked with men, who didn't take me seriously as a professional; to them I was just a pretty teenager.

Working at the diner sucked, but tips were pretty decent, especially from men. I would just bat my crystal blues and flash a smile.

One day, a group of four guys in their very early twenties came into the diner. They were the cocky type. I knew I would probably want to slap at least one of them by the end of their meal, but I marched over to their table anyway. I flashed my brightest smile as I greeted them.

"Hey guys, my name is Cami, what can I get you to drink?"

My eyes fell on the guy furthest from me. I didn't realize just how good-looking he was from a distance. He had longish-brown hair, almost cinnamon in coloring and gorgeous green eyes with specks of gold around the pupil. For the first time in my life, I felt my knees buckle at the sight of a boy. Sure, I had celebrity crushes on guys like Rob Thomas and Dave Navarro. I was always into rock and alternative music—it helped get my frustrations out. Between not having much of a childhood, no friends or family, and losing my mother at seventeen, I had a ton of anger inside me.

Aside from a few celebrity crushes, I never found myself swooning over "real life" guys. I even wondered if I was a lesbian for a while, but then I realized girls irritated me, and I wanted to claw most of their eyes out!

After forcing myself to get into a short-lived relationship with a guy from one of my business classes—I even lost my virginity to him—I wondered if maybe there was something wrong with me. I had no emotional pull to anyone at all. I figured I was just asexual. But suddenly there I was, staring—and I do mean staring—at this beautiful man.

"Um, I'm over here..."

One of the other guys snapped his fingers at me. He actually snapped his fingers! I was infuriated. I managed to tear my eyes off the gorgeous boy to look at another attractive—though slightly thuggish—guy. His blue eyes looked at me and I somehow decided to disregard his rude behavior. If I only knew then what I know now, I would have given him an earful!

"Sorry," I shook my head out of the daze.

"Can I get a coke?" he laughed.

"Sure," I forced my best smile before looking over at the next guy to take his order.

When I turned my eyes on the over-the-top gorgeous guy again, he was scribbling something down on a napkin. Something inside me hoped it was his number.

"Jordan," the bald-headed guy next to him nudged his arm.

Jordan AKA Mr. Absolutely Irresistible stopped writing and looked up at me with a killer smile.

"Sorry. I'll just have water."

I finished taking the other drink order before I began to walk away. I heard the blue-eyed guy say something about my ass and I rolled my eyes to myself. By the time I had delivered the check, I overheard several conversations about music and a show.

Finally, my curiosity got the best of me.

"Are you guys in a band?"

Jordan smiled, "Do we look like rock stars?"

He laughed and I couldn't help but laugh in return.

"*You* definitely do," I nodded with a flirtatious smile.

The guys all made teasing noises.

"What was your name again?" he asked.

"Cami."

"I'm Jordan Walsh," he said sticking his hand out.

I reached across the table to shake it. He winked and I thought I was going to fall flat on the table since I didn't want to let go of his hand.

"I'm Danny DeSano," the blue-eyed guy stuck his hand in my face.

I looked over at him and shrugged.

"I'm not impressed," I smirked.

Again, a round of teasing noises were made. Jordan was laughing hard.

"Wow, I don't think any girl has ever said that to D.," he said.

"You've got to be kidding me," I shook my head. "What do you do in the band?"

Danny smiled, "I'm the drummer and I co-write with Jordan."

"Drummer," I nodded. "Kept in the back a lot, huh?" I glanced over at the rest of the band. "Good thinking."

They all cracked up laughing and Danny looked at me with an embarrassed smile.

"You're a feisty little waitress," he said, trying to belittle me.

"And you're an asshole wannabe rock star."

I flashed the coldest look possible and wondered if these guys were going to get me fired. I couldn't afford to lose my job. Though I didn't want to back down, I didn't want to screw myself over because of some idiot either. I was about to walk away when Jordan called out to me.

"Cami, what are you doing tonight?"

I turned with a goofy smile.

"Nothing."

"Well, we have a show tonight at Arlene's Grocery and…"

"You want me to come to your show?"

I was trying to play it cool; like I would do this band the favor of my presence.

"Of course," Jordan flashed a smile and added a wink, making sure he got me.

I would certainly subject myself to Danny's jerkiness to see Jordan again.

"Would you mind selling some merchandise for us?" Jordan asked. "We'll give you a percentage of everything you sell."

I eyed him, "How much?"

"Five percent," The bald-headed man, whom I was introduced to later as Sebastian, cut in.

"Ten," I challenged.

"Forget her," Danny said. "Who does this chick think she is?"

I leaned on the table toward Danny, knowing his eyes would go straight to my cleavage.

"A good business woman," I said.

Jordan laughed, "Deal."

"Jordan," Danny huffed.

I stood up straight.

"See you boys tonight," I said over my shoulder, looking at Jordan as I walked away.

That night, I sold all of Tortured's band merchandise at Arlene's Grocery—which is a small, somewhat underground music venue on the Lower East Side, and yes, it used to be a grocery store. Tortured was and still is the name of the alternative rock band I met at the diner that day. And they were truly talented. Their music spoke to me, and not just me, but the entire small crowd at Arlene's Grocery that night. It wasn't too hard to sell their stuff, especially to girls. They all wanted something with Jordan Walsh's beautiful face on it.

I had to roll my eyes. Girls. It didn't matter to them if a guy had talent or was a jerk. As long as he was hot, they'd sell their souls. If it were anyone else, I'd be sickened by it—but it was Jordan. It was hard for me to understand this feeling toward anyone, but he was just the total package. He had the looks, the personality and the talent. Maybe it was his easygoing personality that made me like him more than his overconfident best friend, Danny.

I don't know, but all I do know is, from that day forward I began a two-year love affair with Jordan, well in my mind, anyway. Mostly it was just me loving him, but I like to believe a part of him loved me too.

"There's nothing left?" Sebastian asked at the end of the night.

I stood proudly behind the empty merchandise table.

"Well, I do have this one crappy sticker," I frowned, holding it up.

The graphics on it were awful. I knew I could do better. In fact, I had a few marketing tips in the back of my mind.

"I'm impressed," Jordan grinned.

"Me too," I said, nodding toward the stage. "So, why am I not selling your music to these Tortured fans?"

"Demos cost money," Darren, the bass player chimed in.

I picked up the tackle box with all the cash in it and handed it to Jordan.

"Done," I smirked. "I already took my cut."

Jordan laughed and Danny spoke up.

"Who the hell is this chick?"

"Cami Woods, your manager."

The band went silent and looked at me questionably. I knew it was crazy to think I could manage some fairly unknown band at just seventeen-years-old with no real experience. They didn't know me yet, but I knew who I was. I knew when it came to making deals and selling something, I could do it. And Tortured was an easy sell.

"Manager?" Danny laughed. "Right. Nice try little girl."

"What do you know about managing a band?" Jordan asked. "How old are you, anyway?"

He turned quite serious with the question. It made me swallow since I only saw a carefree attitude from him so far.

"Well, I have a degree in business and marketing," I said, trying to keep my confidence. Who cares that it was only an Associate's and not a Bachelor's degree? I figured it was best I left my age out of things for the time being.

"...And I'm interning at Mega Music Management. I'm learning a lot and...you just have to trust me," I said, smiling and making my eyes pierce.

I knew no one could say no to me, but I was wondering if there really was a first time for everything. Instead of saying yes or no, no one said anything.

"We'll get back to you, Cami," Jordan said. "Great job tonight."

Just like that, I was dismissed. I didn't leave with a job or a date with Jordan, which is what I was hoping for. I went home that night and stared at my rundown apartment with very little furniture.

Before I knew it, I was crying. Sobbing was more like it. My heart hurt. I missed my mother. I wanted to make her proud and live the life she should have. Even though I didn't think I liked anyone very much, I wanted to have friends or even a husband someday. The husband dream was definitely my mother's dream for me, and maybe not so much mine. I wanted a great, empowering job. I didn't want to be some weak woman who had to depend on a man. That didn't get my mother very far. She wound up pregnant with me and broke!

In my apartment that night, I felt especially weak and alone. And I didn't feel quite as beautiful as everyone always told me I was.

Jordan didn't seem to be fazed by my beauty. I shouldn't have been surprised—he was the first person I met that had me beat looks-wise. Yes, I was extremely conceited about my beauty. I needed something in life to feel good about!

Two weeks had passed and I hadn't heard from Tortured. My internship had ended with Mega Music Management in that time after I had tried to secure a job with them. They basically told me I was too young and to contact them in a couple of years. The president of the company gave me his cell phone number and told me to call him when I was twenty-one. He had the nerve to wink at me in a creepy way. I had enough. I accepted all of the inappropriate comments while I interned there at the hopes that I would prove myself as more than teenage eye candy to the company.

I found myself crumpling the president's number up and throwing it at him.

"I'll just start my own company then," I said with a smug smile.

I stormed out of the office, not saying goodbye to anyone as I gathered my things and headed to the elevator. I was shaking. I was angry and upset and scared. I crossed myself and prayed to my mother. We weren't really practicing Catholics, but we still believed in the core of it.

That night, after my shift at the diner I went home and looked through my contacts I had made at Mega Music Management. The next day, I sat at an internet café and contacted everyone I knew. I invited them all to Tortured's show at The Bowery Ballroom. I promised free tickets to everyone. I made enough in tips that week to cover it.

I still didn't consider anyone a friend, but I was the intern that went the extra mile for clients, press, and booking agencies. Most of them thought more of me than the people in my office did. They wanted to help me out. Besides, I talked Tortured up to the point where I had people wondering, how anyone could be *that* good.

I'll never forget the look on Tortured's faces when I walked into The Bowery Ballroom with a photographer from *The Village Voice*, a big time booking agent and Matt Porter, teen heartthrob from the boy band Sound Wave[†]. Of course, no one recognized the other guys, but they did recognize Matt Porter, even if they hated

---

[†] Sound Wave is a fictional boy band from Sandy Lo's novel LOST IN YOU, which is also available to purchase.

his music, or would never admit to finding some Sound Wave songs catchy.

Matt had been hitting on me for weeks. He was in New York to record his solo album and was represented by Mega Music Management. I thought he was cute and all, but I wasn't into him. Maybe I didn't like blondes, or maybe there was something wrong with me since every teenage girl in the world had been drooling over him. I had allowed Matt to take me to lunch a couple of times, but I have warded off his attempts at kissing me. I knew most girls would think I was crazy for turning Matt down. I probably *was* crazy.

The band was still doing sound check. I also knew some people at The Bowery Ballroom that allowed me inside early. Jordan stopped checking his microphone and hopped off the stage. Danny, Sebastian and Darren quickly followed.

"How'd you get in here?" Jordan asked curiously.

"I know people," I shrugged. "This is Harold Armstrong from *The Village Voice*."

"Cami's said some great things about your band," Harold said, holding his hand out to Jordan, who shook it looking dumbfounded.

"This is Jon Mason of Artist Mayhem Agency," I continued introductions.

"And I'm sure you all recognize Matt Porter," I finished with a smile.

Matt and Jordan shook hands, almost sizing each other up. I stifled a laugh. Danny was even worse. It looked like he tried to break Matt's hand off when he shook it. Matt is six-one, but Danny has him beat by a couple of inches. While Matt was a bit lanky, Danny was solid.

"Can we talk alone for a second?" Jordan asked, in a low voice, turning my attention away from the dueling blue-eyed ego maniacs.

I swallowed. Jordan's voice really was an extension of his looks. We walked away from everyone. I looked over my shoulder to see Danny's eyes following me. I thought he hated me. He later on claimed he was baffled and intrigued by me. I wasn't like other girls he knew. Sometimes, as much as Danny says he was in love me, I wondered if he was threatened by me; intimidated even. At times, even now, I wonder if he downright hates me.

Anyway, back to the private conversation Jordan and I had…

"What is all this?" Jordan asked, nodding toward Matt Porter and the other two guys that came in with me.

"I have five more industry people coming tonight," I said matter-of-factly.

"Why?"

"To prove myself to you."

Jordan sighed, "Maybe we don't want a manager."

"Maybe you don't, but you need one."

He laughed, "Says you? Listen, you're impressive. I'll give you that, but this is our band and we're doing fine—"

"How much merch do you usually sell at shows?" I asked, interrupting him.

He sighed and shrugged.

"That's what I thought. And that crowd that I saw, are they the same crowd that'll be here tonight?"

"I'm sure there will be some new faces. Word of mouth is powerful," Jordan said, trying to sound convincing.

"Yes, it is," I agreed. "In the same city, at the same three venues, how fast do you think the word is going to spread?" I raised my eyebrow.

Jordan stared at me.

"*The Voice* is willing to run a piece on you guys—if you're as good as I told them you were—which we both know you are."

Jordan stared at me blankly. I was smugly smiling.

"What do I have to give you?"

Now, that was a loaded question! There was so much I wanted from Jordan at that moment. A job. His lips. His heart.

"A chance."

He broke into a smile.

"You've got a chance. I mean, how much money are we talking?"

"How about ten percent of every show I book you? If you guys book it yourselves, you owe me nothing. Once we get a record deal and sell a million albums, we'll renegotiate," I chuckled.

Jordan laughed and his smile blinded me.

"Is that a deal?" I asked, sticking my hand out.

Jordan shook it and Danny walked over to us.

"Why did you bring that douche bag to our show?" Danny asked.

I rolled my eyes, "He's here to support you."

Danny furrowed his eyebrows, a look I oddly found attractive.

"We don't need him. Are you crazy or something?"

I smiled, "No, I'm your manager. And trust me, take a picture with Matt Porter for *The Village Voice*, and his fans become your fans," I said patting his chest before walking away.

"Did she just say she was our manager?" I heard Danny ask Jordan as I headed back over to Matt.

"D, she can help us."

"You didn't even talk to us about it!" Danny hissed.

"Seb and Darren think it's a good idea," Jordan said with a sigh before walking away from him.

Matt nudged my arm.

"That Danny kid is a douche."

I snickered at him and looked over at Jordan, who smiled at me. I smiled bigger and Matt sighed next to me.

"So, you brought me here to impress a guy?" he whispered.

I looked over at Matt and he looked offended and hurt.

"Matt, that's not it. I brought you here to help me land a job."

"Or land Jordan."

"No," I said through gritted teeth. "Stop with the bruised ego. I'm just not interested in dating right now. I want to be friends."

Matt nodded, "Okay."

Danny was staring at us as Jordan talked to the photographer. I decided if I was going to be the band's manager, I better smooth things over with the drummer. I walked over to Danny and took his hand. I pulled him to the bar.

"I know you don't like me, but I promise you I want to make Tortured a success."

Danny sighed, "I'll admit this is all kind of impressive."

I smiled, "I'm the one impressed by you guys."

Danny returned my smile. He really was handsome. There are times when he would look at me and something inside me wanted to jump on him. Still, I found myself falling for Jordan long before I ever thought about Danny as anything more than pent up sexual tension.

CHAPTER TWO

Over the course of the next six months, I worked hard. I still held down my job at the diner and got a second job on weekends working at an independent music store in the East Village. Of course, I used the music store as an outlet to promote Tortured's shows. I also worked hard promoting Tortured on the street. The band and I would hand out flyers in Times Square and on NYU's campus with a free download of their song "Break The Mold".

They now had two songs recorded. I helped find the band a studio with a discount and we have started selling the two songs on iTunes and at shows. The band didn't regret hiring me at all, which was a relief for me. I wasn't making too much money from being their manager, hence the other two jobs, but I knew it would pay enough eventually. Besides, I loved every second of working with the band. It gave my life purpose. I was doing something I was passionate about. Plus, I was starting to feel like I had actual friends. Jordan, Sebastian, Darren and yes, even Danny were my best friends. I didn't know how they felt about me, but I even began to think of them as family.

Actually, I had quite a few friends at that point. Most of them were guys, though, Matt Porter being one of them, but beggars can't be choosers. Girls just didn't like me much, or maybe I didn't like them. Most girls have jealousy issues, in my experience. One thing is for sure, I am most certainly a jealous creature. Growing up, I was used to having all of my mother's attention. Now, when I get close to someone, I don't like anyone getting in the way of that closeness.

Danny and Darren had gotten girlfriends and I found myself giving them dirty looks without realizing it. I started banning any outsiders from rehearsals. I thought it was reasonable. Girls were distractions to the guys.

For my eighteenth birthday, the guys took me out to dinner followed by going to Carney's Pub, which was our hangout—thank God for fake IDs! I wasn't one to dress up, mostly because I didn't have a ton of nice clothes. I was more of a baby doll tee and skinny jeans type of girl. As a birthday present to myself, I bought a new dress. It was a black and red corset dress that laced in the front. It was kind of punk with a touch of Goth. It was true to my style at that time, but showed off more skin than I was used to. The skirt of the dress was poufy but short. The top was strapless and pushed up my boobs to reveal cleavage I didn't even know I had.

I could tell the guys didn't know I had it either. Four pairs of eyes went straight to my chest when I walked into the restaurant that night. I think sometimes they forgot I was a girl. I really did become one of the guys—probably because I didn't giggle at everything they said all the time and I cuss like a sailor. I didn't take their crap either. I dished it back.

By the time we were at Carney's, I was fairly drunk. I know, I know—I wasn't twenty-one, but it was my birthday and at eighteen, you think drinking is cool. Even worse, you think getting wasted is really cool. Besides, I had four guys buying my drinks all night. Was I about to refuse? Nope. Especially not when one of those guys was Jordan Walsh and especially not after he made the most amazing toast to me.

"To Cami, without you, Tortured would still be stuck in the same spot. From the bottom of our hearts, thank you for pushing your little butt into this band."

I laughed, "My butt's not *that* little."

For a generally small person, I had a big butt. I wished my boobs were a little bigger. They were a full B-cup, but I wanted a C. Jordan raised his eyebrows at my not so little butt comment. He smirked before peeking his head around me.

"No, I guess not."

Everyone laughed and called out, "To Cami", before drinking their beer. My eyes stayed locked on Jordan's. My crush on him had intensified with every month that I got to know him. I think anyone would agree, the more you were around Jordan Walsh, the more incredible he became.

At the end of the night, Jordan offered to walk me back to my apartment since the other guys were crashing at Sebastian's place, and he didn't want me walking alone so late at night. We walked in silence. The night had consisted of plenty of flirting between Jordan and me. I usually flirted with everyone, but something happened that night that brought it to another level. Maybe it was the alcohol or my dress, but I was making my intentions known, and Jordan seemed to go right along with it.

"Hey, Landry is coming to town next week," I said to him.

Landry was Jordan's favorite band in the world.

He smiled, "I know. I'll be up in Boston."

He lived in Boston for the most part. I didn't know why. He was from New York. His father and brother were still here, but his mother and aunt had lived up in Boston. He didn't say much about it. I thought the traveling back and forth might be hard on him. He was really close with his brother, Andrew. I met him a couple of times. He was an adorable kid and a charmer, saying all kinds of flirty comments the few times I had met him. Andrew definitely takes after Jordan in both the looks and personality department. However, his brother was definitely more like me when it came to flirting. Even at his young age, he obviously tried to flirt while Jordan wasn't quite as blatant. Jordan was just smooth with everyone. I wish he was a little more forward and not so aloof. I wanted to know what he thought of me, but he was a hard person to figure out.

"Do you ever think about moving back to New York?" I asked as we stopped outside my building.

"You know I do," he nodded.

I heard the sadness in his voice.

"I can't stand my dad," he shrugged. "Besides, my job up in Boston pays pretty decent."

"You don't have to stay with your dad," I offered.

"Look, I don't want to talk about it."

"Okay," I said, wishing he would open up to me.

Darren and Sebastian knew nothing about why he was attached to Boston, either. Danny did, though, but he wouldn't speak about it.

"Do you want to crash here?" I asked, knowing it was late and my neighborhood wasn't exactly the safest to be walking through.

Jordan looked at me and his eyes dipped down to my cleavage.

"I better not..." he started to say, but I took his hand in mine.

"I won't bite unless you want me to."

I couldn't believe I said that with a straight face. Before I knew it, I was laughing hysterically. Jordan began to laugh as well. Just as I was recovering from my ridiculously cliché line, Jordan pulled me into a kiss.

This was what I had been waiting for! I wrapped my arms around him as his amazing mouth devoured mine. Crap, he was a good kisser. I knew I was in trouble for sure. I never felt anything like what I felt for Jordan. It was scary and exciting and sexy. We hurried into my apartment, tripping over things, throwing pieces of clothing aside.

When we were completely naked, we looked over one another approvingly. Afterward, Jordan fell asleep quickly. As I dozed off, I thought about how good-looking of a couple we would make. I imagined us being a power couple like Brad Pitt and Angelina Jolie. With Jordan's rock star persona and my young business mogul ways, we'd be unstoppable.

I woke up to Jordan putting his jeans on.

"Are you skipping out on me?" I asked, with my best seductive look.

Jordan turned and looked at me with a smile.

"I have to head up to Boston."

"Maybe one day I can come up there with you," I smiled.

Jordan didn't respond to that. He sat down on the bed.

"About last night..."

"It was the best birthday I ever had," I grinned, rubbing his thigh.

"I don't want this to affect our professional relationship."

"It won't."

"Promise?"

"I promise," I smiled. "Can I get a goodbye kiss?"

Jordan leaned down and kissed me.

"You taste like alcohol," he shook his head at me.

I hopped out of the bed butt naked and ran to the bathroom; listening to Jordan chuckle and whistle as I did. I walked back out a moment later and struck a pose.

"Are you sure you want to leave right now?"

I walked over to him, enjoying his eyes looking me over. He smirked and placed his hands on my hips as he kissed around my bellybutton. He finally left my apartment two hours later.

I was on cloud nine for the next six weeks. Though Jordan was in Boston for half the time, our sexual activity was intense. Around the rest of the band, we were pretty normal. Danny knew, though. I could tell. He just looked at me differently, almost coldly.

One day, I was working out with Danny at the gym. Sebastian was his usual workout partner, but he got called into work. I was surprised when Danny asked me. We were on side-by-side treadmills when Danny spoke up.

"So, what are you doing with Jordan exactly?"

I looked at him with a silly smile.

"What do you mean?"

"I know you're sleeping together."

I blushed, though I'm sure he couldn't tell with my tan skin.

"Wow, way to embarrass a girl," I said stopping the treadmill and wiping my face with a towel.

"Look, Jordan's my best friend. Don't hurt him, okay?" Danny said, not looking at me.

I had to laugh. Me? Hurt Jordan?

"Why would I hurt Jordan?"

Danny stopped his treadmill before turning around to look at me.

"You weaseled your way into the band and we love you, Cami, but...if you're using Jordan..."

I was quite offended.

"Using Jordan?" I scoffed. "For what?"

"I don't know," Danny sighed, scratching his chin. "I'm just protective."

I looked at him and saw something I never saw in Danny DeSano prior to that moment. He was caring and loyal. Maybe not to me, but to Jordan, for sure.

I smiled, "I won't hurt him. I love him."

The words just fell from my lips and I couldn't take them back. Danny and I stared at each other, both in shock.

"I love you, and Darren and Sebastian, too," I tried to cover it up, but we both knew what I meant.

"Well, I guess I should tell you this, Cam," Danny said, looking into my eyes. "Don't get attached to Jordan. He's not going to fall in love with you."

I stepped back from him. I had never been so angry.

"Screw you, Danny."

"I'm not trying to hurt you. I just know Jordan better than you. He's complicated and... Just don't expect too much emotionally."

"Thanks for the advice," I said with a clenched jaw.

No girl wants to hear that the man she loves will never love her back. Sadly, Danny was right, though. My six-week affair with Jordan turned into three months and still, we were nowhere close to an emotional connection. We'd sleep together and laugh together and do band-related things together, but Jordan and I were simply friends with benefits. Even those benefits were becoming less frequent. I chalked it up to Jordan being busy and tired from traveling back and forth.

I figured maybe I should tell Jordan how I felt. Maybe if I made the first move, he would reciprocate my feelings. This was the 21st century after all. Girls could initiate more. I was almost feminist in my beliefs, so why shouldn't I put myself out there?

I invited Jordan over my apartment for dinner. I made my mother's lasagna, one of the three things I knew how to make. I knew no man could resist it. Jordan devoured three helpings of it. After dinner, he began to talk business. I had to interrupt.

"Can we talk about something else tonight?"

Jordan looked at me blankly, "Uh, sure."

I always loved to talk business, so I'm sure that took him by surprise.

I smiled, "You know, the other day was our three-month anniversary."

Jordan made a funny face.

"Anniversary?"

"I know we don't really celebrate, but I've been thinking about us more. I lo—"

"Cami," he sighed. "Look, I don't want anything serious."

Wow. He didn't even let me finish! I was ready to pour my heart out to him and he was ready to dismiss me. I just nodded and took a sip of my water, trying my hardest to swallow that down, along with my feelings.

"Maybe we shouldn't..." Jordan began. "You know, anymore."

"Why?" I asked numbly.

"Because. It's not right," he shrugged.

I looked at him, with a hurt expression on my face. I felt myself wanting to cry. I never cried in front of anyone before. I never had a reason to. I never had anyone before! Now, the only boy I ever had feelings for was telling me he didn't want me—not even for sex anymore.

My bottom lip trembled and I couldn't speak.

"Cami, I think you're amazing. You're beautiful and smart and funny and..."

"Don't, Jordan," I said, my voice shaking. "Can you just go?"

Before he could respond, I stood up and hurried to my bathroom. I looked up at myself in the mirror. I didn't look like the headstrong business woman. I didn't look like the beautiful, tough Italian girl my mother raised. I looked like a lonely little girl. And I hated this girl. I hated being that vulnerable. I sat down on the toilet bowl lid, not wanting to look at myself any longer.

A half-hour later, I walked out of the bathroom. My cell phone was blinking. I secretly hoped there would be a text or voicemail from Jordan, but I knew better. The jerk didn't use his cell phone—only for emergencies. Half the time, he didn't even carry the prepaid piece of garbage around with him.

Instead, I had a text from Danny.

U ok? J asked me 2 check on u.

I didn't respond. I began cleaning the dinner dishes and wrapping up the leftover lasagna. About an hour later, there was a knock on my door. I sighed, hoping it wasn't one of my crazy neighbors. I looked through the peephole and I was surprised to see Danny standing on my doorstep.

I pulled my hair back into a ponytail and wiped underneath my eyes to make sure I had no makeup running down my face. I swung the door open and put on my best fake smile.

"Hey. What are you doing here?"

"You didn't reply to my text," Danny sighed, pushing past me.

He looked so tall in my small apartment. Heck, he was tall—six foot, three.

"Sorry, I'm okay," I smiled again.

"You can talk to me, you know," he sighed, plopping down on my loveseat.

He looked even more like a giant on the small piece of old furniture. He patted the spot next to him and I sat down on the edge.

"Really, I'm fine," I lied.

"Your pretty blue eyes are red," he sighed, touching my cheek with the back of his hand.

Before I knew it, Danny was holding me in his arms. I began to cry into his chest, surprised that I was allowing myself to. I knew it wasn't just because of Jordan. I was letting out years of pent up emotions on Danny's shirt, and he just allowed me to. We fell asleep together on the couch. We didn't even talk much. The next morning, we both woke up with cramped necks and backs.

"Can I take you to breakfast?" Danny asked, as he got his shoes on.

"Sure," I nodded.

I threw a hat on my head and a hooded sweatshirt on. We went to a nearby diner. I felt much more secure walking with Danny in my neighborhood than by myself, although I never would admit that to anyone. I always walked with confidence and attitude in the area, knowing muggers and rapists preyed on fear.

We were seated in a booth and I looked into Danny's eyes. He smiled at me and I finally saw a softer side of him. It made me smile in return.

"You deserve a good guy, Cam," he said.

"You don't think Jordan is a good guy?"

"He is. Just not the guy for you," Danny shrugged with a smirk.

"So I'm waiting for you to rub in my face that you were right."

"I'm not going to do that," Danny shook his head. "I'm not happy I was right."

"Thanks," I sighed. "I was stupid to believe he could fall for me," I rolled my eyes.

"Whoa, where is this insecurity coming from?" Danny asked in total disbelief.

I shrugged, "It's not insecurity. It's the pain of rejection. I know I could find a guy to love me."

Danny laughed. He always loved when I was cocky, mostly because he was the cockiest person I ever met.

"But?"

"But it's rare I find someone I can love in return."

Danny stared at me. I shouldn't have said that, but it was too late. I had already accidentally admitted to Danny I loved Jordan once before. I suppose he knew I always would love Jordan in some way.

The next band meeting, I was concerned how Jordan and I would act around one another. He pretended like nothing happened, and I think that just hurt me, though looking back on it, I'm glad. I tried my hardest to make it awkward, but Jordan ignored it. Sadly, I was not the bigger person. I wanted him to feel some of the hurt and discomfort I was feeling, but it never worked, which just frustrated me.

As the months passed, Danny and I started hanging out more—just the two of us. We had a playful friendship. Yes, we flirted, too, which I did more around Jordan out of spite. Danny and I always had that element about us. We liked to argue and challenge each other. It was inevitable really—Danny and me. I didn't see it then since I was still so hung up on Jordan.

Soon, my bruised ego and emotional attachment did begin to get in the way of me managing the band. I began to get jealous of other girls hanging around Jordan; more so than usual. I was jealous of fans at shows, receptionists at the recording studio, and even waitresses at bars. I was completely out of hand and I know that now. I had an insane jealous streak to begin with, but with Jordan and I ending—it was out of control. We would fight constantly. It all came to a head one night when a fan grabbed Jordan, kissed his cheek and wouldn't release him from a hug. I practically ripped her off of Jordan and yelled some inappropriate names at her.

Jordan dragged me backstage and was furious with me.

"Are you insane, Cami?!?" he screamed. "You're supposed to be encouraging fan interactions not trying to fight them!"

"I'm sorry! She was all over you!"

"I can fucking handle myself!" Jordan screamed. "I've put up with your immature behavior long enough. We're done!"

I just stared at him, not sure what to say.

"You promised! You promised you wouldn't let us come between the band!"

"I thought I could handle it," I mumbled.

"Well, you were wrong. That's it, Cami. You're fired."

"Jordan, no," I said, grabbing his arm. "I'm sorry, please..." I pleaded.

He ripped his arm away from me and stormed out. I paced back and forth for a moment, convincing myself Jordan was just angry and he would get over it. When I walked back to where the band was, Jordan wasn't with them. I looked over at Danny, Darren and Sebastian. The three of them looked at me like I was on death row.

"You okay?" Danny walked up to me.

"No," I sighed.

"Come on, it's late. I'll pay for your taxi."

Danny guided me outside. I turned around and threw myself into his arms. I don't know why it was so easy to be vulnerable around Danny. He was good at nurturing me when I was upset. I felt his hand on my back, rubbing up and down; trying to soothe me as I breathed deeply.

"He fired me," I sighed heavily.

"He's mad. Give him time to calm down. He can't fire you without talking to the rest of us," Danny assured me.

"He hired me without your consent!" I whined, and I felt Danny chuckle into my hair.

"Cam, just try to get it together a little around him, okay?"

I pulled away from him and wiped my tears. The truth was I was even getting more jealous those days when girls were flirting with Danny, too. I nodded and Danny wiped my tears.

"I'll talk to him," Danny smiled and kissed my forehead.

He stared into my eyes and I found myself wanting him to kiss me. He didn't. Instead, he turned away and hailed a taxi.

Obviously, Jordan didn't fire me. Danny smoothed things over for me and though there was still some tension, business continued as usual. My friendship with Danny intensified. After several months of flirting and hanging out, things progressed. It was a beautiful late spring day and I thought it would be nice to have lunch in Bryant Park. Danny and I were sitting on a park bench. He had mayonnaise on his lip—he was a messy eater—and I leaned over to wipe it off. He caught my hand and sucked the mayonnaise off my finger. He smiled as he moved in and kissed me softly. He pulled back, waiting for my reaction.

I stared down at my sandwich for a moment. I was scared to get involved with someone again. If Danny hadn't been there, I don't know if my feelings for Jordan would have dulled as much. I was definitely feeling more for him than friendship. If Danny didn't develop feelings for me, however, how would I make it through? How would I face the band after falling for two members, who didn't see me as anything more than someone to pass time with?

I looked over at Danny, wondering what exactly he felt toward me. Was it merely attraction? Lust? Or just another friends with benefits situation?

"Cami, I know this won't be easy. We work together and whatever went on between you and Jordan..." he waved his hand in the air. "But I really like you," he added, smiling stupidly. "I have since I first met you."

I laughed, "You were so rude to me that day!"

"I'm stupid around girls I like!"

"Damn right," I shook my head with a smile.

"I know I'm not the one you wanted first, but..."

That actually hurt me, hearing him say that. Why didn't I want Danny first? Well, I know why. He was being stupid! He showed me a different side of him though. I knew it would always be a battle with Danny. I'd either want him or want to throw him out a window.

I moved closer and kissed him, deeper than he had kissed me. I ran my tongue along his bottom lip and he allowed access. He ran his fingers through my hair before trailing them down the side of my neck. He was good and I wanted more. When he pulled away from me, he smiled at me and I just pulled him back into a kiss. We forgot all about our sandwiches as we made-out for quite a while.

CHAPTER THREE

Breaking the news to Jordan was left entirely up to Danny. Judging by Jordan missing the next rehearsal, I took it he was pissed off. Little did I know he wound up having bus trouble on the way down from Boston. Little did I know, he also brought a girl back from Boston. When Jordan showed up late to rehearsal the next day for a big Battle of the Bands thing I had booked him, he was cold to me. I wasn't any better. I was angry he missed rehearsal the day before and late to another one, especially when it was for such a big gig.

Jordan was even colder to Danny. I hate to admit it, but it gave me great pleasure to think maybe Jordan was jealous and regretting not wanting more with me. Maybe he missed me. He didn't want to talk to us about it that day. Danny said to give him time. I feel like that was the way everyone always dealt with Jordan. No one ever talked to him about anything. They just let him cool off. As a girl, it was kind of frustrating since I rather find out what flew up his ass every once in a while. In that moment, however, I didn't really want to talk to him about what was going on between Danny and me anyhow.

What I was not prepared for was meeting Haley Foster that night. She was backstage. Jordan had never brought anyone backstage, except his brother once, and here he was bringing some pretty little blonde rich girl! I was furious! Who was she and why did he seem so protective of her?

Needless to say, I gave the girl the coldest shoulder I was capable of. No one seemed surprised, especially not Danny—thankfully. I was trying to curb my jealousy, but it was difficult and he understood my emotions were still raw, even though it was almost a year since Jordan and I had been together physically.

Tortured won the Battle of the Bands that night! It eased some of the tension between us all. It was the happiest moment in all of our careers so far. The band would win money, radio airplay and an opening spot for a major music artist—who turned out to be Landry, Jordan's favorite band. It was a huge deal! Everyone but Jordan thanked me for booking them on it. Even though it was the band's performance that won, I still felt entitled to a thank you or some kind of credit.

48

Jordan was too busy rescuing Haley after she passed out at the meet & greet session. I hated her for it—for getting all of Jordan's attention when that night should have been about the band. Jordan claimed he and Haley were barely friends. He was doing someone a favor by showing her around the city, but no one believed him—least of all me. It turns out that someone he was doing a favor for was Tasha Torres, a girl I had met at a few of the shows and I didn't like much. She was loud, flirty and had the boobs I always wanted—plus she could dance like one of those girls in the music videos, another thing I couldn't do. Anyway, back to my jealousy of Haley. My list of girls I was jealous of is quite long...

I saw Haley as nothing but a distraction for the next few days. Then, something changed. I'm not sure what. I think part of it was Danny. The night after the Battle of the Bands, the whole band—and little miss blondie came too—celebrated at Carney's.

Danny and I continued the celebrating in my apartment. We were making out pretty heavily and as I reached for his pants, he stopped me. That was a first. I looked at him worriedly. He was looking at me with this serious look. I thought he was going to end us—just like Jordan did.

"What's wrong?" I asked.

"Nothing. Everything is perfect," Danny smiled. "I'm falling hard for you, Cam."

His smile replaced the contemplative look. Even his eyes were smiling. I absolutely loved when his eyes looked like that. They were boyishly adorable.

"Good," I grinned and moved into kiss Danny again.

He pushed me away, "Good? That's all you're going to say?"

I laughed, "I'm falling hard for you too, Danny. Can't you tell?"

He rolled his eyes, "It's hard to tell when you're shooting daggers at Jordan and his new chick."

"Eh, I'll get over it. I just hate not being the only girl around."

I did in fact get over it. The next couple of days, I loved being officially in a relationship with someone, especially Danny. He was so sweet and had this romantic side I never thought he would have! As for Haley, she kind of grew on me. She wasn't at all like I thought she was. She wasn't an airhead bimbo. She wasn't a rich snob. She was down-to-earth and truly cared about Jordan. I could see that. She supported the band. And Jordan wrote "Haley's Letter" about her, which would become Tortured's first number one single on iTunes.

Haley became a fixture in the band and one of the only girls I ever truly considered a friend. She checked on me after every stupid breakup Danny and I had. She was my maid-of-honor at our wedding. When I had a miscarriage six years ago, she cheered me up and let me cry on her shoulder. I couldn't imagine going through that terrible time without her.

Anyway, that summer seventeen years ago, Tortured went on its first tour. I got Haley a gig doing photography for it. She was incredibly surprised by the gesture. I guess I really was a bitch to her. I was glad I wouldn't be the only girl on tour. It was a great experience for all of us.

Danny and I fell deeper in love, as deep as I was capable of anyway. Jordan and I buried the hatchet. I found out why Jordan lived in Boston, too. His mother was in some kind of mental facility up there. He and I had similar personalities when it came to dealing with things in life. We liked to shut people out. As much as I had wished I could have opened him up, I was happy he had Haley. I was happy to be with Danny, too.

The summer was beautiful. Tortured was gaining more momentum. Danny and I were in that new love stage where everything was perfect. We didn't even fight anymore.

That fall, however, our little heated arguments came back. We didn't mind though. Make-up sex was amazing! Unfortunately, that over-sexed, angsty, puppy love faded fairly quickly. Before our two-year anniversary, we almost broke up a couple of times. Our fights were pretty brutal since we both had quick tempers and said things we didn't mean in the heat of the moment.

After one particularly big fight, Danny asked me to move in with him. I stupidly said yes. Looking back on it, I doubt we were ready. Hell, we had no business getting married! We were so young, impulsive and plain old dumb.

I don't know if we felt we had to keep up with Jordan and Haley or what. They had a baby girl right before Danny and I moved in together, and were married soon after. A few months after their wedding, Danny proposed to me. Again, I stupidly said yes. I was twenty-two and loved the idea of planning a wedding. It was the control freak in me. I don't think I thought too much about planning a life, though. I spent almost two years planning the lavish party and no time planning my life outside of work.

"Do you and Danny want kids right away?" Tasha asked at my bridal shower.

Tasha was still Haley's best friend, as much as I wished to take her place. What was worse was she ended up becoming Sebastian's wife. I still didn't like her much, mostly because she was gorgeously buxom with a personality to match. Tasha was Haley's maid-of-honor and the Godmother of Aylin, Jordan and Haley's daughter. I'm still pretty bitter toward her over that.

"I think we're going to wait for kids a while," I answered Tasha, reminding myself to play nice. "My career is still taking off..."

It was, too. I began managing a couple of other artists along with Tortured and spent a lot of time traveling.

By the time I was twenty-four, Danny and I were married in lavish, typical celebrity fashion. We even had a four-page spread for *InStyle Magazine*. We honeymooned for three weeks in the Virgin Islands, and it was perfect.

For the next five years, we were fairly happy. Our careers were still skyrocketing. We had enough time together, but still a good amount of time apart to not drive each other too crazy.

At thirty, something changed. I wanted to slow down and have a baby. I wanted to be in one place with my husband for a longer period of time. Tortured was having time off before they were going to start writing the next album in New York. That meant Danny would be home for a good six-months.

I sat Danny down and told him I wanted to have a baby. Thankfully, he felt the same way. I knew Danny would be a wonderful father. He was always great with Jordan's brother, Andrew—even though he wasn't that young when I met him. Danny was just as great with Aylin. We would babysit for Jordan and Haley from time to time.

Within a few months, I had gotten pregnant. I was delighted and so was Danny. Within two more months, I had lost the baby. I was devastated and Danny didn't know how to help me. I was depressed for weeks. I had gone numb, just like when my mother passed away.

After getting the okay from the doctor, we began trying again. We tried for five years, even using fertility drugs, and nothing worked. We were both miserable. I was driving Danny crazy. We started fighting more than usual.

One night, Danny didn't come home. We had fought and threw blame at one another for why we couldn't have a baby. He went too far by saying he wasn't even turned on by me anymore. We both said some pretty nasty things to each other before, but that killed me. I began to cry; the fertility drugs made me extra emotional on top of it. Danny tried to hug me and apologize, but I pushed him away. I asked him to leave, but I didn't think he wouldn't come back.

I called Jordan the next morning. I could tell I woke him.

"Is Danny with you?" I asked.

I had barely slept.

"Cami, it's five in the morning..." he said, gruffly before it hit him. "Wait, Danny didn't come home?"

"No," I said, letting out a shaky breath. "We had a bad fight. He's not answering his phone."

"He probably crashed on Darren's couch," Jordan said with a sigh.

An hour later, I heard the door slam. Danny walked into the bedroom and I stared at him. He threw himself on the bed. He reeked of alcohol. He looked up at me and put his hand on my knee.

"I'm sorry."

I just nodded and lay down next to him, allowing him to wrap his arms around me, even though I wanted to throw him in the shower.

For the next couple of months, Danny disappeared a bunch of times. He always came home. I just couldn't get a hold of him for hours at a time. He was never with Jordan, even when he told me they were writing together. I would call Haley and she'd tell me unknowingly how Jordan was at the movies with Aylin or home with her.

Danny was extra nice to me, though. He would make me dinner or take me out. Our sex life was still fairly active, maybe not like it used to be, but we were still trying to have a baby.

Then one day, I took a pregnancy test expecting it to come out negative as usual. I stared at the test for five minutes before fully processing it was positive. I began screaming and Danny came into the bathroom freaking out. I showed him the test and we hugged, both relieved. I was planning to be extremely cautious with this pregnancy, not wanting to have another miscarriage. Unfortunately, my joyful news wore off when everything blew up in my face. Or should I say, it blew up in Danny's face.

I had just gotten back from the doctor. I was four months along and still thinking the baby would make all of our problems go away. I thought we could finally stop pretending like we were happy when we weren't, and actually be happy.

The phone rang before I could call Danny. Tara James, the publicist for Struck Records, Tortured's label, was on the line. She wanted to know what kind of statement she should release in response to the photos in *Razz Magazine*. *Razz* is the top tabloid magazine that enjoys exploiting a good scandal, whether it's true or not.

"What photos, Tara?" I asked.

"Oh, uh...you haven't seen them?"

I wondered if they were photos of Danny drunk or high since he's known to party a little too much from time to time. It was something I accepted about him over the years, but I still didn't like it. His sometimes excessive partying was the cause of many fights and even a couple of break-ups in our early years. Danny was definitely known as the bad boy of Tortured. I started to wonder if there was another photo circulating of him doing a shot off some waitress' neck.

I was pretty upset about the photo, but he swore it was all in good fun, and he didn't do anything with the waitress. Danny was big on doing things for show. He wanted to look like a real rock star. It always did bring more press to the band. Either Danny was a marketing genius or a sleazy jerk. I always thought he was a little of both, but he'd have to tone down things a bit for our baby's sake. Tara James was hesitant to describe the article in *Razz Magazine* to me.

"Cami, maybe you should talk to Danny about this first."

"Maybe you should tell me. I am the band's manager, Tara. I need to know about anything that's going to affect their career," I sighed, already getting angry with my husband.

I had a feeling that anything in *Razz* was most likely not going to affect Tortured negatively. That was how things went—especially with guys. They could get away with starting fights in bars or getting sloshed, where as if this was some female pop princess, she'd be destroyed.

Instead, whatever was published in *Razz* would most likely destroy our marriage. I was sure of it. Maybe it was something like him licking a shot off a girl and I could get past it in a few weeks. My gut told me otherwise, though.

"Well, basically the magazine says Danny is having an affair. They have pictures..." she trailed off.

My voice caught in my throat. I knew it. I knew it was going to be bad.

"Pictures?"

"Danny and Anastasia Milos. They met at Fashion Week, right?"

I swallowed, "Anastasia?"

This is not happening! Anastasia Milos is just as bad as when everyone thought Jordan was dating rich, party girl Bippy Reynolds again! Anastasia Milos is a Greek lingerie model! She is everything I'm not: tall, red-haired, and a D-cup—even if they were fake! She had dated every A-List celebrity, including my friend Matt Porter—the guy I lost touch with because Danny hated him.

"They were probably just having a friendly lunch or something," Tara said, trying to smooth things over. "Talk to Danny and we'll retaliate."

"Okay Tara. I have to go," I said, quickly hanging up the phone.

I felt nauseous. I was literally sick to my stomach. It might have been morning sickness, but I think it was my life crumbling. I threw my sunglasses on and headed to the nearest newsstand and purchased *Razz Magazine*, hating that I was supporting them when they could possibly sabotage my marriage.

Sure enough in the upper right corner of the cover was a photo of my husband walking arm in arm with the slutty Greek bitch! I hurried back to my apartment, furiously flipping pages while in the elevator. I walked through the door just as I saw my two-pages of humiliation. There were photos of Danny leaving Anastasia's apartment building. There was a photo of them walking together, both with hats and sunglasses on, as if either of them could disguise themselves! She was almost six-feet tall and he was well over it! Plus, her flaming red hair stuck out of her hat giving her away.

I barely got through the first sentence of the article before running into the bathroom. I threw up and cried, but I felt anger more than any other emotion. I was embarrassed by the world knowing my husband was having an affair, and with a model no less!

I did not call Danny. He was actually writing with Jordan that day—not just pretending to. I decided to see Haley. I needed to get out of the penthouse before I destroyed it. As soon as Haley opened the door for me, she knew something was wrong.

"You look pissed," she said, allowing me to come inside.

"I guess you didn't see *Razz Mag* yet."

"Oh no, what's in it?" Haley sighed, running a hand through her hair.

The month before, they had posted a photo of Jordan with Meghan, Haley's friend, having a drink together; meanwhile, Haley was simply in the bathroom.

I pulled the magazine out and showed it to her. She just laughed.

"Remember, don't believe everything you read," she rolled her eyes. "Especially in trash like this."

"I believe it," I said seriously.

"Cami," Haley said as I followed her into the living room.

"Things have not been good, Haley," I said, my eyes becoming watery.

Ugh, I used to be so good at controlling my tears. The older I got, the easier it was for me to show my emotions. Danny used to be the only shoulder I cried on, but as years went on, he became less of a comfort to me. Haley had been the one to wipe my tears more than anyone lately.

Haley grabbed my hand and just then, the door opened. I heard a bunch of male voices.

I could pinpoint Jordan and Danny's voices anywhere, but someone else was with them. He had a voice that sounded a little deep, but still light somehow. To my surprise, it was Andrew Ashton, Jordan's little brother. They walked down the hallway and entered the living room.

I sometimes forget Andrew isn't a kid anymore. He is in his late twenties and played major league baseball. His dream of playing for the Yankees came true and Jordan couldn't be more proud of him. He was almost a spitting image of his brother aside from his paler skin tone, darker eye color and the cutest dimples I had ever seen. I hadn't seen him in a while, other than watching baseball games on TV, since we all had busy schedules.

"Drew!" Haley yelled, jumping up and giving her brother-in-law a hug.

"Hey Cami," Andrew walked over to me and I stood, forcing a smile on my face as I avoided eye contact with everyone, especially Danny. "Congratulations on the baby."

He kissed my cheek and I accidentally looked into his big brown eyes. He smiled at me and I was sure he could tell I was upset. I was trying to hold it together, but it was fairly impossible for me to hide anything was wrong.

"Hey babe," Danny said, slinging an arm over my shoulders as if he didn't know about *Razz Magazine*.

Jordan and Haley were in a kiss. Danny and Drew teased them, but I was jealous. I knew Jordan would never cheat on Haley. I knew Jordan would never say such awful things that Danny had said to me when we fought. Why couldn't it have been me that Jordan loved like that? Why did I end up with a two-timing jerk of a husband?

When Danny and I got home, he plopped on the couch and turned on the television.

"What's for dinner?"

That was all it took. I lost it. I pulled the magazine out of my purse and threw it in his lap.

"Ask Anastasia."

Danny looked up at me and laughed.

"Come on, you don't believe this, do you?"

I put my hands on my hips.

"You don't think I'm that stupid, do you?"

"Anastasia and I are friends…"

He didn't even sound convincing.

"Danny, just stop," I snarled. "Tell me. This isn't going away. If you love me at all, you'll tell me the truth," I sniffled.

He sighed and moved toward me, taking my hands off my hips and pulling me down onto the couch.

"I've been having an affair."

His blue eyes burned into mine and I wanted to slap him. Instead, I just nodded.

"Just one?"

He just looked down and back up at me. His eyes told a tale of several women.

"Wow..." I said in disbelief. "So, this whole time we've been trying to have a baby, you've been with how many women?"

"Baby," Danny said, swallowing.

He only called me "baby" when he was in trouble.

"I've been very unhappy."

My bottom lip trembled, "And you think I'm happy?!?"

I stood up and wouldn't allow my tears to fall. Danny didn't deserve to see me cry anymore. He didn't deserve to see he got to me.

"I'm fucking miserable, but I would never cheat on you, Danny!"

"I'm sorry, okay? Look, no more..." he grabbed my arms. "I love you, Cam and I love our baby. We finally have our family. Don't ruin it," he tried to kiss me and I smacked him away.

"You ruined it, asshole!" I yelled before pacing. "You love me?" I snickered. "What's to love? Anastasia isn't gaining any baby weight and she has the boobs you wanted me to get," I sniffled.

"Cami, I was joking about the boob job!" He huffed.

"Right. I looked the other way when you flirted with other girls because we're both natural flirts, but I can't look the other way now."

Danny stared at me, "Why not? I look the other way every time you stare at Jordan."

I shook my head, "We both love Jordan, don't you throw him in my face."

"I don't love him the way you do, that's for sure," Danny said.

"Oh, so you want to turn this into your jealousy over Jordan?" I asked. "Maybe you should have been a loyal husband like he is! I would never make a move on Jordan because I love him and Haley together and I love you!" I smacked his arm. "I want you out of here."

"Cami, don't throw us away," he said, grabbing onto my shirt.

I pushed his hands away.

"I didn't throw us away. You did."

"We should never have let us go on this long," Danny sighed.

I looked back at him. It hurt to hear that, but he was so right.

CHAPTER FOUR

The knocking on the door startled me awake. I panicked, looking around the room for my baby. I looked down and he was asleep in my arms. I kissed his forehead, got out of bed, and placed him in his crib. My cell phone began ringing. I picked it up off the nightstand. I looked at the screen to see it was Jordan.

"Hey," I answered, my voice sounding gruff.

"I'm at the door. I brought lunch," he said.

"Give me a few minutes."

Last week, it was Haley that showed up. I could tell they were worried about me. I couldn't blame them. My entire pregnancy was spent arguing with Danny. When I wasn't arguing with him, I was fighting off paparazzi trying to get photos of Danny DeSano's estranged pregnant wife AKA me.

I didn't sleep well during my pregnancy either, since I constantly had nightmares of miscarriages. I gave birth three weeks early and to my relief, Ben came out healthy and beautiful. I have been a ball of emotion since. I had a serious case of postpartum depression, or maybe it was just plain old depression. On top of that, I was unable to breastfeed like I had wanted due to a low milk supply that was most likely induced by stress.

I walked into the bathroom and I almost jumped at the sight of my reflection in the mirror. I had bags under my eyes. My skin was broken out and my hair was a mess. I pulled my thick, dark brown mane back into a ponytail, and brushed my teeth. I looked down at my leftover pregnancy belly and I wanted to cry. I stopped feeling attractive before my pregnancy, thanks to the insecurities being married to Danny gave me, but now, for the first time in my life, I felt downright ugly.

I finally opened the door for Jordan and forced a smile at him. He didn't seem fazed by the phony gesture as he kissed my cheek and walked inside.

"Where's little Benvenuto?"

"Sleeping."

Okay, so I named my son Benvenuto. Benvenuto Gian DeSano. I don't know how I became a typical Italian-American who is so proud of her heritage to name her son something so overly ethnic, but I did! Benvenuto means "welcome" in Italian and it is something people name their child if they had a hard time conceiving. I liked the special meaning behind his name. I wanted Ben to go through life knowing how much he was wanted, in spite of the circumstances.

Aside from being true to mine and Danny's Italian roots, we were being typical celebrities by naming our kid something different. I just hoped our little Ben didn't hate us some day.

Jordan told me to sit at the table as he grabbed what he needed from the kitchen. Normally, I would be anal about people going through my cabinets, but I just let him. I didn't have the energy to argue. Who would have ever thought that me, Cami Woods, wouldn't want to argue? Jordan sat down across from me and placed a sandwich in front of me. Turkey and Swiss with lettuce, tomato and honey mustard. I had to smile at that.

He remembered what I liked. Of course, I knew things like that about him and the rest of the guys, too. When you toured together as much as we did, you knew details like favorite sandwiches. I knew that Sebastian liked hot sauce and cherry peppers on everything. Darren couldn't handle spicy food. Jordan loved roast beef, only if it was rare. He also had an unhealthy obsession with peanut butter and was allergic to bananas. As for Danny, I knew too much on what he liked and disliked. I was good at remembering details. I really wish I could forget the particulars on him.

"Thank you," I smiled at Jordan as he took a bite of his roast beef sandwich.

"Don't mention it," he said, though it was muffled by the food in his mouth.

We didn't speak much while we ate. I devoured my sandwich, realizing I hadn't eaten since yesterday afternoon. Jordan smiled at me as he wiped his mouth and I couldn't help but smile back.

"So are you excited to see how the summer tour is going to sell?" I asked.

He shook his head, "You're always thinking about business."

"It's all I have besides Ben," I shrugged.

"Cami, don't say that. You still have Haley and me."

"I was worried you'd take Danny's side."

"Come on," Jordan swatted his hand through the air. "He's my best friend. I love him, but I don't approve of what he did. I am not going to stop being his friend and I'm not going to stop being yours, either."

I smiled.

"Besides, we're in this thing together. We're family. You and Danny are still family regardless..."

I rolled my eyes.

"He is not my family, Jordan."

"You have a son to think about. Do you want Ben to grow up knowing you hate his father?"

"Ugh," I huffed. "Why couldn't Danny just move somewhere else and send a card to Ben twice a year?"

Jordan gave me a look.

"Is that really what you want?"

I stared at him. That would be more than what my father did for me. I never even got cards. I should be grateful Danny wants to be such a huge part of Ben's life, but it hurt seeing him. It felt like Ben was all I had now and I didn't want to share him with my cheating soon-to-be-ex-husband.

"Look Cam, I know it's hard. Take all the time in the world off to be with Ben, to mend your heart..."

I looked at him coldly. I didn't want to admit my heart was broken, especially not to Jordan—the first man to ever break my heart. I hated being weak. I hated the look of pity on Jordan and Haley's faces. Even Danny looked at me like that from time to time—when he actually felt remorse.

Suddenly, I wondered if Jordan was trying to fire me. Was this his sweet way of doing it? I narrowed my eyes at him.

"Colin can take care of everything."

Colin was Tortured's tour manager. He worked for me. Still, when it came to Tortured, I was hands on with them more than any of the other acts at Out of the Woods Entertainment, my company.

"Oh, I see...so you're firing me?"

Jordan rolled his eyes and laughed.

"I am not firing you. As your friend, I'm ordering you to take time off."

"And as *your* friend, I'm warning you to not tell me what to do. It's for your own safety," I smirked, standing up and grabbing our garbage.

I took it into the kitchen and Jordan followed me as I tossed it in the trash.

"Look, I'm watching out for you and for the band. You need time to be with Ben. When Haley had Aylin, she decided she wanted a home business so she could be with her," Jordan explained.

Oh great, so now I'm a terrible mother for wanting to go back to work!

"Jordan, I still have a business to run. I'm not abandoning Ben," I snorted.

"I know. Maybe you need time away from working with Danny, too."

Jordan was being careful with his words and I had to laugh.

"Come on, it's been rough. Band meetings are like presidential debates only worse," he explained. "You and Danny just argue—and sometimes I worry that your resentment toward him is going to overflow to the rest of us..."

I rolled my eyes, "I'm not going to destroy Tortured! I would never do that to you or the other guys."

"Good," Jordan smiled.

"I just might suggest a new drummer," I tilted my head to the side and shrugged my shoulders.

"Cami..."

"Kidding. Do you think I want the father of my child to be a washed up rock star? He just better stop being the bad boy of Tortured. He's a dad now."

Jordan rubbed my back and his beautiful green eyes stared into mine.

"And you're a mom. Set a good example for your son and play nice."

I watched his lips as he spoke. God, he was incredibly gorgeous. How did Haley get so freaking lucky? If I cared nothing for her, I might be tempted to make a move. I would really lose everything then. For one, Jordan would never be stupid enough to allow anything to happen between us. Secondly, he would never mess with his best friend's wife. Thirdly, I wouldn't want to destroy a family I cared so much about. Having my home just ripped to shreds by an affair, I wouldn't put anyone through that—least of all Haley and Aylin. Nope, I'll just envy what the Walshes have and live vicariously through Haley.

"I'll be fine," I smiled at him. "Sure, I'm a mess now."

Jordan laughed, "You're not a mess."

"I'm a mess. I know you and Haley are worried. I'm too proud to let a man ruin me," I teased.

"Yes, you are," Jordan kissed my cheek.

Just then, Ben began to cry.

"My Godson," Jordan said with a gasp.

I smiled and patted his arm before going into my bedroom to retrieve Ben. My son was looking up at me with those crystal blue eyes of his. They were the lightest blue eyes I had ever seen on a baby—they were the same color as mine. I picked Ben up and brought him out to Jordan, who reached for him immediately.

I chuckled as Jordan gushed over my son. Standing there, watching Jordan hold my baby boy, I began to weep. I walked away quickly, not wanting Jordan to see. It was hard to explain why I was crying really. It was largely due to hormones, but underneath that guise, my tears had to do with the fact that I wish Jordan Walsh was the father of Ben. I know that's an awful thing to feel. I couldn't help it. The admiration and love I had for Jordan as a person, a husband and a father was so great sometimes that it was hard for any man to compare—especially Danny. I'm sure that was partly why I couldn't make him happy.

The next day, I was just finishing giving Ben a bath when there was a knock at the door. I groaned. There were several people on mine and Danny's list to be allowed up to our apartment automatically. Of course, that list was under the pretense that we would be expecting said people. I will have to destroy that list since no one calls before showing up at my door anymore. I hate drop-in visitors, especially now that I just wanted to be alone with my son and my depression.

I wrapped Ben up in a towel and kissed his cheeks before placing him on my shoulder. He was developing a pattern of falling asleep after a bath. It was intriguing learning his schedule and his little personality. I walked to the door, hoping I didn't look like hell—I could use a shower myself. I looked through the peephole and I saw three people, but I could only make out Haley's wavy blonde hair. I wasn't surprised it was her, and was even happy to see her, but I wasn't in the mood for any other visitors.

I opened the door and Haley dropped whatever bags she was holding and grabbed Ben out of my arms. I tightened my robe and was relieved to see Aylin, Haley and Jordan's daughter, opening her arms to me. I hugged her.

"How come you're not in school?"

"Aunt Cam, it's Saturday," Aylin laughed.

She is such a pretty girl. She has the best features from both her parents. At almost sixteen, she has a maturity not many girls her age have. She is lighthearted and witty, like her father, and she is thoughtful and intuitive like her mother. Just don't pronounce Aylin's name wrong. It's "A-lin" not "Eye-lin". She's pretty touchy about it.

My third visitor was the only one I wanted to slam the door on—the curly haired Tasha stood in my doorway with a look of pity on her painted face.

"Hey Cami, I brought a present for Ben," she said, holding out a gift bag.

I sighed, "Don't look at me like that Tasha."

"Like what?" she laughed, walking inside.

I shut the door behind her. Haley and Aylin were busy with Ben.

"Like you feel sorry for me."

Tasha rolled her eyes, "Well, I do."

"Gee, thanks," I said.

"Cami, I'm trying to be your friend."

"Did Sebastian send you here?"

"Ugh, no. I care about you," she said, shoving my arm. "Even though you hate me for whatever reason."

My jaw clenched. I didn't have a reason to hate Tasha really. I guess I hated her because she was just as feisty—if not feistier—as me.

I shoved Tasha's arm back roughly.

"Fine, come in. It's so nice of you to visit," I forced a smile.

Tasha laughed, "Go shower while we play with Ben. You stink."

I gave her the finger, but decided she was probably right. I headed to the bathroom. I even took my time washing my hair, something I felt I hadn't done since before Ben was born.

As I was walking to the living room, I noticed Aylin staring at the photos in the dining room. She looks at those photos every time she comes over. I walked over and glanced at them with her. I was so used to the décor in my apartment that I never stopped and looked at the photos anymore. The dining room was basically a timeline of my career with Tortured. It was Danny's idea really. I didn't like the idea of tour photos in the dining room, but he somehow won that argument.

Aylin was smiling as she looked at a photo of herself as a baby sitting on Jordan's lap while he strummed a guitar. It was always her favorite photo. I made a mental note to give her a copy—maybe for her Sweet Sixteen. Her eyes moved to a photo of Jordan, Danny and me a few months after I started managing the band.

I was standing in the middle of them. Although you can't tell in the photo, I knew my hand was on Jordan's butt. It's something that always makes me laugh. I sometimes wonder if Jordan remembers that at all. I often wonder if he remembers anything about us when we dated—how I felt, how I looked, how I made him feel.

I shook myself out of these thoughts as I looked at Aylin—the man of my infatuation's child with another woman—a woman who was one of my only friends.

"Maybe you and Uncle D. will get back together," she said with a sympathetic smile.

Apparently all Aylin saw when she looked at the picture of me in love with her father was that I was probably in love with her uncle from day one.

I slung an arm around Aylin's shoulders.

"I don't think that's going to happen, A."

Aylin looked at me with sad eyes and she hugged me. I squeezed her in my arms. I know it was hard for her to understand how something that's been one way her entire life could change. As a teenager, you believe everything will last forever. That includes school, boy bands, hard times and love, especially love.

Until now, Aylin didn't have anything to dispel that. Her parents were more in love than anyone I knew. I wouldn't be surprised if the end of my marriage made her worry that someday it could happen to her parents as well. Aylin didn't know the disastrous rollercoaster that was my marriage. To her, Danny and I were a second set of parents—aside from Andrew.

Although Andrew was probably more of an older brother than an uncle. He spoiled Aylin rotten and let her get away with murder. He snuck her out of the house when she was twelve to go late night bowling with the Yankees on a school night. No one would have known, either, except for the fact that an autographed bowling pin hit the floor as soon as Aylin snuck back into the apartment. The pin hitting the hardwood floor was enough to have Jordan and Haley jumping out of bed at four-am, which was two-hours before Aylin had to be up for school.

It was impossible for Jordan to stay angry at Aylin, though—or his little brother. They were both pretty charming in their own right.

Aylin pulled out of the hug and smiled.

"You can bring a date to my sweet sixteen, Aunt Cam," she said.

I laughed, "Thanks. I think I'm a long way off from dating."

I couldn't even think of dating. Aside from not wanting to leave the apartment, I simply no longer saw myself as someone attractive. I had a belly that probably wouldn't go away. My face looked puffy; my skin splotchy and broken out. My boobs, now a C-cup like I always wanted, felt heavy and gross. I just felt plain, old disgusting. I am a washed up middle-aged woman raising a baby, whose husband left her for a supermodel. What guy my age—or any age—will want me now?

"Well, Uncle Danny is stupid. I love him, but he's a jerk for being with that model. She's not even that pretty," Aylin rolled her eyes.

I smiled, "I love you, A."

Later that night, Danny came over. He said he wanted to see Ben, but also wanted to talk to me. I was not looking forward to whatever it was he wanted to talk to me about. What made things worse was he was wearing blue—my favorite color on him. He looked good, damn him, and happy, screw him!

"How ya doin', Cam?" he asked me, sitting down next to me with Ben in his arms.

Those blue eyes of his looked so deep. His lips looked incredibly sexy. I don't know if it's because my hormones are out of whack or that I was just truly horny...or maybe that I actually missed my husband—a man I spent most of my adult years with, but I wanted to beg Danny to come back suddenly. I hated myself for feeling so pathetic and needy.

"Oh, I'm doing great," I forced a smile. "It's surprising, huh? Considering I get no sleep and I haven't left the apartment in almost three weeks."

Danny reached over and put his hand on my knee.

"Why don't you let me take Ben for a few days?"

I pushed his hand off my knee.

"You're not taking my son away from me."

"Cami, it's just for a few days. Don't be selfish and keep him to yourself."

I scoffed, "Selfish? I'm selfish? I don't want you taking *my* son over to your slut's place for you two to play house together!" I screamed, which caused Ben to start fussing.

I immediately grabbed Ben away from Danny and he stood up.

"This isn't healthy for our son."

"You bringing him around your mistress? No, it's not."

"I meant us fighting," Danny sighed. "I don't want to fight."

I looked at him and saw that vulnerability on his face that I fell in love with so many years ago.

"Neither do I," I wiped away a tear, hoping he didn't see it.

"Obviously you're not ready for me to take Ben overnight. That's fine," he nodded, coming closer.

He reached his hands out and I reluctantly placed Ben back in his arms.

"I'm getting my own place," Danny explained. "I won't bring Ben around Ana until you're ready for me to."

Ana? Now, it's Ana? Great, they're already going by nicknames. I wonder what the Greek nympho calls Danny. Probably something sickening like her little baklava. I never had a problem with Greeks or their cuisine—in fact, feta is my favorite kind of cheese. Now, I just don't think I can bring myself to be associated with anything from their culture. The Greeks have Anastasia Milos to solely thank for this.

"Danny, I will never be ready for that woman to be around my son."

"Our son," he corrected.

"Did you carry him for nine months? No. You were screwing that bitch while I was hanging onto us."

He let out an aggravated groan.

"Cami, we both knew it was over!"

"Did we? Because I sure didn't until a tabloid told me!"

"Okay, we are not going through this again. There is more we need to talk about."

Of course he doesn't want to have this conversation again. He knows he is wrong. Like a typical man, he expects me to just forgive and forget. I will never forget. Never. As far as forgiving, I don't think I can do that, either. I know I'm supposed to be civil for Ben's sake, but how am I going to pretend I like his father when I can't stand him anymore?

"What do we have to talk about?" I rolled my eyes as Danny smiled down at Ben, who was making cooing noises at him.

Why couldn't my son instantly dislike his father and only want me?

"The band."

I put my hands on my hips.

"Jordan already spoke to me."

"Cami, I know you."

"Yeah?" I raised an eyebrow.

"I know you're going to throw yourself back into work. You're going to force yourself to be around me and I know you can't stand me right now."

Danny was right—he did know me.

"So?"

"It's not good for you."

"Don't tell me what's not good for me," I huffed, pushing my hair away from my face. "I love work."

"You've been working since you were a kid. You need a break. I already talked to your team."

"You did what?!?" I yelled.

"Everyone agrees you need time off. The band, the staff, your other clients."

"You contacted my other clients?" I gasped.

"Your work has been divided. We want you to take an extra month or so off."

"Fuck you!" I yelled.

I would have probably shoved him if he wasn't holding Ben.

"How dare you tell me what to do at my job! How dare anyone tell me what to do with my company!"

"Calm down," Danny sighed. "You know you've been kind of bitchy at work lately..."

Lately? I haven't even been at work for a month and a half.

"I was hormonal the last time I was at work! And my husband and his concubine were plastered all over the tabloids! I think I had reason to be a raging bitch, don't you?"

Danny shut his eyes and looked at me with that vulnerability once more.

"I'm sorry," he mumbled.

I rolled my eyes.

"I just don't want you to take out your feelings on everyone and eventually ruin your standing in the industry. There were already several instances where the other managers had to smooth things over for you."

I tried to interrupt, but Danny continued.

"Some people think you're on the verge of a nervous breakdown," he said hesitantly.

"What!?!" I screamed, which caused Ben to start crying.

Danny cradled him over his shoulder, trying to quiet him.

"Can you calm down? You're upsetting Ben."

I scowled at him. I love how this man comes in and acts like I'm the crazy lunatic who can't handle anything—like my son or my job—when he couldn't even handle being faithful to his wife!

"Maybe I can take him off your hands tomorrow for a few hours," Danny suggested.

"Alone?" I scoffed.

Danny gave me a dirty look.

"Yes, alone. I am his father, Cami."

I dropped my hands from my hips, trying to remember the fact that I should want my son to grow close to his father.

"He's just so little still," I said, my voice sounding so small. "I haven't been away from him yet."

Danny smiled softly.

"You're great with him," he said, walking over and kissing my forehead.

The gesture, that I once found incredibly endearing, conflicted with my emotions. Part of me still found it sweet while another part of me wanted to head butt his lips off me.

"It'll be good for you to have a break, though. It's healthy to have some time to yourself."

I looked into Danny's eyes and it became clear to me that it wasn't everyone who thought I was on the verge of a nervous breakdown. It was Danny who thought it. I closed my eyes, willing myself not to cry and not to get angry. Sadness and anger seemed to be the only emotions I could express lately.

I reached out and grabbed Benvenuto from Danny.

"It's time for him to be fed," I said sternly.

Danny sighed, "Cami, please. I only get a couple hours with him a day. Do you think this is how I pictured fatherhood?"

I laughed at him.

"Do you think I pictured being a single mother?"

His lips curled angrily.

"You are not a single mother! I am here!"

Ben started crying and I tried quieting him. I was about to walk into the kitchen to prepare Ben's bottle when Danny called out.

"I'll be by to pick him up at noon. If you could have some bottles prepared, that would be great. I'll bring him back to you at five."

I looked over my shoulder and saw he wasn't going to budge.

"Fine," I choked out before he left the apartment.

As soon as he shut the door, tears ran down my face. I looked down at Ben and he was about to cry some more. Five hours without my son tomorrow. Five hours without the only thing keeping me alive. Five hours of worrying about him. Five hours of wondering if Danny introduced our son to Anastasia. Five hours of nothing but the dark depression I have fallen into.

CHAPTER FIVE

I looked myself over in the mirror. No matter how much make-up I caked on or hairspray I put in my hair, I still looked distressed. I even had on my most flattering black dress, but it just made me look pale—which for me was still kind of tan, but not my normal hue. I pulled my hair back into a ponytail and threw on a baby blue cardigan, hoping to make my eyes pop like they normally did when I wore blue, or anything really. Lately, though, the crystal effect of my eyes has dulled significantly. I was sure of it. New mothers are supposed to glow, not fade.

Danny had taken Ben, as planned, and I fought every urge to stay in bed. I knew I would just stare at the clock until Ben returned. I decided to stop by work and see what the situation really was like there.

The doorman hailed a taxi and I noticed the weather had gotten significantly colder. The last time I had been outside, it had been rainy, but not cold yet. Fall weather in New York could be unpredictable.

As I rode in the taxi toward Midtown, it was obvious winter was almost here. Trees were looking more and more barren. Many people walked with heavy coats on along with gloves and scarves. I was underdressed. I just had on a jacket that was more appropriate for September than November. For some reason, the cold air felt good, though. It made me feel like I could breathe again.

When I walked into the building that held the Out of the Woods Entertainment offices, I felt as if it had been a lifetime since I had been there. I never took days off. Ever. Even on my wedding day, I still checked e-mails on the limo ride to the church and had a conference call that morning while my hair was being done.

I didn't know how to relax or take time off. The past few weeks were torture for me. I had no energy; and no brain power left to work from home as much as I wanted to. Between the depression, the exhaustion and how completely enamored I was over having a baby, I couldn't work. Apparently, no one had wanted me to and maybe that's why it was so easy for me not to—I don't remember seeing any urgent e-mails or getting any phone calls now that I thought of it. I think I was being blacklisted from my own company!

When I got to the fourteenth floor, I marched myself into the office, unzipping my jacket as I did. Tracy, the main receptionist, stood up in utter surprise. She looked alarmed to see me.

"Cami, what are you doing here?"

"Relax. Just saying hi."

She forced a smile at me.

"How are things here?"

"Oh, just fine," she smiled wider, not quite as forced.

"Is Colin in his office?" I asked.

Colin Houlihan is an import from Dublin, whom I hired ten years ago, and I haven't regretted it so far. He was sharp, a great negotiator and took care of my clients while on the road—especially Tortured, who were always my first priority and everyone knew it.

"Uh," Tracy said uneasily. "No..."

"I'll find him," I waved her off; knowing Tracy wasn't exactly on top of things.

She spent more time talking on the phone to her boyfriend and getting star struck any time Jordan or Rad Trick walked into the office. Rad Trick is our newest success story. He's a pop-rocker—which translates to wannabe rocker—who reached number one on Billboard two months ago, and who did not use a stage name. What mother would name her son Rad? Oh wait, I named my son Benvenuto. Who am I to talk?

I walked further into the office, plastering a smile on. I passed by one assistant's desk, who almost choked on her lunch.

"Hey Cami," she smiled, more forced than Tracy. "How are you doing? Congratulations on the baby. Did you get the balloons we sent?"

"Fine. Thanks and yes, they're deflated now," I said, not slowing down as I walked and talked.

I waved to a few other people in the main office before heading to the managers' offices. I knocked on Colin's door first and got no answer. I opened the door and he wasn't in there. I then knocked on Lisa Ann's door, a blonde from Georgia, who seemed as sweet as a peach, but when it came down to business—she gave me a run for my money. She was a tough cookie. When she yelled out to come in, I opened the door.

"Hey. Meeting," I nodded my head toward my office.

"Oh hey Cami," Lisa Ann boomed, jumping up as if she were going to give me a hug, but I just walked onto J.J. Fowler's door.

J.J. was my least favorite manager that worked for me. He was also the youngest and newest. At twenty-five, J.J. was a wisecracking, smug, little jerk that wanted the world handed to him on a silver platter. I threatened to fire him three times in the past six-months. He mostly handled Rad Trick and traveled with him. Rad had such a bromance with J.J. that I felt I would lose him as a client if I fired the punk. In fact, they were both punks that hit on anything with a skirt, and got on my every last nerve.

"Cami Woods!" J.J. slung an arm around me. "How's the sexy new mama doing?"

He may have been trying to make me feel good, but even if the compliment was genuine, which it wasn't since I noticed him glance at my leftover belly, any attempt at flattery from J.J. was disgusting.

"Where's Colin?" I asked, looking between Lisa Ann and J.J. who were following behind me.

"He should be around somewhere, hun," Lisa Ann said. "Why didn't you bring little Ben with you? We want to meet him."

"He's with Danny," I explained, not looking behind me as I headed toward my office.

Normally, I was a little bit more for small talk with Lisa Ann, but I usually kept things about business. I never wanted things to turn personal in business, ironically. Maybe I should have thought about that before marrying one of my clients! Never again will I make that mistake. No more dating clients for me. Business is strictly business. I know everyone was scared of me, and maybe even hated me, but that's kind of what I wanted. Business is about getting a job done, not about making friends. I pay them well enough. They don't have to like me.

I opened the door to my office surprised to see Colin Houlihan sitting in my chair, with his feet on my desk and speaking on my phone! When he saw me, he plastered on the biggest smile and waved me in, as if he were giving me permission to enter!

"Joe, I'll call you back. We'll finalize the details for the Midwest next week," Colin said in his cute Irish accent that almost made me forget I was about to blow fire.

"Cami!" Colin stood up with his arms in the air. "How's motherhood treating you, love?"

I scowled and folded my arms.

"Why are you in my office, Houlihan?"

"Well, I just thought...you know I always loved the view of the city in your office. I figured you wouldn't mind since you're not using it," he flashed a bright smile.

"I'm calling a meeting. Now," I demanded before shutting the door and looking at my team.

Lisa Ann looked slightly concerned while J.J. looked like I was wasting his time. In true Colin-fashion, he looked calm and collected. Nothing ever seemed to shake this guy. He handled himself well in every situation and everyone loved him. I just couldn't dislike him for outshining me personality-wise like I had wanted to.

"Is everything okay?" Lisa Ann asked.

I ignored her question and cut to the chase. Crossing my arms, I scanned the three faces before me as I spoke.

"My soon-to-be ex-husband informed me you all had a little meeting about me."

J.J. rolled his eyes, "Look, you and Danny need to leave us out of your personal life."

His Long Island accent was thick; worse than my Brooklyn one I tried to get rid of over the years.

"I am trying, J.J. Danny should not be calling a meeting to discuss your boss," I huffed. "This company is none of his business."

"Actually Cami, I called the meeting," Colin raised his hand and flashed a sheepish smile.

"You called a meeting to talk about me without me?"

"The staff has been concerned about the amount of stress you're under with everything going on," Colin said in a pitying tone.

"I can handle myself, Colin!"

"Listen, you've been a bitch to everyone!" He yelled back.

I should have been offended, but being a bitch was sort of my thing.

"What's so new about that?" I asked.

J.J. and Lisa Ann snickered.

Colin sighed, "You know it's worse than usual. Besides your attitude, you haven't taken a real vacation practically ever."

"I'm your boss. No one is my boss. You can't bully me out of my own company."

"No, we can't," Colin shrugged.

I smiled, knowing they would have to back down.

"But I'm prepared to quit if you don't take time off. And so is Lisa Ann and J.J., right guys?"

I scowled at Colin. He was bluffing. He wouldn't quit. I then looked at Lisa Ann and J.J. who looked terrified as they nodded. They were definitely bluffing.

"Right," I laughed. "You're not going anywhere."

I walked past him and over to my desk.

"Mega Music Management offered me a sweet deal, Cami," Colin spoke up.

I turned and stared at him. The same company I started my career in was trying to steal my best employee?

"You're lying."

"I can start as early as next week. I don't want to leave, but I won't work in an environment with a dictator any longer. And you know if I leave, it's only a matter of time everyone else will, too."

I stared at Colin, no longer finding his accent appealing as it spoke to me with a silver tongue. The man was backing me into a corner and I hated not being in control.

"Lisa Ann, J.J., please leave," I said, still staring at Colin.

Once the other two managers left, I sat down at my desk.

"Why are you doing this to me?" I asked.

Colin pressed his palms on my desk.

"I am not trying to do anything. As hard as it is to believe, I care about this company and I care about you," he sighed. "You may not think we're friends, but I think of you as family.

I think of all the guys in Tortured as family and we're all concerned about you. I know Danny hurt you, but he is worried about you. He's worried about your son."

I bit my bottom lip to keep myself from having an emotional outburst.

"I'm a good mother, Colin."

"I know. We want to keep it that way. We want to give you more time with him and for you to mourn your marriage properly."

Mourn my marriage? I wanted to punch Colin. I wanted to punch Danny. Hell, I think I would knockout anyone I could get my hands on at this point. I wasn't in mourning. Or maybe I was, but I wanted to appear strong like I always did. Everything that was going on was just proof to me that I'm not strong. My weakness is painfully obvious to everyone around me that they're backing me into a corner at work!

"You win," I said, defeated.

"It's not about winning," Colin said as he walked around the desk and put his hand on my shoulder.

I shrugged him off and stood up.

"You better take care of things, Colin," I smacked his chest.

"I promise, love."

He pulled me into a hug and I pulled away immediately. I was on the verge of tears and I had to get out of there as quickly as possible. I didn't make contact with anyone as I rushed out of the office with my head down. I heard some people throwing out goodbyes or asking me things, but I ignored everyone.

When I stepped outside, I was breathing heavy. I had all this pent up energy that I wanted to use toward hitting someone, preferably Danny, but I wouldn't see him for a few more hours. I called Haley, but it went straight to voicemail. She was probably in the middle of a photo shoot. I bet no one that worked for her would force her into time off she didn't want. Then again, Haley would never be in my situation. She would never be on the verge of a divorce and if she was, she would never take it out on her employees.

I decided if I couldn't punch anyone and I had no one to talk to, I would walk off my frustrations. I kept my hands tucked away inside my pockets since they were going numb from the cold. At first, I took a walk through Bryant Park, but then I found myself walking past Times Square. Before I knew it, I was at 59th Street. At that point, I realized I should just walk home. I trekked over thirty blocks, which was the most movement I had done in months.

As I took the elevator up to my apartment, my phone rang. I figured it was Haley, but it was a 954 area code. I guessed it was a business call and thought to let it go to voicemail. I should direct them to Colin instead. If he wanted me to take a hiatus, along with my so-called favorite clients, Tortured, then Colin better be prepared to take on the entire workload. Let's see if the Irish schmuck can handle that!

I answered the phone with a professional greeting, trying to sound chipper and not bitter. I was never any good at faking it. Danny can attest to that, especially in recent years.

"Hey girl."

It took me a moment, but I recognized the cocky voice of Matt Porter. It had been a while since we spoke. We would run into each other sometimes at events, but our encounters were always brief and made awkward if Danny was around. He isn't very good at hiding jealousy—neither am I, but I wound up getting over my jealousy enough to befriend Haley. I never even dated Matt and Danny didn't want me to be his friend.

"Matt," I gasped, partly from being tired and cold from the walk, and partly because I was truly happy and surprised to hear from him.

"How are you, babe?"

"Oh wonderful," I laughed.

"I can't believe that douche of a husband left you for my ex-bitch of a girlfriend."

The way Matt Porter spoke was as if we were stupid teenagers. It wasn't as frivolous as that. Danny was—I mean still is—my husband! We created life together! I couldn't expect Matt Porter to understand that, though. He was a serial dater. A player. He was the only member of Sound Wave still single.

I stepped off the elevator and dug my key out of my purse.

"He's an idiot, Cam. Anastasia is nothing but a rich-class skank. You are incredible and should have married me instead," he cackled.

I laughed, "Right. You wouldn't have broken my heart."

I unlocked the door and entered my apartment. It was weird coming home to an empty apartment. I never liked the feeling. It reminded me of how alone I felt after my mother passed away.

"I would never," Matt chuckled in my ear. "How's the kid doing?"

"Ben's a good baby. I'm exhausted, but I love him. He's the only thing keeping me going."

"And work?"

"I've been laid off for a few months."

"Huh? It's your company," Matt said confused.

"Well, my employees and some of my clients, mainly my husband's band, decided I could use a break to get my shit together."

"Wow. And you're standing for this?"

Matt was just as surprised as I am for taking it. My son and work were all I had, though. If I lost all my employees and my clients, what would I have? What if I did lose my mind from this depression I'm in and Danny took Ben away from me?

"For now I am. I've been working since I was twelve and I think it's time I took some time for myself," I explained.

"Good girl. You should come to Tampa and visit me."

"Tampa? I thought you were living in L.A."

"I gave up on that whole Hollywood thing years ago. I have a house in Tampa."

"Good. Florida is where you boy band guys belong," I teased.

"Shut up," he laughed. "So are you going to visit?"

"Sure."

"When?" he asked.

"Uh, I have a kid now. I don't know," I said, thinking his offer was just a nice gesture that would never actually come to fruition.

"I have plenty of room. Bring your son along. Stay for a month if you want to. I miss you, girl, and I'd be happy to help you take a well-deserved vacation."

I plopped down on the couch and was silent for a moment. If I didn't know better, I would think someone let Matt in on my depression, but who would do that? Danny would never and no one else really knew him. Then again, I wouldn't be surprised if Jordan didn't somehow have contact with Matt.

"Did someone put you up to this?" I asked with a sigh.

"No! Look, I miss my friend. When I saw all the crap in the tabloids about Danny cheating on you and you just having a baby, I just figured you could use an old friend."

Matt was so right. I needed a friend, but to go to Florida for a month with my son? How would that work? Danny would never let me take Ben to Florida.

"Danny won't allow me to take Ben and I won't leave him..."

"Well, Danny will be traveling at some point. He won't be able to see Ben everyday anyway. Just think about it."

I did think about it for the rest of the afternoon. Sunny Florida sounded nice while the weather was turning frigid in New York. Getting away from my apartment was definitely something I could use. I was sick of staring at the photos of Danny and me, or of the ones with Jordan in them, reminding me how I lost him. I was definitely sick of sleeping in the bed where Ben was conceived—the bed Danny and I shared. I definitely missed making love—not just sex, but the emotional feeling to go along with it. Danny and I hadn't had that in a few years. Besides all of that, it would be nice to reconnect with Matt again. It makes me mad when I think about all the years I lost with him because of my stupid, jealous, cheating husband. It makes me sick.

Danny brought Ben back around dinnertime. To my dismay, he looked perfectly pulled together. His clothes were neat—no noticeable spit-up stains. He didn't seem frazzled in the least and that just angered me.

"How'd it go?" I asked, grabbing Ben from him and kissing his cheeks as if I hadn't seen him in months.

"Great. He started to fuss at first, but he got used to me," Danny said, all smiles, as if I would be happy hearing that my son didn't need to rely solely on me.

I didn't bother to respond.

"How was your day?"

"Well, I went into work," I sighed, placing Ben in his bouncy seat.

"Cami," Danny sighed.

I glared at him.

"You can't tell me what to do."

He looked frustrated at that.

"I'm not trying to tell you what to do, but I still care about you."

I rolled my eyes and went to walk away, but he put his hands on my shoulders, keeping me in place.

"I don't want you to burn yourself out. I know you're in a funk and..."

"I'm in a funk because of you," I said hatefully. "I'll be fine though. Don't you worry," I said pushing him away from me.

It just hurt more that Danny felt sorry for me and knew how much pain I was in. I wanted to be strong enough to at least fool him into thinking I could move on and be happy. Maybe Florida would be a good idea after all. After the holidays, Tortured would be traveling a bunch. I could go to Florida then. Danny would think I was having some spring fling with Matt Porter. He would flip! The more I thought about Matt's offer, the more appeal it had. Matt seemed more appealing, too. He had aged well and although I never felt any real attraction to him in the past, I found myself wondering if that could change now.

"Well, I guess I'll go," I heard Danny say as I busied myself with taking bottles out of the diaper bag.

"Danny?" I called out to him.

"Yeah?" he turned as he opened the door.

"When you start the tour, I'm going to take a vacation in Florida with Ben."

He smiled, "That'll be good for you. If you wanted to go by yourself, I'm sure my mom would be happy to watch Ben."

"Well, I plan to be gone for a few weeks. I don't want to be away from Ben that long."

"I know how you feel," he nodded. "I think it's a great idea."

"I wasn't asking your permission. Just letting you know," I shrugged.

Danny laughed and walked over to me. He leaned down and kissed the top of my head.

"I will always care about you," he said.

I wanted to spit in his face. I wanted to cuss him out. At the same time, I wanted to kiss him—just once more. I didn't though. I stared at him, once again on this stupid day, trying not to cry.

As soon as Danny left the apartment, I did cry. I grabbed a throw pillow and tossed it across the room before crumbling to the floor. I hated myself for crying and for still wanting Danny in some way. I hated myself for feeling pain, anger, love, hate, nothing and everything.

CHAPTER SIX

The holidays had come and gone. Haley and Jordan went up to Vermont to spend Christmas and New Year's with her family. Danny and I fought a ton about the plans for Ben for the holidays. He wanted me to come over to his mother's house for dinner on Christmas Eve. I really didn't want to, however, I went anyway for everyone else's sake but my own.

New Year's Eve, I decided to sleep through, even though I was invited to Sebastian's party and numerous industry parties. I didn't want to risk running into Danny and Anastasia, and who was I going to get to sit for Ben anyway?

I spent most of January planning to be away for a month in February as well as baby proofing the apartment. It felt like Ben was growing up so fast! I know he was only four-months-old, but he was starting to nap less and was becoming more alert. I even decided to redecorate a bit. While I would be away in Tampa, the kitchen was going to be expanded, and the bathroom redone with a spa-like tub, which included bubble jets!

Danny's game room slash gym was also being redone. I was putting in a wet bar and taking out the gym equipment. We had a gym facility in the building, if I needed to work out, which I was trying to do at least three times a week. I felt the need to renovate something in my life. My body and my apartment seemed like a good place to start!

The night before Tortured left for the European leg of their tour, there was a kick-off party at our old hangout, Carney's Pub. I wasn't going to go, but Haley enlisted Aylin to babysit Ben. As reliable as Aylin is, it kind of made me nervous having a teenager sit for my baby since I'm still technically a new mother who hasn't been away from him much. But Haley and Jordan insisted I go to the party. Aylin wasn't even sixteen yet and Ben just turned four-months-old. I was pretty protective and Haley understood, but assured me Aylin could handle it. Aylin loved kids. She always wanted a younger sibling, but with the complications Haley had while pregnant, it wasn't safe for her to have any more children.

I was surprised I was able to fit into one of my pre-pregnancy dresses. I didn't even look bad in it. Even though I was exercising more, I had given up hope I would ever look good again. I mostly exercised to help combat depression. Plus, I wanted to have more energy for Ben when he was old enough to crawl and walk. I guess the long walks with Ben, the Zumba DVDs I did, and swimming laps in the building's pool paid off in assisting me back into a size six.

After Aylin arrived, I gave her a laundry list of information and made sure she had my cell phone number before leaving. As soon as I got to Carney's, a million people greeted me. Someone shoved a glass of wine into my hand. I hadn't had a drink since before I was pregnant.

As soon as I tasted the wine, I realized how much I had missed a glass after a long day or a fight with Danny. As I sipped on the liquid, I wasn't really listening to Rick Rogers, a popular DJ, talk about getting some on-air time with Tortured and Rad Trick.

"So, can you work something out?" Rick asked.

I just smiled, "Well, I am on maternity leave. You'll have to speak with Colin and J.J. about that."

Rick frowned. He spent fifteen minutes schmoozing me for nothing. I have to admit, it's quite liberating to leave responsibilities to someone else. My only responsibility was Benvenuto Gian DeSano—the new love of my life. I decided I was going to put my all into being the best mother I could be. I was not much of a nurturer, but that all changed once I looked at my baby boy.

By the time I found Haley, I had finished my first glass of wine and had obtained another one. Haley gushed how good I looked. I wasn't sure if it was genuine or not. Haley definitely looked gorgeous. No one could deny her that. She had something purple and sparkly on, in true Haley fashion.

She pulled me over to Tasha and Darren's latest girlfriend—Jodi or Joanie, whatever her name was. Tortured were off making their rounds while Colin was berated with requests for Tortured from various press and show promoters.

Idle girl talk was being made and I tried to be a part of it, but really I was wondering if Anastasia Milos was at the party. I finished another glass of wine by the time I saw the six-foot model walk into Carney's.

"There she is," I seethed.

"Cami, easy," Tasha said. "You don't want to make a scene. There are all kinds of press around."

I wonder if Tasha would care about the tabloids if she were in my shoes! Suddenly, all the photographers in the room snapped pictures of Anastasia before Danny made his way over to her. He kissed her, almost for show, but in greeting as well. I felt my chest tighten and I stood up, but felt pretty woozy from the wine. I hadn't eaten dinner, on top of my tolerance being fairly low since I hadn't drank in a long time.

"You okay?" Haley asked.

"Stupid question," I sighed before heading toward the bathroom.

I almost tripped when a blinding flash went off in my face. A photographer with a dumb looking soul patch on his chin took my picture! I smacked his camera away almost causing him to drop it before continuing my way to the bathroom.

I stared at myself in the mirror. I felt so ugly, so alone, and like no one knew how I felt. I just couldn't see the confident, beautiful woman I used to think I was. Next to Anastasia, I was gross. Next to Haley I was even more disgusting. Haley not only glowed all the time, she had the likeability factor going for her. Me on the other hand scared people away or ripped their heads off for no good reason. More people pretended to like me than people who actually did like me.

Suddenly, my uncontrollable emotions hit and I was crying. Just great, like I could afford to be splotchy on top of everything else! The bathroom door opened and Haley walked in.

"Oh Cami," she said going to hug me.

I put my hand up to hold her back.

"I'm fine, Haley," I sniffled, wiping my tears, which just smeared my eye make-up.

"You had to know Anastasia would be here," Haley said softly.

I glared at her, "She shouldn't be here!"

Haley jumped at the volume I raised my voice to.

"Or maybe I shouldn't be here," I said, crying all over again.

She pulled me into that hug she wanted to give me before and I cried on her shoulder. I'm sure Haley wasn't used to seeing me such a mess. The only other time I remember tearing up in front of her and Jordan was after his mother passed away. Between seeing Jordan so broken up and the memories of my own mother's death coming back to me, I couldn't control my tears.

I know the alcohol definitely had something to do with the release I was having in the bathroom, but my breakdown was also a long time coming. Other than Danny, I hadn't cried or discussed how upset I was in front of anyone else.

Haley rubbed my back soothingly. I felt paralyzed there, but my mouth just kept talking. And then, it happened—word vomit.

"I just..." I sniffled. "I don't get why I got Danny and you got Jordan."

Haley stopped rubbing my back.

"What do you mean?" she asked.

"I am so jealous, Haley. Of you. Of what you have. Of *who* you have."

Haley pulled away from me and she didn't even look angry. I would have killed her if she said something like that to me.

"Cami, you have a wonderful life. I know it may suck now, but you have a beautiful baby boy—"

"But I will never have Jordan," I said, tears falling.

Haley giggled, "Cami...you're drunk."

I laughed, "A little bit. Why aren't you slapping me?"

She smiled, "Because I always knew you still loved Jordan in some way."

"And you're okay with that?" I asked, confused.

Haley was so weird!

She shrugged, "I'm not threatened by it. I just think there is someone out there for you who will love you like Jordan loves me. Danny just wasn't that guy."

I nodded, sadly.

"And Jordan isn't that guy, either, in case you are having misguided ideas of being a home wrecker," she smirked, in warning.

I smiled in return.

"I wouldn't do that to either of you."

"Good," Haley nodded. "I can accept that you love my husband as long as you know he's mine."

"I know," I said.

At that moment, knowing how much Jordan loved Haley hurt me just as much as how many years Danny and I tried to make our relationship work. After hanging out in the bathroom a little longer to fix myself, I plastered on the fakest smile ever and headed back to the bar.

Sebastian spotted me and wrapped me into a hug. He pulled me along with him, asking questions about Ben and how I was doing. He stopped when we got to the back table, the one we had always sat at when we went to Carney's. I saw red—literally. Anastasia's red curly hair was the first thing to register. I just couldn't be social with her. I looked at Danny and he immediately stood up and walked over to me.

"I want to introduce you to Anastasia," he said.

"Are you a moron?" I asked.

It was a serious question, too. Danny was always pretty smart. Why the hell would he think I wanted to meet the other woman? I'm sure she didn't want to meet me, either.

"Cami, I'm trying to be civil. You're making it impossible!"

"I don't think introductions are necessary, you cheating bastard," I said, shoving him.

Jordan rushed over.

"Cami, don't do this here."

I glared at Jordan.

"Me? I'm the problem?"

Jordan sighed, "Just don't make a scene."

I rolled my eyes, "Fine. I'm just going home."

"Fine," Danny threw his hands up and walked back to the table.

Anastasia was giving me the evil, slutty eye as Jordan tried to talk me out of leaving. I knew if I stayed, I'd wind up attacking either Anastasia or Danny. It was best I left. Besides, I already missed Ben. I much rather spend some time with him and Aylin.

The next morning, I was awoken by Ben crying. As I fed him a bottle, I thought about my breakdown in the bathroom at Carney's. I couldn't believe I said all those things to Haley. As if I couldn't be any more pathetic, now she knew that I was pining away for her husband. I just needed to stop loving men who didn't love me like I love them. Or maybe I just needed to forget love and just use guys for fun. I never thought like that before. I either had no interest in sex or no interest in sex without love. Maybe it would be good that I'll be around Matt Porter in a few days. He was all about sex and not love. For once, I was willing to give that to him.

An hour later, I found myself arguing with Danny about the night before and then watching him tearfully say goodbye to Ben. That did break my heart despite my excitement to be rid of seeing Danny's face for a while. I hope Florida helps clear my mind. I want to spend time just relaxing, having fun with Ben, and maybe have a few spontaneously provocative nights with Matt.

CHAPTER SEVEN

Upon arriving in Tampa, I was frustrated. Traveling with an infant was not easy. Between carrying my diaper bag, Ben's boppy, my lap top and Ben himself, I was a mess. My hair was falling in my face, I had spit up on my shoulder, and Ben was not a happy traveler. I went into the bathroom to change Ben and call Matt.

I looked at my reflection and sighed. How the hell was Matt going to find me attractive now? I looked like a frumpy mommy not a sexy mama! Granted, I was never one to go out of my way to be sexy. It wasn't until I started making money that I slowly upgraded my wardrobe from t-shirts to dresses and blouses. Even now, I tend to go for more of a simple, comfortable look. Matt wanted me back in the band t-shirt days, though, so I guess I shouldn't feel too out of my league, even though I definitely feel like I am.

"Hey, I'm at baggage claim," Matt answered his phone. "People are starting to stare at me."

"Sorry, I had to change Ben. I'll be there in a minute."

I finished changing the diaper and fixed my hair a bit before juggling everything toward baggage claim. At first I didn't see Matt, but then I noticed the crowd of people—mainly girls—surrounding someone. As I walked closer, I could clearly see Matt's face, since he was so tall; he rose above the crowd. He looked really good, better than I ever remembered.

I figured I wouldn't interrupt him with his groupies. I waited for my baggage to show up before looking over again, not able to handle everything myself. He waved to me and told the fans he had to go. It was as if the crowd parted for him as he gave me a huge smile and hugged me, careful not to squeeze Ben. He looked down at Ben and took him from my arms.

"Hi little guy," Matt cooed. "Cami, he looks just like you."

I shrugged, "I see a lot of Danny in him."

Matt made a face at the mention of Danny and I laughed. It felt good to laugh.

"You look good," he smiled.

I rolled my eyes, "Thanks, but you're lying."

"I'm not lying," Matt said.

He was definitely lying. I was older, depressed, frazzled, and flabby. At least I managed to lose fifteen pounds in the past two months, which was not easy to do with the holidays.

"You look amazing," I cut in. "Age agrees with you," I gave him a flirty smile.

He blushed and handed Ben back to me. I unfolded the stroller and put Ben inside. Matt grabbed my suitcase and lap top from me. We headed to his Mercedes truck and put Ben's car seat in.

On the drive to Matt's place, I glanced at the palm trees, so happy to be out of the brisk weather and barren trees.

"So how's life?" I asked, looking over at Matt.

He went on to talk about Sound Wave and how they'll be going back in the studio in a couple of weeks. He also said they got rid of their old manager, which I'm pretty sure was a hint toward me, but I let it go for the time being. Then Matt said something that caught me off guard.

"Other than that, just been busy planning the wedding."

"Who's wedding?" I asked.

Matt laughed, "Mine, dummy."

"You're getting married?"

I was completely upset at the thought! There went my provocative nights or any chance at fun. I know myself and I know girls. I can guarantee that Matt's fiancée will hate me, and I'm sure I'll hate her.

"The wedding is in September," he smiled.

"Who are you marrying?"

"You really don't keep up with me, do you?" he laughed.

"If you mean, do I read tabloids or go to the Sound Wave website, no, I don't," I said.

"Her name is Laura. We've been together for seven years."

I thought back and vaguely remember seeing Matt with a gorgeous brunette at the Grammys a couple of times. Back in Sound Wave's prime years if Matt was dating someone, it was highly publicized, but that was when he was dating other celebrities.

"What took you so long to propose?" I asked.

Matt shrugged, "We weren't in a rush. Marriage wasn't so important to us; we both come from broken homes... But since we made it this long and with the baby coming..."

"Baby?" I gasped.

He grinned, "I'm going to be a dad. I love Laura so much and we're going to have a baby."

I stared at Matt. This couldn't be the same guy I knew as a young punk player. I tried not to show it, but I wanted to cry. I was jealous of any happy couple I came into contact with. I was jealous of anyone who was happy. I knew I needed to find happiness for Ben's sake, but it was difficult. I didn't know what to be happy about other than him. He should be enough, but as much as he made me happy, he also reminded me of Danny and our failed marriage. It also convinced me nothing lasts. Matt and his fiancée could be divorced in a year! Danny and I had been married for eleven years and look at us now...

"That's great," I said through my teeth.

Matt gave me a funny look.

"Why are you being a phony? I've never known you to be phony, Cami."

"Well, you haven't known me recently. I faked the last few years of my marriage. I fake being happy, being strong. I pretend I'm not hurting. And I'm terrible at being phony," I said, covering my eyes with my hand.

How the hell was I crying yet again!? I hardly ever cry and not in front of people! I'm losing control and I don't know how to get it back. I knew my out of whack emotions had a lot to do with me going back on birth control and leftover hormonal issues from the pregnancy. I also knew it mostly had to do with me realizing how alone I felt inside.

Matt reached over and rubbed my back.

"You *are* terrible at being phony," he agreed.

Guys are the worst at being comforting!

"Thanks a lot!" I said, still not looking at him.

"You don't have to be phony around me. You need to allow yourself to grieve and to move on. You and Ben can stay with us as long as you want. I just hate what Danny did and hate him even more for ruining my friendship with you."

I looked up at him and gave him the ugliest, most pathetic smile. I was an emotional mess, and so touched by Matt's words. I can't believe I pushed him out of my life all because of Danny! I wasn't the one with the wandering eye. In fact, I never even looked at Matt in a non-platonic way until recently, and now, that was squashed.

Though, I do wonder if my love for Jordan, even if never acted on, was considered to be adulterous. I would have to say yes, but I tried not to love him. Besides, it wasn't like I was willing to leave Danny if Jordan returned those feelings or…wait, would I have left Danny if Jordan returned those feelings? Sadly, yes, I would.

Great, so not only was I pathetic, but I was a cheating whore just like Danny! I'm unfaithful and disloyal and indecent. Pretty much any negative word that begins with "un", "dis" or "in" could describe me!

By the time, Matt pulled into his driveway; I was touching up my make-up. Matt helped me unload Ben and all my things. He opened the door for me and we were instantly greeted by two pit bull mixes. I kind of gasped and held Ben back protectively as the dogs started sniffing him.

"It's okay. They're sweethearts," Matt said shooing the dogs away so we could enter the house. "Baby! I'm back!" He yelled.

He went back outside to bring in the rest of my things as I glanced around the large beachside condo. It was absolutely gorgeous and huge! I felt so tiny inside the house, with all the high-ceilings. I was used to New York City and all of its clutter and apartments, even though mine was larger than most.

The gorgeous brunette I remembered seeing on Matt's arm in the past came down the stairs. Her dark brown hair reached her shoulders in big wavy curls. Her blue eyes were big and bright; her smile warm. She had a pretty fit body to go with the beautiful face, except for a small, rounded baby bump.

"Hi Cami, I'm Laura," she walked right up to me and hugged me, taking me and Ben by surprise.

He looked at her with furrowed eyebrows and pursed lips. His father often made the same face when he was thinking hard about something. Ben was probably just pooping, though.

"It's really nice to meet you," I said, but she was no longer focused on me as she cooed over my son. "This is my little Benvenuto."

"Can I hold him?" she asked, pleading with her eyes.

I allowed Laura to take Ben from me. He continued to stare at her. She started in with a flurry of questions about his eating and sleeping habits. I, in turn, asked about her pregnancy and all of the nuances to go with it. It felt extremely difficult to connect with people lately. I didn't have much in common with anyone. I was the only one I knew, at this point in my life, who was getting divorced and had a baby to take care of.

Although Laura wasn't divorced, she was going through changes in her body that I had just experienced. I found it easy to talk to her. She reminded me of someone—Haley. Once Matt came back into the house, and I saw him kiss Laura with all the love in the world, it both sickened me and made me swoon.

Maybe there was something to being a nice girl after all. Bad girls like me, the ones who are over confident, bitchy, and know she can get what she wants are great at landing the guy. At keeping the guy, well, I was starting to think I sucked at it, despite Danny staying with me for so many years. If I were sweet like Laura and Haley, maybe I would have a man so madly in love with me that he'd look at me like Matt and Jordan looked at those girls. Ugh, I'm too old to change.

Matt and Laura gave me the tour of the condo. There were five bedrooms, three bathrooms, a game room, fitness center and a big yard with an in ground pool. After Matt brought the last of my things to the room I was staying in, which overlooked the ocean, I plopped down on the bed and sighed.

"This is how you live?" I asked.

He laughed, "Come on, you have enough money for all this."

"Yeah, but this is nicer than our vacation house in the Hamptons."

"Thanks," he grinned.

I smiled, "Laura seems great, by the way."

"She is great. I'm glad you like her. Do you need a nap or anything? We'd be happy to watch Ben for you."

"Since when did you become so sweet?" I asked.

He shrugged, "I've always been sweet."

"Eh," I moved my hand back and forth.

"Bitch," he hissed.

The rest of the day, I took it easy. I napped, took a long, relaxing bath and had dinner with Laura and Matt. We watched a movie before they went to bed. I went up to my room with Ben and put on the TV as background noise as I rocked him to sleep for the night.

As I dozed in and out of sleep from the sound of the waves crashing onto the shore from the window near the bed, something on the television caught my attention.

"As the New York Yankees get ready for spring training here in Tampa," the newscaster began. "The team likes to mix work and play around the city. Last night, Andrew Ashton was spotted at Publix buying groceries, most noticeably a big tub of peanut butter. The former rookie of the year was also seen at a few night clubs earlier in the week where he entertained patrons with his goofy dancing and bad karaoke."

My eyes opened and a smile formed on my face. I forgot about spring training. I didn't even think how I would be in the same city as Jordan's little brother, Andrew. I would have to try and get together with him. It had been so long since I'd seen that kid—other than the few minutes I saw him the day I found out Danny was cheating on me months ago. Drew hasn't gotten to meet Ben yet, though he sent a gift, which was sweet.

I made a note to myself to get Drew's number from Jordan tomorrow.

CHAPTER EIGHT

The sounds of the waves hitting the shore woke me up. I immediately checked the portable crib to see if Ben was asleep. He was, to my surprise. Ben just begun sleeping through the night, but since he was in a new environment I expected to be awoken a couple of times.

It was seven-am. I headed to the bathroom and freshened up. When I got back into the bedroom, I heard Ben starting to fuss. He opened his eyes and looked up at me with the smallest, cutest smile. I smiled back and began speaking to him in silly, cooing tones.

I heard laughter from the doorway as I picked Ben up. I turned to see Matt standing in pajama pants and a tank top, leaning against the doorframe with his arms folded.

"I can't believe my ears," he said, still chuckling.

"What?"

"Cami Woods, the toughest chick I know, has gone soft and mushy."

"Hey, I am still tough," I pouted.

My lips said those words, but my head was beginning to think differently. Maybe I did go soft. Motherhood and heartbreak has turned me into a pathetic sap. Soon I would start crying over Folger's Coffee commercials and Lifetime movies.

"It's not a bad thing," Matt shrugged. "It's nice to see you have a heart and soul," he winked. "Laura made breakfast if you're interested."

Matt walked out and I thought about his words. I used to think cold and heartless were good things; it showed unstoppable strength and that I could remain unharmed. I guess I failed at being made of stone, though. I allowed myself to love the wrong men, and I allowed their inability to fully love me crush me. How could they love me? Did I even really love who I was? Heartless didn't show strength; it just came out mean and uncaring.

I looked down at my little baby in my arms. I imagined Ben meeting some girl like me, and I feared for him. Even though I was good to Danny, I was also selfish and cruel at times. Don't get me wrong, so was he, but other than the fact that I didn't physically cheat on him, was I any better? I hugged Ben close and decided he deserved a warm, loving mother that would teach him how to treat others.

After breakfast, I was antsy to get on the beach. Laura offered to watch Ben for me. I went for a run along the water, feeling the wind, and the mist hitting my face, and the burn in my legs. I was still out of shape and I was determined to change that.

When I got back inside the condo, I was desperate to get in the shower. Laura wasn't throwing Ben back to me, so I headed into the bathroom. Just as I was getting out of the shower, my phone rang. It was Jordan. He explained there were two passes for me at George Steinbrenner Field.

"That was nice of Drew," I said, thinking Matt would flip.

"How are things going in Tampa?"

"Good. Matt's been really attentive," I explained, wanting that to get back to Danny. "How's the tour?"

"Good. It feels a little weird without you here, I have to admit."

I smiled, "Aw, are you getting sentimental on me?"

"I'm used to you pushing everyone around. It's way too mellow around here."

I know Jordan was trying to cheer me up, but really, it kind of hurt my feelings. I never cared what people thought, but now I wonder if everyone just talked about me behind my back. They're probably saying how much of a crazy bitch I am.

That night, I was decked out in a Yankees cap and the number twelve jersey, Andrew Ashton's jersey, of course. I filled out the navy blue tank top underneath way more than I did the last time I wore it. I glanced over myself in the mirror skeptically. I never thought big boobs could be a bad thing, but they just made me feel heavier, which I was.

"Are you ready?" Matt asked, grinning like a child going to Chuck E. Cheese's.

He was more of a Marlins fan, being from Florida, but he did like the Yankees as well. He wore a simple navy t-shirt with the Yankees logo on the left-side of his chest.

"Is Laura really okay with watching Ben tonight? Maybe she should go with you…"

"Cami, Laura and I want you to have fun while you're here. Neither one of us minds watching Ben. Take advantage of us. This is a once in a lifetime opportunity we're offering you. That kid is yours for the next eighteen years," Matt patted my back.

I smiled at him and hugged him.

"What was that for?"

"Being a good friend to me even though I was terrible to you," I said, trying to keep myself from getting emotional.

"You were never terrible to me," he waved me off.

"I turned you down every time you asked me out, pretty rudely actually."

Matt shrugged, "I was a cocky kid. You were just keeping me in check."

"Then I kicked you out of my life," I sighed, with my hands on my hips.

"Your husband hated me, it's understandable. We're here now. Luckily, my fiancée is secure and will allow me to keep you around," he winked.

"If she knew the old me, she wouldn't," I said, knowingly.

Matt didn't argue, which proved my thoughts.

The entire drive to the baseball field, Matt would not shut up about what might or could happen—what players we would meet, where we would sit, etcetera, etcetera. I was starting to regret taking him and not Laura.

"Do you think Topaz will be sitting with the wives?" Matt asked.

Topaz is a twenty-two-year-old singer and occasional actress. She has light blue hair and wears outrageous stage costumes. I met her once or twice while escorting Rad Trick around at some teen awards show. She seems nice enough, but she sure loves to be looked at.

"Why would Topaz be there?"

"Uh, she's dating your friend."

I still looked at him confused.

"Topaz and Andrew Ashton are speculated to be one of the new hot A-List couples. Where have you been?"

"I don't pay attention to any tabloid trash unless it involves one of my clients. I have people who read that stuff for me," I rolled my eyes.

He just laughed, "Well, excuse me..."

Matt parked the car and we walked up to the box office. We were allowed into the stadium to see the players warm-up. We found our seats, which were right behind the dugout! As a Yankees fan, I was pretty excited, even though I'm a girl who gets All-Access passes to The Grammys. Baseball was still a magical thing for me. Knowing Andrew Ashton since he was a kid didn't take away the novelty of the game yet.

Spring training felt more intimate. Maybe Matt's energy was rubbing off on me. I felt as much excitement as I possibly could for someone going through a depression, which meant I probably still looked miserable to everyone else. Matt kept asking me if I was okay, which was my first hint. I decided I better plaster on my fake smile to convince him.

As the players got onto the field, it was hard to spot who was who since everyone had hats on; the Yankees didn't believe in putting names on the backs of jerseys either. I looked for number 12 and couldn't see him. I noticed one player bending over to fix his cleats. I couldn't help but notice how nice his butt looked. Damn, it was probably the hottest butt I had ever seen on a guy—Jordan and Danny included.

Hot Butt stood up and took his hat off. He ran a hand through his tousled blondish-brown hair before putting his hat back on. It still didn't click until I saw the number on his back. Oh crap, I just checked out Andrew Ashton, Jordan's little brother!

My mouth just hung open. I know it hasn't been that long since I had seen Drew, especially since I keep up on Yankee games every season. Still, every time I see him, I forget he is not a little boy anymore and I also forget how good-looking of a man he has become. I had seen him in his baseball uniform plenty of times.

I just never noticed that butt or the way it moved as he jogged onto the field.

"Cami," Matt nudged my arm.

I turned toward him, blinking a few times.

"I asked if you wanted a hot dog..." he said, looking at me funny.

I did want a hot dog, but I also didn't want to feel weighed down from it.

"No, thanks. I'll just have water."

Matt headed toward the concession stand as I leaned against the hand rail in front of me. I fell into a relaxed state sitting there in the warm weather, watching the Yankees throw the ball around and take swings with the bat. I didn't even realize how long Matt had been gone until the team started heading back to the dugout.

I turned around seeing if I could spot Matt and noticed a large group of girls by the concession stand. I rolled my eyes. Groupies got him, figures.

"Cami!"

I whirled around toward the field and saw Andrew standing a few feet in front of me. I waved like a fool, which translated to my arm being raised high and vigorously whipping it back and forth, as if I was trying to signal the guy piloting the blimp over the stadium. What is going on with me? I did not get star struck frequently, but that's what it felt like and I had no idea why. Maybe it was the fact that the best baseball team in the world, in my opinion anyway, was right in front of me. Or maybe because their star player was calling out to me. But he was not some star to me. This was Andrew—the sarcastic, witty, sometimes irritating kid I tolerated because I was in love with his older brother.

Drew climbed up the wall and hugged me with one arm.

"You look good," he smiled, showing all of his teeth.

I laughed, "Right."

He looked at me funny, "After the game, wait here. We'll hang out."

Drew smiled again and I just nodded. After he walked away, Matt finally made it back to his seat with plenty of stories about his trip to the concession stand. The game started about ten minutes later.

When Drew was announced to the field, Matt and I cheered like we did the other players, but I guess I got a tad bit more vocal because Matt was holding his ears.

I smacked his hands away.

"Stop. I'm not being that loud."

"Cami, you just screamed louder than the teenage girls and their moms who saw me at the concession stand did," he said.

I shrugged, "I'm just supporting Drew."

Matt cracked a smile, "I think he has enough support."

He nodded up at the giant television screen. Three girls, who looked like they were in college, were wearing navy t-shirts that read "Take Us Home, Drew!" and had number 12's painted on their faces. They were flailing about like crazy for the camera.

Andrew Ashton was no longer the little boy envious of his brother. He had his own career, his own spotlight, and apparently, he could pick any girl he wanted. I don't know why, but I found it all upsetting. I mean I'm depressed, so I find everything upsetting.

Looking at Drew, though, I was thinking of how young he still was, and how innocent he used to be—even though he was a pretty big flirt as a teenager. Now, that boy is gone and he was probably having sex with a million women, doing steroids, and thought the high he was on was going to last forever.

I snapped out of my cloud of gloom when Matt started clapping. I looked at the field to see the game had started and the Yankees already had a runner on second base. I tried to focus on the game, but found myself worrying how Ben was doing with Laura, or how Tortured's tour was going, or I would just completely zone out.

Every once in a while, Matt would nudge me and I would look over at him with forced smiles. The only time I didn't have to force having a good time was when Drew got a hit or made a sweet play as short stop. As soon as the moment was over, I was back to being depressing Cami, and I know Matt could feel the change in me.

After the game was over, I debated just going back to the condo. It felt too long to be away from Ben.

"We should go," I said, as the crowd began to clear.

Matt shrugged, "Don't you think you should say hi to Drew? Thank him for the tickets at least?"

"I already spoke to him," I said.

"And he said he wants to see you after the game," Matt said, looking at me as if I had four heads.

I know Matt was excited to meet the team. I thought about offering to take a taxi back to his place and allowing him to hang out.

"But Laura's at home stuck with Ben."

Matt laughed, "Is that how you feel about your son? You're stuck with him?"

I frowned. I was angry at that remark. It made me wonder if I did feel like that, though. Maybe once in a while, but Ben was also my reason for getting up every day when I just wanted to sleep my life away.

"How about this," Matt said. "I'll go home and help Laura out—although I doubt she'll need it, and you spend some time with Andrew. I think it'll be good for you."

Matt spoke to me as if he were trying to be delicate, as if I were a child. He was worried about me just like Haley and Jordan and every other friend or foe to come into contact with me recently. I'm terrible at pretending to be happy! Ugh. That was the worst part about this. There are people in this world that can put on a show and pretend nothing was wrong, but I am just not one of those people. Even when I was happy, I still looked like a bitch. When I'm miserable, I just look mopey and sad—not much bitch in sight—and that had people worried. How crazy is that?

"Matt, I just want to see my son," I said, exasperated.

"Cam, he's going to be right where you left him in a few hours," Matt said, putting his hands on my arms.

"Psst!"

We both turned to see Andrew peeking out of the dugout. I plastered my fake smile on and Drew smiled, with no teeth this time. He saw through me. I could tell by his expression.

"You still up for hanging out?" he asked.

I was about to tell him no, but Matt spoke for me.

"She is, but I'm going to head home. Pregnant fiancée wants ice cream," Matt laughed. "Thanks for the tickets, man."

Drew hopped onto the fence and shook Matt's hand.

"No problem. It's nice to meet you. Don't tell anyone, but I like some of Sound Wave's music."

I had to laugh. Jordan would torment Drew if he ever found that out. I think Drew said it just to be nice, though. That's the kind of kid he was.

Matt laughed, "Come on, I have to tell someone. Like *Razz Magazine*."

I groaned. *Razz Magazine* was a sore spot for me since it was how I found out my marriage was over.

"Sorry, not a fan of that rag," I smirked.

Matt and Drew both were silent for a moment, which assured me they knew what I meant by the comment.

"So, I guess it's just you and me," Drew said. "The guys are going to this pretty cool lounge if you're up for that."

"Uh, sure," I agreed, not knowing what else to do.

"Great," Matt said, kissing my cheek. "See you at home. I won't wait up," he winked.

I turned toward Andrew and he jumped down from the fence.

"I'm just going to shower and change really fast. Wait by the security entrance. I'll tell them you're with me so they don't kick you out," he said, running back into the dugout and disappearing into the clubhouse.

I turned to walk up the stairs and a bunch of number 12 fans were about to storm toward me. I guess they caught a glimpse of Drew before he went back inside. I looked at my outfit and thought how embarrassing it was to be going out with the Yankees covered in team gear.

I could kill Matt for leaving me. I could kill myself for not thinking about bringing a change of clothes. Yes, I am a huge Yankees fan, and there was nothing to be ashamed of. However, in my line of work, integrity is important. I wouldn't wear a Tortured t-shirt if I were out to dinner with Danny. That would just be odd and draws attention. What was even worse was the fact that I had the name "Ashton" on my back with Drew's number. I hate groupies and that night, I was one!

I hurried into the bathroom to see what damage control I could do before meeting up with the team. I took off the baseball cap and shoved it into my purse before pulling my hair out of its ponytail. My hair had no volume to it and was fairly frizzy, even after I fluffed the hat head look out of it. I decided to braid it quickly. I touched up my make-up before pulling off the pinstripe jersey. In my tank top and jean shorts, I looked like I wasn't wearing enough clothing! I put the jersey back on and decided supportive fan was a better look than white trash groupie.

About forty minutes later, I was standing by two security guards watching the team start to file out of the clubhouse. I guess I *am* a groupie since I found myself stifling the need to get an autograph or a picture with every single player to walk by.

I am used to being surrounded by celebrities. I stood next to Nicole Kidman on the red carpet before. I ate dinner with Lady Gaga twice. John Mayer hit on me a few times, big surprise there, which caused a huge, public feud between him and Danny. Still, there I was star struck over the New York Yankees. I suppose I wasn't used to being around professional athletes. On top of that, being from New York and growing up watching baseball, these players are practically royalty in our eyes.

Andrew was the last player to come out. He was dressed in black slacks and a white collared dress shirt, that had the first three buttons undone. His hair was slicked back somewhat, but mostly because it was still wet, making it look darker than usual. I couldn't help but notice the silver chain around his neck that disappeared into his shirt. It drew my eyes to the peek-a-boo he was giving of his chest. I hadn't realized how muscular he had gotten until now. The last time I had seen him, he had a jacket on. He wasn't very tall—5'10" according to his stats online—yes, I knew a lot of facts like that about the Yankees. Even though Drew wasn't all that tall compared to the other players, he was solid and toned. He had the body of an athlete, which I wasn't used to being around.

I couldn't help but compare him to Danny in that instant. Danny was really tall and soft in spots from too much partying. As Drew walked closer to me, I found myself mentally comparing him to Jordan as well. They were close in height probably, but Drew definitely grew into a more muscular guy with a boyishly handsome face while Jordan had a more defined jaw line and intense eyes.

When Drew smiled at me, once again, I couldn't help to genuinely smile back. He pulled me into a hug—with both arms this time—and I sunk into his broad chest instantly. It was the best hug I had received in such a long time; I didn't want him to let go, but he did.

"Tonight, we are going to party like we're twenty-one!"

I laughed, "Aren't you twenty-one?"

He smirked, "I'll be twenty-nine in July."

"Wow, you're getting old," I teased.

"Me? You must be pushing fifty!"

I scowled, "Thirty-seven in September."

He smiled, "You look much closer to my age than that."

I rolled my eyes, "I wish. You look amazing. Been working out?"

I squeezed his bicep, and let my fingers linger on his arm. He wasn't huge like, a wrestler or one of those muscle head gym rats, but for a guy of his stature and his frame—he was big with broad shoulders. I was never into muscular men, but Drew had the perfect body. He looked at me for a moment. His brown eyes were searching mine for something—I didn't know what, but I stared right back into his eyes.

"I'm not on anything, if that's what you're thinking."

I dropped my hand and I stared at my shoes. That whole steroid idea went out the window hours ago. That was just me being cynical. Obviously, he was sensitive about it, though.

"I didn't..." I said. "I mean, I wasn't judging you if you were..."

Great, I couldn't even lie anymore!

Drew laughed and slung his arm around my shoulders.

"You're not the only one who thought it."

I looked up at him, amazed he was smiling.

"Some stupid gossip website posted that I was on steroids. Jordan even asked me about it, too. It just makes me mad that he would think I would do that to myself. I already worry I have the temper of Chuck Ashton inside me, I don't want 'roid rage on top of that," Drew winked.

I smiled, "Well, you'll have to tell me your workout secrets."

"It looks like you don't need my help," he said, glancing down my body to my legs for a moment.

I felt extremely self-conscious under his gaze, knowing he was just trying to flatter me.

"Thanks, but I know you're just being nice like always. I gained some weight since the baby and the separation," I sighed.

"You look great, but if you need a workout buddy, call me up if I'm in town."

I smiled and a moment later, he directed me toward his car. As soon as we got settled inside, Drew turned on the radio. Funny enough, a Sound Wave song was on, and we both laughed. What was even funnier was Andrew actually sang along—to every word! The song came out while I was in high school, but I only knew the chorus.

After the song was over, I just stared at Drew with my mouth open.

"What?"

"You weren't lying when you told Matt you were a fan..." I gasped.

Drew blushed, his smooth baby like cheeks, turning red.

"It's fun music. It puts me in a good mood."

I smiled and tried to keep from chuckling. Drew looked over at me and squeezed my knee, which made me spasm a little. He laughed before staring at my jersey.

"Is that my jersey?"

He was trying to catch a glimpse at the name on the back.

"No, I paid for it," I grinned.

He laughed, "You're a groupie."

"Shut up," I said and reached over to squeeze his much larger knee, but it didn't have the same effect on him.

He just cackled at my attempt and I scowled.

"There's the Cami I know," he winked.

I looked over at him.

"What do you mean by that?"

He pulled into the parking lot of the lounge and put the car into park. He turned off the engine and faced me.

"Cami Woods was always tough. You're feisty and put people in their place, especially guys. You didn't pout or dwell..."

I stared at him.

"And now I do?" I asked, trying to remain calm.

I was about to lose it on him and I didn't want to take my drama out on sweet, untainted, but the very forward Andrew Ashton, but it was going to happen.

"Well, you just look miserable. From what I hear, you don't want to do anything or go anywhere...and you're not yourself."

"From what you hear?" I asked. "From who? Jordan? Or Danny? Maybe Haley? Who are they to discuss my business with anyone? Who are you to butt your nose into my business, Drew? Am I supposed to take advice from a hot shot kid who doesn't know one thing about love or pain?" I yelled, infuriated at this point. "Of course I'm not myself! I just had a baby with a man who cheated on me! Will everyone just give me a fucking break?"

Drew swallowed and didn't say anything.

"Take me to Matt's house. Obviously you were put up to this whole getting me to go out thing," I huffed.

"No," he mumbled.

"No? You won't take me to Matt's?"

He looked over at me and shook his head.

"I'm sorry, Cami. You're right, it's no one's business and I understand you need time to heal. I want to be here with you, though. I know how much you love the Yankees. And as much as we don't see each other, we are family."

I looked over at him, and was grateful no tears were coming out, though they felt like they would.

"Danny was your family first."

He was like a second big brother to Andrew.

He sighed, "Do I have to choose who I keep?"

I smiled at him and unbuckled my seatbelt. I kissed his cheek. Drew was one more thing I had Jordan to thank for. It hurt so much knowing without Jordan, I wouldn't have a career, or had Danny, which means I wouldn't have Ben, and I certainly wouldn't have any friends.

"Let's go in there and have a good time," Drew said.

I smiled and nodded. And now I had Jordan to thank for Drew, who was allowing me to party with my favorite sports team. Maybe life wasn't so terrible, but why did all that was good in the world have to be from Jordan, the man of my dreams that I would never have?

CHAPTER NINE

I woke up to the sound of birds chirping and the sun shining in my eyes. I opened them and immediately wanted to close them again. My mouth was dry and my head felt like it was weighing me down. I tried to sit up, shielding the sun from my eyes, and realized I wasn't in the same room I was staying in at Matt's house.

I looked around, squinting, trying to focus on something, like the room, or how I wound up in it, and how I got home last night; or where Ben was. I immediately looked around for Ben's portable crib before glancing at the clock—it was a little before six-am.

I thought about the night before, remembering going into the lounge with Andrew. I remember doing shots with the team, whom by the way were really cool. They found it hilarious that I knew way too much about the players' lives thanks to *Yankeeography* on YES! Network. By the time I was on my third beer and fifth shot, I turned into one of the guys, except for the being super flirty part. It didn't matter who it was—from the waiter to Billy Lotto, who was really the only guy on the team who wasn't attractive physically or personality-wise. I remember some of the players' wives and girlfriends giving me attitude when I would make a flirty comment or touch their man's arm.

I, of course, being wasted and becoming my normal "don't back down" self, would get an attitude back. In order to diffuse the situation, Drew kept me close to his side and made jokes about what an awful drunk I was. At some point, I could barely hear him say something to the women about how much I had to drink and that they had nothing to worry about because I was with him. I saw him add a wink and a flirtatious smile of his own.

I remember liking the sound of me being *with* Drew for some reason... I remember liking the sound of Drew's voice in my ear telling me he always thought I had the prettiest eyes he had ever seen. I remember thinking he had the sweetest smile with luscious lips that were so soft against mine...

Holy freakin' crap! Drew and I kissed last night. Oh, we did more than kiss last night... I can still feel the rough skin on the palms of his hands on me, in particularly my extra sensitive, post pregnancy boobs! Oh. My. God. I went to get out of the bed and I was stark naked. Oh shit!

As I searched for my clothes, the entire night came rushing back. Drew's muscles, his long eye lashes, his butt—God, that butt. I can't remember what it looked like, but I remember what it felt like in my hands.

I found my bra and panties and as I put them on, I thought more about his body—how he looked shirtless with that silver chain with the number 12 diamond encrusted pendant, and how that pendant tickled between my breasts as he laid on top of me and kissed me. I couldn't help the dumb smile that crept across my face. I just plopped down on the huge bed. Was it Drew's bed? Yes, it was.

We took a taxi back to his place because I was too drunk to remember the address of Matt's place. I wish I could remember how it all started. I know alcohol was definitely a catalyst, but I couldn't for the life of me remember what was said or who made the first move. Was it weird at first? All I remember was how amazing it was!

This was like steamy, romance novel amazing sex—raunchy, hot and sexy as hell. We were up against the wall, on the floor, on the bed. I looked back at the bed. Where the hell was Drew? Was it going to be weird for us now? What was I thinking? Of course it was going to be weird! I'm so much older than he is! I knew him as a kid! He's Jordan's little brother for crying out loud!

I finished getting dressed and looked for my purse. I dug my cell phone out and I had a bunch of text messages. One was in response to the message I sent Matt around one-am.

Matt Porter: Your message doesn't even make sense! Ha. Don't worry. We got Ben. Just have fun with Mr. Baseball ;-)~

Oh great, Matt definitely thought something was going on between Drew and me. I would have to swear him to secrecy so it never got out to Jordan or Danny. There was a message from Jordan saying something about seeing me on TV at the game and hoping I had fun. There was another message from Danny asking how Ben was doing. Finally, there was a text message from Andrew.

Morning. I had an early meeting. Sorry to leave you there. I left you money to take a taxi to Matt's...if you can remember the address. I'll call you.

Oh man. I just slumped back down on the bed. That "I'll call you" was like the kiss of death in dating! Or whatever last night was... it wasn't a date, I know that much. It was sleazy, trashy, fun actually, but it wasn't a date, and it wouldn't happen again. I just hoped things wouldn't be awkward whenever mine and Drew's paths crossed.

I called a taxi from my phone, which was just about dead at that point and waited outside, not sure how I should lock the door. I responded to Drew's text.

Hi. I didn't know how to lock your door. Hope you don't get robbed. You can save your taxi money. I'm not a whore, thanks. See you at Aylin's Sweet 16 in a few months. We can pretend this didn't happen.

I was kind of mad by the time I got inside the taxi. I didn't know if I had any right to be, though. I was a consenting adult the night before, even if I was blasted and going through a depression, and maybe Drew took advantage of that situation. And maybe he was just being thoughtful by leaving me money for transportation; it sure made me feel like he took the walk of shame and left me there, just wanting to get rid of me.

From what I understood, Drew was into casual hook-ups and nothing serious. Haley worried he was turning into Darren—a heartbreaking player.

When I got to Matt's, whose address I still barely remembered sober, I was doing my own walk of shame. My hair was disheveled, my make-up half on, and I reeked of alcohol. On top of that, I felt so irresponsible for leaving my baby with Matt and Laura overnight. I wanted to take a shower and pretend that night didn't happen.

I peeked into the living room and Matt was lying on the couch with Ben asleep on his chest. The sight made me smile, but it also made me sad. Laura was lucky to have a guy who would be there for their child, and her as well.

Danny may be good with Ben, but he wasn't there for me. He was the last person I wanted to see, and that was so hard for me. I once thought he was my best friend. I could tell him anything—even my feelings for Jordan to an extent.

I took two aspirin before going into the shower. The warm water felt good on my skin, washing away some of the tawdriness of the previous night. I couldn't help but think of Drew once again, though. Gone was that little boy I had known as he wrapped his large arms around me, and I wrapped my legs around his midsection. I wish I could remember more of the details, though, even if it was a night I should forget. It might be the last time I would have sex for a long time. It upset me that I couldn't remember things, like how he looked completely naked, or how he felt inside of me. Those things were important to me. It scared me to think I was too drunk to remember a night of intimacy, even if it was a one-night stand.

I looked down at my body and suddenly, I was crying. I saw the stretch marks and pouch of belly I still had. My boobs are actually the size I wanted them to be now, but I didn't feel good about them. How unattractive Drew must have thought my body was. I couldn't believe I had the hottest sex of my life and I felt worse than ever.

Once I was out of the shower and dressed in a t-shirt and sweatpants, I went downstairs to retrieve Ben. He was starting to squirm in Matt's arms. I carefully picked him up, trying not to disturb Matt, but it was no use.

Matt startled himself awake as soon as Ben was out of his grasp.

"Sorry," I said, with Ben nuzzled against my chest.

I figured he was hungry and retrieved a bottle from the refrigerator. Matt followed me into the kitchen.

"So, you have a good day?" he asked, a sleazy tone to his voice.

I rolled my eyes and sat down at the table to feed Ben. I didn't answer Matt.

"Oh come on," he said sitting across from me. "I missed out on hanging with the Yankees to make sure you did. You have to give some details."

"You can't tell anyone about this," I sighed.

"Who am I going to tell?" Matt laughed.

"Jordan? Danny?"

"Oh right, like I talk to Danny?" he laughed harder.

"Just keep your mouth shut, please."

"You're ashamed?" he asked surprised.

"No, I'm proud of getting so drunk and shacking up with a Yankees short stop who just happens to practically be the little brother of my husband while I left my son for the night!"

Matt sighed, "You're just being dramatic. You needed a night out."

"Maybe so, but hooking up with Andrew Ashton? Big mistake! He's a kid to me. I took him to the zoo once," I threw my hand down on the table, startling Ben.

I rocked him a little as I held his bottle.

Matt laughed, "Cami, you definitely weren't looking at him like a kid yesterday at the game. I saw you checking him out."

I blushed, "I was not."

"You were. In fact, the only time you looked truly happy since I picked you up at the airport was when you were looking at that boy."

"See, even you call him a boy."

"I'm in a boy band, everyone is a boy to me. I'm still a boy," he shrugged.

"That's for sure," I sucked my teeth.

"Just answer me yes or no to the following questions," Matt began. "Did you have fun last night before the sex?"

"Yes," I nodded.

"Did you like the sex?"

I swallowed, "Of what I can remember, yes."

I couldn't control how breathy my voice became and Matt chuckled.

"Do you want to do it again?"

I looked away and mumbled a yes.

"So, what's the problem?"

"The problem is that I can't just sleep with Drew. He's too young for me. I'm a mom now. And he's practically family."

"Age is not that big of a deal. He's in his twenties, almost his thirties and you're in your thirties…"

"Almost my forties," I pointed out.

"Whatever, you're still a few years away from that. And so what if you're a mom? Moms can't have fun? I think Ben will grow up a lot happier if you got laid once in a while, and weren't miserable with pent up emotions, don't you think?"

I had to giggle a little at that, even in my ashamed state of mind.

"As for the family thing, big deal. You're not related. You're not even in-laws. Your client's little brother is fair game. And your husband's best friend's brother is definitely fair game."

I sighed, "Is your ex-boyfriend's little brother fair game, too?"

"Huh?" Matt asked confused.

"I dated Jordan."

"When? Like twenty years ago?"

"Close."

It frustrated me to know that most people didn't remember my fling with Jordan Walsh all those years ago. If they did remember, they thought of it as just that, a meaningless fling.

"Please, Jordan is a happily married man. You're on vacation. Enjoy some ass."

I laughed, "One problem..."

Matt rolled his eyes.

"Drew doesn't want my ass."

"What?" Matt asked.

"Come on, I don't exactly have the body I used to. And we both know my personality leaves a lot to be desired..."

"Cami, I don't think Drew has a problem with your body or your personality when you're not being as difficult as you are now."

"He knows what I look like naked. He left before I woke up," I explained.

"Maybe he had some place to be," Matt shrugged.

"He regrets last night, Matt. Just like I do," I said before concentrating on Ben drinking his bottle.

As much as I enjoyed the night—drinking, Yankee mingling, hot Drew sex and all—I definitely regretted it just as much. I felt sick with myself and worse than ever.

CHAPTER TEN

I was playing with Ben on the floor of the living room while Matt and Laura were snuggling together on the couch with both pit bulls. ESPN was on the TV and it flashed to the Yankees at a press conference from this morning. Matt threw a piece of popcorn at my head.

"See, your boy did have something to do this morning."

I stuck my tongue out at him, "Matt, it was a one-time thing."

Laura gasped, "Wait, you and Drew 'Take Me Home' Ashton?"

"Take Me Home" was a famous phrase yelled at Drew by teammates and fans. Drew was legendary for hitting triples and homeruns. He had a league record for the most RBIs as well as grand slams. The starting catcher for the Yankees, Francisco Rodriguez, used to yell to Drew while he was at the plate, "Take me home!" His voice would carry so much that the TV cameras could pick up the sound. Soon, it became Drew's thing. When he gets up to bat, fans begin to chant it.

"Way to keep a secret, Matt," I scowled at him before standing up and taking Ben with me.

"Come on, Cam, I won't tell anyone else," he said as I just walked past him.

About an hour later, Ben was sound asleep. I grabbed the baby monitor and attached it to the waistband of my yoga pants and announced to Laura and Matt I was going for a walk on the beach. I stepped onto the sand, barefoot, and walked down to the water. I allowed the water to lap at my toes as I strolled through the wet sand. It was a breezy night. The wind combined with the sound of the water had a soothing effect.

I tried not to think about anything as I walked, but that was hard to do. For once, I wasn't thinking about my anger toward Danny or my dull yearn for Jordan. I wasn't even thinking about work. I was thinking about lust. Something set me off the night before. I hadn't felt such desire in a really long time. There were times with Danny where it was hot and animalistic, but those times were far and few between, and years ago. The first time with Jordan was pretty sizzling; I was also an inexperienced teenager back then. But last night with Drew—it was like he was made for sex. Even with a fuzzy memory, that much I knew.

I guess he had a lot of experience being the All-Star athlete he is, but man, even drunk, he kept my toes curled for quite some time. I sighed loudly and decided to turn back toward the house. I needed to put an end to my impure thoughts for the young short stop I had a one-night stand with—that was never to be mentioned again.

As I turned around, I saw someone walking toward me. I couldn't make out his face in the dark, but he looked kind of intimidating. I was prepared to smash his face with the baby monitor on my hip. The device was a little heavy, pulling the lightweight material of my pants down slightly. It was getting windier as I walked closer to the condo and the approaching man. My hair kept whipping into my face, making it hard for me to see.

I caught a glimpse of the man's face once I was a few feet away. I swore he looked just like Andrew Ashton. Wow, was my mind really playing tricks on me like that? Did my night with Drew really consume my mind this much?

"Hey," his voice said.

It sounded deep, like the word was caught in his throat. I brushed my hair away from my face, and Drew was in fact standing there. He wasn't a hallucination, a side effect from sleeping with him. He wore basketball shorts, a grey hooded sweatshirt and a backwards cap.

"What are you doing here?" I asked.

"I called, but you didn't answer."

"You called?" I stared at him.

"Twice. I thought you hated me after what you texted."

I knew I was a little too harsh in my text, but I felt his text was cold too.

"My phone died and I left it on the charger on silent," I explained.

"It took me an hour to find out Matt's address," he said, sticking his hands in the kangaroo pocket of his sweatshirt. "He told me you were walking out here when he answered the door."

He had that boyish look to him again. It made me smile.

"Was Matt even listed?"

"Of course not, but I know people. In Tampa, Matt Porter is not too low-profile," he winked.

I laughed, "No, he's not. Neither are you, huh?"

He shrugged before stepping closer to me.

"You're not a whore, so you know."

I laughed, "Thanks."

"I didn't want to leave like I did, but you were snoring and..."

Oh great... I flashed him an annoyed look and he laughed.

"That's not why I left," he chuckled through the words.

I couldn't help but laugh, too.

"I had a bunch of stuff to do for the team..."

"I know. I caught some of the press conference on TV," I said, letting him off the hook, not that he really owed me an explanation, but I'm glad he gave one.

"Last night..." he began.

"Don't Drew," I waved my hand in the air, forcing a smile. "It's forgotten," I shrugged.

I grabbed the elastic band off my wrist and wrapped my messy hair into a ponytail to keep in from blowing in my face.

"Forgotten?" Drew asked, narrowing his eyebrows, which made his brown eyes almost puppy-dog like.

How could one man look sexy in one instant and adorable in the next? Most guys I knew were one or the other, not both! It just didn't seem fair.

"Yes, forgotten. I'm not one of those girls—you don't have to smooth things over. I'm fine with what happened and can totally just be friends," I said.

And I did mean that. I knew I could do it. Sure, maybe I would think about his smooth, bare chest with the happy trail of hair down his belly button from time to time, but I wasn't blind. There were plenty of guys I found good-looking that I thought about on occasion sexually... Okay, maybe not. Let's face it; I was not a normal person. Aside from Jordan and Danny, I didn't fantasize much. I just wasn't physically into anyone unless there was a deeper feeling behind it.

It was getting windier and goose bumps were beginning to form on my arms.

"Okay," Drew nodded. "So we just pretend it didn't happen?" he asked.

"Right," I shrugged.

"Cool. So I'm going to the gym in the morning. I wanted to know if you were really interested in working out with me?" Drew asked with a small smile.

I couldn't believe it! Why didn't Drew just come out and tell me I was flabby and disgusting? He saw me naked and now he wanted me to workout with him! I wanted to climb under a rock.

"I see you noticed I need it finally," I said, trying to make it sound like a joke.

I guess he picked up on the expression on my face. I felt the color drain from it.

"No! Cami, I mean—I just thought it would be something we could do together—you said you wanted to..."

He was stumbling over his words and I know I was looking at him like I wanted to punch him. I've been told I could be quite frightening, though it was hard to believe that Andrew Ashton could be intimidated easily. He always seemed so self-assured, especially during interviews. It was moments like these that I got to see the sensitive, caring little boy he used to be appear in the man he is now.

He glanced down and swallowed. I shivered and realized my chest was reacting to the cold through my t-shirt. Drew was staring and I rolled my eyes, shoving him. He laughed and blushed.

"Sorry."

"You're still a pervy thirteen-year-old!" I laughed.

He smiled, "You didn't seem to mind last night."

I groaned, "Is this your way of pretending it didn't happen? By making jokes and ogling my boobs?"

Drew didn't say anything as he took his sweatshirt off, the tank top he wore underneath hiking up as he did so. I swallowed as I stared at his abs. His hat fell off in the process and he offered the sweatshirt to me.

"So you're not cold and to keep me from ogling," he winked.

I blushed and took the piece of clothing from him. I slipped the sweatshirt over my head. It was so warm and huge on me. Drew had bent over to get his hat and now I was staring at his magnificent butt. Drew stood up quickly and I tried too hard to divert my eyes toward the ocean.

Drew slid his hat back on and stepped really close to me.

"Still cold?" he asked, his eyes looking into mine.

I shrugged, just looking into his big brown eyes. The wind picked up even more and his hat flew off, but this time, he didn't retrieve it.

"Your eyes look amazing out here with the moon and the ocean..." he said.

I couldn't help to think he was being cheesy, but at the same time, I wanted to fall into his arms. I watched his hair blow in the breeze and I wanted to run my fingers through it.

"You don't have to flatter me to make up for the gym remark."

Drew put his hand on my jaw. His thumb rubbed against my cheek while his pinky unconsciously tickled my neck.

"I just wanted to work you into a sweat again," he said, his voice husky.

My throat went dry and before I could stop him, his lips were on mine. And this time, we were both sober...I think! I knew I was and Drew didn't taste like alcohol as his tongue slid against mine. My toes curled into the sand and my hands reached up to play with his thick, wavy hair. It was so nice to make-out with someone not an entire foot taller than me! I could barely reach Danny's hair when I used to kiss him because he was so tall.

Drew wrapped his arms around my waist and I practically slammed my hips against his. I heard a groan from him.

"What was that?" he asked with part of his mouth leaving mine.

I laughed, "The baby monitor. It's in case Ben cries…"

"Oh, I was going to say…I don't remember that being there last night," Drew said.

I cracked up laughing.

"You were drunk, who knows…" I said with a raised eyebrow.

Drew laughed, "I was drunk? You were trashed!"

"I still remember everything last night, though," I said, biting my bottom lip.

He grinned and began kissing my neck.

"So do I…" he nipped my skin and I jumped. "The way you smelled, the way you felt," he said, moving his hands under his sweatshirt and up to my breasts.

I moaned as I felt him harden against my leg. He felt so big; I didn't quite remember how big until that moment.

"The way you sounded," he smirked against my skin after hearing the noise I made. "I still can't believe you crawled into my bed naked…"

I pulled him by his hair lightly.

"I what?" I gasped.

He looked at me funny.

"When we got back to my place, you just kept taking clothes off and you got into my bed..."

"I did?"

I didn't know how we made it to his bed. I remember making out all over his condo, but I figured it was a mutual, gradual thing, moved by the heat of the moment. The way Drew made it sound was that I just stripped suddenly!

He nodded in response to my question, "It was hot. I mean, I've had girls throw themselves at me before, but..."

I pushed him away and sat down in the sand, placing my head between my knees.

"Cami, what's wrong?"

I pushed my hair back and looked up at him.

"I'm a groupie slut."

Drew laughed and plopped down next to me.

"Na. You were horny. So was I," he said, putting his hand on my bent knee and sliding it upward.

"I was drunk," I pushed his hand off. "You took advantage of me!"

"What?!" Drew yelled. "I didn't force you or...you made it very hard for me to resist," he said with suggestive eyes.

"Ugh," I said and looked away from him.

We just sat there for a moment. The wind was starting to settle down. After a couple of minutes, I felt Drew's hand on my back.

"Cami, last night was...wow. I never thought you could be like that."

I shot him a look, showing I wasn't exactly happy with myself. He instantly tried to pull me into a hug.

"Don't touch me."

"Cam, please...I wasn't—I was pretty drunk, too. All I saw was this absolutely gorgeous girl in my bed..."

I smiled that he called me a girl instead of a woman; the gorgeous part was an added bonus.

"I've been with a lot of women, but..."

I scowled at him and he stopped.

"Not *that* many, but you were something else," he smirked.

I couldn't help but smile at the somewhat offensive compliment.

"I've been so lost, Drew. So stressed and sad... I can't believe I have become that woman who is so pathetic to seduce a younger man," I shook my head. "I'm a cougar!"

Drew chuckled, "You didn't technically seduce me! I thought you said you remembered everything?"

I looked at him confused.

"In the taxi, I started kissing you first...you couldn't help yourself after that," he shrugged, with a cocky grin.

I smacked his arm, but we both laughed. I looked at the tattoo on his arm, vaguely remembering it last night. It was the Celtic symbol for brotherhood. Drew and Jordan got matching tattoos when he turned eighteen.

"We were both all over each other," Drew explained. "I didn't want to take advantage of you, just so you know. That's why I slept in the guest room."

I blinked at him a few times. I could tell he was slightly offended at my accusation of him taking advantage.

"Wait, you didn't sleep in the bed with me after we had sex?"

Drew began to laugh, "Cami, we didn't have sex!"

My mouth dropped. I thought back to the previous night and no wonder I couldn't remember certain details! I vaguely remembered Drew saying we should stop. I remember myself saying we should stop, until finally we both reluctantly did. I was already naked at that point, and Drew was in his boxers. I smacked myself in the head as I felt a mix of emotions—regret and relief were definitely involved. Part of me wish we did go all the way while the other part was happy we didn't. The regret outweighed the relief, I think, which surprised me. I looked over at Drew, who was sitting down next to me with crossed arms, probably trying to hide the fact that he was cold.

"God, I'm sorry I'm being such a temperamental chick right now. My hormones are still out of whack."

"No apologies needed," Drew put his arm around me and I placed my head on his shoulder. "Danny is the most idiotic person I know."

I smiled and looked over at him.

"Most people probably think he's smart for leaving me. All we did was fight. I'm not exactly a bed of roses all the time. Your brother will tell you."

Drew shrugged, "You're tough, but there's definitely more than meets the eye with you."

I just laughed. Great, so I'm a tough bitch who is almost a great lay... I guess that was better than nothing. I might as well put my assets to use. It was funny how men will overlook personality for a piece of ass. Drew was no different I guess, but hey, I might as well enjoy myself while I can. I was on vacation, after all, and Jordan wants Drew to show me a good time. I hate men. All they want to do was tell me how to feel and when to feel it, and in the end, they all leave me for someone else. I just had to accept that and detach myself. The only man in my life that has my unconditional love is Ben.

CHAPTER ELEVEN

At five-am, my phone alarm went off. I groaned and just lie in bed, wondering why I would agree to Andrew Ashton's fitness boot camp! He somehow talked me into getting up before the sun to go to the gym. I agreed after he pulled me into a giant hug. There was no kiss goodnight—that would have felt too much like a date. The hug was almost as good, though. It sounds cliché, but I fit into Drew's arms like a baseball rests inside a mitt.

I did want to get into shape, so I guess I didn't protest too much. I wanted to get back to who I was—before my marriage fell apart, before pregnancy took over my body, before I lost control emotionally and physically.

It was a daunting feeling to be working out with Drew, however. I mean, *Fit Magazine* voted him #3 on their "Best Body" list, and there were plenty of other lists he made it on having to do with his physique. No wonder he was so cocky sometimes!

His cockiness wasn't arrogant, if that makes sense at all. Confident men were a turn-on, but arrogance was not. Drew, like Jordan, was fairly confident in who he is and how people perceive him.

I was used to being around really good-looking men. Danny and Jordan made lists of their own. Jordan was voted *Cosmo's* sexiest man of the year more than once now, and Danny was featured in a non-nude piece for *Playgirl* a few years ago. Danny had more of an arrogance about him, and that was something that always pissed me off.

Drew stood apart from most men I knew. He actually worked at his body. Yes, Danny went to the gym, like every other New York Italian. He would work out hard and drink protein shakes for a month, and then the next month, he'd eat wings and fast food, taking a week or two off from the gym.

Jordan and Darren didn't go through the extremes Danny did. They weren't gym rats or obsessed with their body either. They are the type of guys who play basketball with some friends on the weekends, and go the gym two times a week.

From what I heard about Drew, and what I can tell about his body, he probably has no body fat, is in the gym for three hours a day, and eats next to nothing. His spring training regimen with the team alone was rigorous, and he *still* worked out on top of that! He must have thought I was a pig the other night when I polished off a plate of quesadillas and a side of French fries!

I rolled out of bed after ten-minutes of debating on whether to cancel on Drew or not. I checked on Ben and he was sound asleep. I walked into the bathroom and tried to make myself look halfway decent for this time of the morning and trying not to overdo it with make-up for a workout.

I slipped a loose black tank top over my hot pink sports bra. I looked at myself in the full-length mirror. My legs looked pretty decent in my leggings at least. The top was baggy enough around my belly to conceal it. I felt like my boobs still looked too big, even though sports bras usually act as a minimizer. Instead, the bra was pushing my flesh upward to emphasize more cleavage!

I peeked in on Ben once more. He was smiling in his sleep and it made me smile in return. I felt guilty sometimes—for hating Ben's dad so much, for hating what pregnancy did to my appearance and hormones. I just didn't want Ben to ever think I resented him. I wouldn't trade him in for anything in the world!

Laura offered to take Ben with her to her brother's house for a play date with her seven-month-old niece. She was too sweet! I had only been staying with Matt and Laura a few days, and they have both been more than happy to take Ben off my hands. It was nice, but at the same time, I was starting to miss him.

I received a text from Drew saying he was outside. I checked my appearance one last time before leaving the house. There was a black Jeep with the top off in the driveway. Drew grinned at me through the windshield. He reached over to open the passenger side door from the inside for me.

I had to do some maneuvering to get into the jeep because of my height, and Drew laughed.

"Shut up," I pouted.

He squeezed that sensitive spot on my knee, like he had done the other day, and I twitched.

"Stop that!" I smacked his arm before trying to find the same spot on his knee.

Again, like the other day, I failed. Drew pulled out of the driveway. The wind began to whip my ponytail around. Drew's hair looked great as it blew in the wind.

"How'd you sleep?" he asked.

"Not bad. You?"

"I didn't get a lot of it," he shrugged. "I guess too much on my mind."

"The upcoming season?" I guessed.

"Yeah," he nodded with a smirk.

"What's that look about?"

"Nothing."

I didn't prod more, but I wanted to. About ten minutes later, Drew pulled into the gym parking lot.

"Explain to me why you work out so early again," I said, seeing there weren't too many cars in the parking lot.

"Less people bother me at this hour," he said, turning off the engine. "Most of the time, I have a full schedule ahead of me, so it's best to get my workout over with."

"So, how long will we be working out?"

Drew stared at me after getting out of the car.

"Why so many questions?"

I shrugged, "I just want to know what to expect from the Drew boot camp."

He laughed, "Boot camp? Cami, I work out for an hour most days."

I looked at him skeptically and he rolled his eyes.

"Get out of the jeep. I'm not a male Jillian Michaels or anything."

I stepped out of the car and walked toward him. He looked at me amused before slinging an arm around me.

"Why do you look worried?"

"I'm not as in shape as you are...I didn't know what you had in store for me."

We got to the entrance of the gym. He smiled and slid the arm around my shoulders to the exposed space between my sports bra and tank top.

"I think you look pretty shapely," he winked before dropping his hand from my side to open the door for me.

Once more, I felt a cross between attraction and being offended. I couldn't tell if Drew was giving me a compliment or not. My self-esteem was that low these days that I couldn't tell.

We walked inside the gym and were greeted by a perky blonde behind a high wraparound desk. She was dressed in a sports bra and booty shorts, leaving a ton of exposed skin. I was envious of her tight, toned twenty-something-old body.

"Morning Andrew!" She squeaked.

"Hey Kelsey, this is my friend Cami," Drew introduced us.

"Hi," she waved, looking disappointed to see a girl with him.

I responded with an almost inaudible hello. I wasn't good at being friendly to females, especially attractive ones. Drew walked through the gym and I followed behind, watching his butt move in his basketball shorts. I didn't notice when he stopped at the elliptical machines. I wound up bumping into him and he laughed at me. I laughed too, blushing, and hoping he didn't know what I was distracted by.

We spent a half an hour on the elliptical machine. Drew tried to make conversation with me, but I would get short of breath after a while. I was just glad I had been doing some kind of exercise back in New York, or else I probably would have been on the floor by now.

When we got off the elliptical machine, Drew led me to a mat to stretch followed by a bunch of squats, crunches and weights. I couldn't stop looking at Drew's body. It was actually making working out enjoyable, no matter how out of my realm I felt.

As we finished up walking on the treadmill, I was able to hold a conversation.

"Thank you for doing this," I said looking over at Drew, who looked like his eyes were once again focused on my chest.

His eyes looked up at mine, and I couldn't even be mad. I had been checking out his butt any chance I got! I just hoped my now, well-endowed chest was considered attractive and not an odd monstrosity people couldn't help but stare at—like some kind of deformity.

"It's not a big deal," Drew said. "It's nice having someone to talk to."

"None of the guys ever go to the gym with you?"

He shrugged, "Sometimes. Aside from Francisco, the other guys are a bit younger—they're all about showing off."

"Oh, and you're not?" I asked, with a raised eyebrow.

"I can be," he laughed. "But the last time I worked out with Lotto, he wound up straining himself to try and keep up with me. He wanted to be a big shot and prove he could lift more weight than me...and somehow I wound up getting in trouble by Riccardi for our starting pitcher having to be benched."

Greg Riccardi is the head coach of the Yankees. From what I hear from Jordan, Riccardi is harder on Drew and Francisco

Rodriguez since they're the oldest ones on the team. Cisco and Drew were co-captains of the team, and were always told to "look out" for the other guys, which meant any time one of the players did something idiotic while out with them, they'd get blamed somehow. And God forbid Drew or Cisco were late for practice, they were not only fined, but also lectured and razzed for days.

"Besides, I spend so much time with the team, working out is kind of my peace away from them," he shrugged.

"I hope I'm not interrupting that peace," I said.

He smiled, "You're a piece of home to me."

I couldn't help but to allow a big, genuine smile take over my face. Drew almost tripped as he held onto the treadmill.

"Easy with that smile," he said. "People might start to think you're happy."

I rolled my eyes, "Shut up."

He stopped the treadmill and I followed suit.

"I am just glad to see you haven't changed too much," I said, stepping off the machine.

Drew jumped down and looked at me.

"You have."

"I know," I sighed, looking away.

"For the better, I think," he said, walking past me. "I have to go to the bathroom. I'll meet you by the jeep, okay?"

I just watched him walk away. What did he mean by that? I don't see how I could have gotten better over time. I certainly don't feel better. I went to the bathroom before making my way out of the gym. As I passed Kelsey, she practically stared at me.

I got inside the jeep and waited for Drew. He sat down in the driver's seat and looked at me.

"Hungry?"

I was starved, but I didn't want to do too much damage after just working out.

"A little," I lied.

"Do you have to be back for Ben?"

"Matt's fiancée is taking him for a few hours," I shrugged.

Drew nodded, "Good. I can make you breakfast then."

"You cook?" I asked as he started the engine.

"Katie taught me a lot," he said, softly.

Drew wasn't a soft spoken person. He always said things loudly and confidently, even if it came out wrong. It took me a moment to realize what he had said. Katie was Drew's first love, and from what I know, his only love. They dated all throughout college. They broke up because they were on different paths. Katie was a school teacher who wanted a family right away while Drew was traveling for baseball and trying to get drafted to the major leagues. From what I heard from Haley and Jordan, Drew proposed to Katie right after he made it to the Yankees, and she said no. She didn't want a husband who was famous or traveled. He was heartbroken and threw himself into the game more than ever.

I didn't know what to say to Drew about Katie or even if I should say anything. Instead, I put my hand on his knee—not to squeeze it to annoy him, like he had done to me, but to offer him my understanding.

Drew looked down at my hand and then at my face. He smiled as he began to drive. I left my hand there, not really wanting to move it. He didn't seem to mind. There was a comfortable silence as he drove the short distance to his condo.

The place looked bigger in the daytime, but not as big as Matt's. I liked that. The tan building looked like a home, not like a mansion. We got out of the jeep and as Drew opened the door, I smiled to myself, remembering him kissing me while trying to get the key in the door.

We stepped inside and Drew immediately went toward the kitchen. I glanced around the living room. There was a fireplace in the middle of the room with wraparound seating. There was also a skylight. There wasn't much on the walls, but photos of family and friends. I walked closer to one of Drew and Jordan. Drew was wearing a high school baseball uniform. They looked so much alike in the photo.

"Cami?"

I followed Drew's voice to the kitchen. He had taken out eggs and various items.

"Do you like turkey bacon?"

"Sure," I smiled. "This place is really nice."

"Thanks," he said over his shoulder as he began to whisk the egg whites. "It feels so big sometimes. I'm used to New York, you know?"

"Yeah," I nodded. "Can I have the full tour after breakfast?"

"Didn't you see it the other night?" he asked with a laugh.

"I don't think I was paying attention much."

Drew looked over at me and I was smiling stupidly, thinking about us exploring each other the other night more than we did the house.

Drew smirked, "Gotcha."

I leaned my elbow on the island and rested my chin in my hand as I watched Drew cook.

"So how does it feel to not have to work?" he asked.

"Terrible and wonderful all at once," I sighed.

He laughed, "I could relate to that. I wind up getting bored on my time off."

"I don't know anything else but work, you know?"

Drew looked over at me after heating a skillet. I watched the muscles in his arm work as he grabbed the handle, allowing the butter to melt. My eyes drifted to his butt for the billionth time that morning as Drew spoke.

"Well, you deserve a break. How old were you when you started your company?"

"I guess technically seventeen. Before that, I just worked multiple jobs to support myself," I sighed.

"Where'd you get your work ethic?" Drew asked. "I mean, I've always been driven, but that's because I love baseball. What drove you?"

"To start my own company? Music did. I wanted to be a part of it. I never could sing or play an instrument, but selling things—I'm good at that. But I guess survival drove me more than anything else," I said, not realizing I was starting to ramble as I stared at the back of Drew—more so his backside than anything else.

"Survival?" Drew questioned.

I chuckled, forgetting Drew grew up rich. He didn't know anything but money. Jordan shunned his father's money—along with his last name—at a certain age. Drew didn't, however.

"Some of us had to work to get money or a place to stay..."

Drew turned and made a face.

"Wow, sorry. I guess that sounded like a spoiled, rich kid, huh?"

I glanced up at his face immediately, realizing he probably saw me checking him out—again.

"Don't worry about it. I know in spite of the money, it wasn't easy growing up Chuck's son."

Drew shook his head as he continued to cook what looked like an amazing egg white omelet. He didn't look at me, but I heard something in his voice as he spoke.

"It was worse growing up Coryn Reilly-Ashton's son."

"What is your mother like?" I wondered.

Jordan always spoke badly about her, but she was his stepmother so that wasn't surprising.

"Very selfish," Drew sighed. "And money hungry. I don't really see her much or speak to her. Her choice," he said.

I felt bad for him, but I understood the feeling.

"I'm sorry."

"It's fine," he said, looking over at me with a smile.

"I don't talk to my dad. I don't even know him," I said.

Drew slid the omelet onto a plate before starting on the turkey bacon.

"Did you ever try looking for him?"

"He could have found me if he wanted to," I sighed. "I sent him a letter once, after my mom passed away," I said, my throat going dry.

Drew turned away from the bacon and pressed his palms on the island I was leaning on.

"I never knew your mom passed away," he said, with sympathy running through his eyes.

"Right after my seventeenth birthday," I nodded. "She was all I had before I met the guys," I shrugged, feeling myself lose control of my emotions.

It had been so long since I spoke about my past. I don't think Jordan ever knew the details. I told Danny, of course, but we had been dating for some time when I did. I'm not sure why I was telling Drew, but was glad I did when I felt him wrap his arms around me.

Drew had walked around the island and hugged me. I felt stupid for getting sympathy from him for things that happened so long ago.

"Pretty pathetic, right?" I laughed, pulling away from him and not looking him in the eye.

I was on the verge of tears.

"Pathetic? Why would I think you were pathetic?"

I sighed, frustrated with myself, my life, everything.

"Because Drew... I told myself I wouldn't allow anything to get in my way. My mother came here from Italy to make a better life for herself—she thought that better life would depend on a husband who would provide for her. And all she got was knocked up and abandoned," I said. "I promised myself I wouldn't depend on a man for money or anything. Now look at me..." I said looking up at him.

"I'm looking at you," Drew said and he just stared at me for a moment.

"I've failed."

"Are you kidding me, Cami? You failed?" Drew asked. "You don't depend on anyone for money. You started a very wealthy entertainment firm. Without you, my brother and your husband wouldn't be where they are today—and they know that..."

I sighed and shook my head.

"Without Jordan, I would still be waiting tables. He gave me a chance."

Drew shrugged, "I still think Tortured wouldn't be as big as they are without you. Neither would Rad Trick or any of the other acts you manage. You're definitely making your mother proud," he said with such a warm smile.

It made me smile in return, which was good because my tears were becoming noticeable.

"You are the most independent, headstrong, beautiful woman I have ever met," he said, placing a hand on my face.

I looked up at him and though I didn't agree with some of those things, I wanted to believe him.

"I always thought you were sexy…" he said, leaning in and kissing my lips lightly.

"What?" I asked; closing my eyes as his lips kissed my jaw.

"When I was a kid, the first time I met you…you were the first real-life girl I thought was sexy, not just pretty or cute, but…yeah, I was jealous of my brother and Danny for spending so much time with you. I looked up to them and thought they were so cool…" Drew said, in between kisses as my hands went underneath his shirt.

"I couldn't wait to grow up and be with a woman as hot as you," he said, his hands reaching down and grabbing my butt.

I groaned as I grabbed his face and pulled him into a kiss. It was like Drew knew exactly what to say to make me hot. Drew's tongue massaged mine and he lifted me onto the island. I wrapped my legs around his waist and felt him growing against me. I pressed myself against him and he groaned into my mouth. He pulled my hair out of the ponytail it was in and lightly tugged my head back. He kissed down my neck to the top of my cleavage. I moaned, which seemed to fuel his passion. He grew even harder as he pulled my loose tank top down to my waist. He squeezed my boobs and I whimpered.

I started to smell the bacon, but I was too lost in the moment that I ignored it and the smoke that was filling the kitchen. The smoke alarm went off, causing Drew and I both to jump.

"Shit," Drew sighed, running to the stove to turn off the burner.

He then grabbed a chair and placed it in the hallway. He stood on it and popped the battery out of the smoke alarm. A moment later, the loud noise stopped. I pulled my tank top back up and hopped off the island. I took a peek at the turkey bacon and snickered at the charcoaled pieces of meat.

"I hope you like them well-done," Drew laughed, stepping next to me and taking a look.

"I actually hate turkey bacon," I admitted. "If I can't have the real thing, I don't want it at all," I said, looking into his eyes.

He smiled, "I'll keep that in mind."

He moved into kiss me, but I backed away.

"I'm hungry now."

Drew looked surprised. I didn't want to stop what we were doing, but at the same time, I didn't know if we should continue. Sure, I was completely sober now, but Drew was still someone I shouldn't get involved with. He was too young and too close to family.

Drew and I split the large omelet he made along with some fresh fruit and whole wheat toast. We were kind of quiet as we ate.

"Do you want the tour now?" he asked, taking our plates away.

"Sure," I said, standing up.

Drew took me through each room, which was decorated quite simply. I liked his style. Most men overdid it with gaudy things or underdid it with not much furniture. Drew's place felt homey.

"Did you hire a decorator?" I asked.

"No, I did it myself. It's obvious, huh?" he asked as we approached his bedroom.

I shook my head, "No, that's why I asked. You did a great job. If this baseball thing doesn't work out, you might have a career in interior design or as a short order cook."

Drew laughed, "Gee, thanks."

He motioned to the bedroom, "You already saw a good amount of this room."

I nodded, "Show me the yard."

I walked back down the stairs quickly, trying to avoid what was bound to happen in that bedroom. I opened the glass doors leading to the yard and Drew was right behind me. The sun was shining brightly as it danced across the blue water of the gorgeous pool. The backyard looked like a small beach club with a bar, chaise lounges and a gazebo. The pool had two waterfalls and a large Yankees logo on the bottom of the liner.

I looked back at Drew in awe.

"This is absolutely amazing," I said.

He smiled and took my hand.

"There's more."

He walked me up a set of spiral cement stairs that went behind a giant manmade rock garden where the water was falling from. There was a beautiful view of the beach and the ocean, that I could only imagine would be even more breathtaking at night.

I looked over and Drew was smiling, watching my reaction.

"I bet this is quite the bachelor pad, huh?"

He shrugged and pulled me against him.

"What do you think?"

"I think you're smooth, but..." I said pushing away from him, reluctantly. "I'm too old and..."

He rolled his eyes, "Don't even, Cami. Eight years is nothing. And I won't stop."

"Won't stop?" I wondered.

"We started something the other night, and now I can't stop thinking about finishing it," he said. "You're the reason I didn't sleep much last night. Tell me you're not feeling the same way, and I'll try and back off."

He looked into my eyes and he was right. Why was I going to fight this urge? I needed to get it out of my system. I wanted his body—all of it this time. I was surprised he wanted my body, though.

"Let's go swimming," I said, hurrying down the steps, smiling back at him teasingly.

He followed behind me quickly and I dove into the pool. It was much easier to hide my body in the water. I surfaced in time to see Drew taking off his shirt. Oh God, I couldn't wait to kiss his chest. The sun reflected off his number 12 pendant as he dove into the water. He swam over to me at warped speed, it seemed like. I felt his fingers behind my knees as his head came above the water. I yelped as his lips made contact with my neck. My hands wove into his wet hair as his fingers fought to remove my leggings. I laughed at his frustration.

"Help me," he said, nipping my neck.

I hooked my fingers into my pants and tried to pry them off, but I kept falling under the water. Drew chuckled and pulled me over to the shallow end of the pool. Once I found my footing, I was able to get my pants off, even though it was still a struggle. I threw them on the side of the pool before lifting my tank top over my head, leaving me in just my panties and sports bra.

I jumped onto Drew and kissed him, deeply. I pushed him against the side of the pool and began caressing his chest and nipples as I kissed him. I ground myself against him, causing him to groan.

"Cami," he breathed.

Hearing him say my name that way almost sent me over the edge.

"I want you inside me now," I whispered into his ear before sucking on his lobe.

Drew pushed my legs off of him and locked eyes with me while reaching down to pull his shorts and briefs off at the same time. He rolled the pieces of clothing into a ball and tossed them expertly. The soggy pieces of clothing landed close to my leggings with a plunk.

I pulled my sports bra over my head and his eyes were trying to see more of my breasts as I reached down to remove my panties. I threw the small material and my sports bra together; trying to get them to land next to the other discarded clothing, but was unsuccessful. Oh well.

I jumped back onto Drew, wrapping my legs around him. He squeezed me against him, and we both groaned, feeling our most intimate parts rubbing together.

"Sexy," he said before lifting one of my breasts to his mouth.

I moaned loudly and he intensified his lips around my nipple. I reached down and began stroking him with my hand. It was his turn to moan, which felt great against my responsive nipple. He ran a hand down my side to my butt then around to my hip before dipping a finger inside of me, causing me to call out his name.

"Are you ready?" he asked, his lips hovering over mine.

I stared into his playful brown eyes and nodded. I placed his tip at my entrance and he pushed forward, causing us both to cry out.

"You've been such a tease," he said as he thrust forward again.

I gasped, both from the feeling and him calling me a tease.

"What?"

He smirked at me before kissing me.

"Stripping the other night... Last night on the beach wearing that thin shirt..." he said, thrusting further with each word, making me almost go limp in his arms.

"Then this morning," he said, his breathing getting heavier. "Watching your body move...your ass..." he said grabbing onto it, pushing all the way into me.

I cried out and he groaned. I decided to regain some control and began pulling back.

"And you're not a tease?" I asked, licking at his lip and pushing forward, making him let out a whimper.

He turned us around and pressed me into the wall of the pool.

"So you *were* looking at me," he smirked.

I bit my bottom lip and ran my fingers into his hair before kissing him deeply, not letting him come up for air as he began to thrust inside me faster and harder. It wasn't long before we both climaxed together, something that hadn't happened for me in a very long time. It was that amazing, earth shattering release that everyone wishes could happen every time. My heart was pounding as Drew pressed his head against my chest.

On the ride back to Matt's place early that afternoon, I thought about what the hell Drew and I were doing. I looked over at him as he drove, a silly smile on his face. I decided it didn't matter what we were doing. It was obvious we needed this. It doesn't have to mean anything and no one has to know about it.

Sex was easier. I never had any trouble with that, even now that I'm older and not as eye-catching, I can still somehow attract a hot baseball player. Maybe it was some childhood fantasy for him—to bang his older brother's ex-girlfriend, but whatever. I was obviously twisted enough to allow it, and twisted enough to still have leftover feelings for his brother all these years.

My relationship with Danny would have been fine, too, had it not turned into anything more than sex. We would have been great friends with benefits. With Drew, while I was in Florida, I was going to allow this affair to play out, and not ruin it with my inability to love properly. Or maybe guys just couldn't love me properly because I was broken.

Drew pulled into Matt's driveway.

"Same time tomorrow?" he asked, referring to the gym.

We both knew after the workout, we'd have a repeat performance of today, though.

I smiled, "Sounds good."

CHAPTER TWELVE

It was weird. I felt like a bad mother the next morning. I felt bad enough leaving Ben to have a sexy romp in the pool with Andrew Ashton, who is eight years my junior, but now I felt even worse bringing my son along for the ride!

I couldn't leave Ben with Laura and Matt again—that would be taking advantage. Besides, I loved being there when Ben woke up in the morning. Matt had offered for me to borrow his car any time, so I took him up on it.

At five-thirty-am, I loaded up my still sleeping four-month-old. I looked at him in the rearview mirror and wondered what Danny would think of me taking Ben. I told myself I was just taking my son to the gym where he would sleep through my workout, but I knew that wasn't bad. The reason for my guilt was what I would be doing after the workout.

Suddenly, I felt this queasy feeling in my stomach. My heart was pounding on top of it. I didn't just feel awkward about bringing Ben along to my affair. I felt like I was cheating on Danny. Technically, I guess I was, being that we were still married. Considering my husband has a girlfriend and we've already filed for divorce, I suppose it was okay, even though it still felt wrong after all these years of being with the same man, to now be with someone else.

As much as it felt wrong, though, it felt liberating and amazing—like I was actually feeling something again, not the dull ache I had been experiencing for so many years. How many years did I feel that ache? I just kept ignoring it, until that pain slowly ripped me apart. I felt like I was gasping for air once the shit hit the fan. I was mad. I was bruised. I didn't know who I was. I still didn't know who I was anymore. I guess I am trying to figure out who Cami Woods really is—without a husband and without a career to hide behind. She's a mother now, that's for sure. Was it okay for Moms to have affairs?

Staring at Ben's sleeping face, it was hard to answer that. I suppose if I was putting him in a bad situation, it would be wrong. I wasn't bringing him to a bar or sleeping with several men, and bringing those strangers around him. I was going to be with Drew, who Ben would grow up calling uncle. Drew was a good guy—maybe he was a bit wild in the sack and probably had a roster of women he kept in rotation, but again, was that going to hurt Ben? No. Too many people have been telling me that if I was miserable, Ben would be miserable. Well, then I might as well have harmless fun!

I started up the car and punched in the gym's address on the GPS. I am not the best driver, to be honest. Growing up in New York City, I was able to get around riding subways and buses. I couldn't afford a car until I was in my twenties anyhow. Sebastian wound up teaching me to drive and I got my license when I was twenty-four. Still, I didn't drive all that much, unless I was heading to the Hamptons, or out of state.

Driving Matt's Mercedes made me slightly nervous. Driving with Ben in the back made me extremely nervous. I think I was driving fifteen miles an hour! Luckily, there weren't many cars on the road to beep at me. I heard my text messages going off. Afraid I would crash, I didn't dare check them! I knew they were from Drew wondering what was taking me so long.

My phone rang just as I pulled into the parking lot of the gym, where I ever so carefully pulled into a spot. I turned the car off and grabbed my phone. I sent Drew a text letting him know I was in the parking lot before I got out of the truck. I opened the back door and slid the top part of Ben's car seat off. I carried the seat, which was way heavier than my little boy, into the gym.

Drew was leaning on the desk talking to Kelsey, the beautiful blonde from the day before. She was leaning toward him as well. I gripped the handle of Ben's carrier tighter. I tried my best to control the jealousy coursing through me. I had no right to be jealous. I wasn't Drew's girlfriend. Besides, they were only talking.

Kelsey reached over and caressed Drew's arm. I imagined crushing the hand she touched him with by slamming Ben's carrier on top of it! Instead, I calmly and casually walked toward them.

"Hey," I said, overly cheery.

Drew stood up straight and smiled. I felt the jealousy subside completely in that moment. He had the kind of smile that made you smile in return.

"It's about time," he laughed.

Kelsey busied herself with other things once she lost his attention.

"Sorry. Nervous Mommy," I motioned to Ben. "I haven't really driven with him yet."

"Is he asleep?" Drew asked, walking closer. "I want to finally meet the little guy."

"Yeah. He fell asleep kind of late last night so he might be out for a while."

Drew peeked in at Ben and smiled.

"He has your lips."

He looked up at my lips and moved in to peck them softly. I smiled and shrugged.

"I think he looks a lot like Danny."

Drew nodded, "He does, but I see you in there, too."

We walked further into the gym and began our workout. I was able to keep up more of a conversation on the elliptical machine this time.

"You must be beat if Ben didn't go to sleep until late," Drew commented.

I shrugged, "I'm kind of used to the whole losing sleep thing by now. Although, he's a really good baby. He's been sleeping through the night for the past few weeks."

"I give you a lot of credit, Cami," Drew said.

"For what?"

"For being a great mother."

I laughed, "It's only been a few months. Let's see when he's older."

Drew chuckled, "Seriously. You could have sent Ben off to be with Danny or got a nanny even, but it's just you and him. I admire that," he smiled at me.

I knew that's what mothers were supposed to do—take care of their kids. I didn't find being a devoted mother nearly as impressive as Drew did. I know it was because his own mother was anything but devoted.

"Thanks, but I never saw any other way. I wanted a baby for so long and I finally got one under bad circumstances, of course, but Ben's my dream come true," I explained. "We're a team. He's here for me as much as I'm here for him."

Drew smiled, "I would have never guessed you'd be like this."

"Like what?" I asked, not sure if I would like what he was going to say.

"Nurturing."

I shrugged, "I know. I guess I'm even surprised by it. I'm a cold, heartless bitch most of the time, right?"

I was hoping Drew would disagree, but he was quiet for a moment before speaking.

"You never were a bitch to me," he winked.

It wasn't exactly the argument I wanted him to make, but it was better than nothing I guess.

"Your brother could vouch for my bitchiness, I'm sure."

"Hey, Jordan still keeps you around, right?"

I just smiled and peeked over at Ben's carrier to make sure he was still asleep. I wanted to cry at that moment. Why did I care so much what people thought of me lately? I don't think I would have gotten far on being nice in the entertainment industry. In order to prove myself, I had to be cutthroat and cunning. Obviously Jordan didn't care that I was a bitch. Or maybe he did and that's why I wasn't the one married to him.

I then wondered if Jordan found out I was sleeping with Drew—or I slept with him, maybe it was a one-time thing after all—would he still keep me around? Part of me even felt like I was betraying Jordan by messing around with his brother. I know it wasn't like I dated Jordan recently or anything, but I still dated him. Was I breaking some kind of code?

"You're not going to tell Jordan..." I began, looking back at Drew. "About yesterday or the other night...right?"

Drew laughed, "Uh, no? You're not, right?"

"No," I shook my head.

"I don't keep secrets from Jordan usually, but this...what happens in Florida, stays in Florida," he winked.

I laughed, "Good."

After our workout, Drew carried Ben out to the car for me.

"Meet me at my house?" he asked, pulling the door open for me and leaning on it.

"And if I said no?" I asked.

He smirked, "I would think our workout wasn't complete."

"Well, I don't want to back down from the boot camp," I said, running a hand over his chest.

He looked around to make sure the parking lot was empty before leaning down and kissing me deeply. I wrapped my arms around his neck and pressed my body against his.

I got in Matt's truck and watched Drew walk over to his jeep. I tried to follow him to his place, but he drove much faster than I was willing to go. I wound up entering his address into the GPS. Just as I pulled onto his block, Ben began fussing in the back. I looked at him through the rearview mirror and his eyes were opening. Oh crap. Great timing.

"Hi baby boy," I cooed before Ben could cry, which I could tell by his face was about to happen.

He started to fuss even more.

"Hold on, I'll get you in a second," I told him as if he would understand.

I pulled into the driveway behind Drew's jeep. I pulled the diaper bag out and the carrier. Ben was now crying since I still hadn't picked him up. I walked up to the doorstep and before I could ring the bell, Drew opened the door.

"Someone woke up," I said.

Drew smiled down at Ben, taking the carrier from me. I followed him into the house where he placed Ben, who was full on crying now, on the couch.

"I'm coming, Benvy," I said.

"Benvy?" Drew asked.

I shrugged as I walked over, "I'm trying out different nicknames. I don't really like Benny."

Drew was unbuckling Ben and picking him up before I could get to him.

"Oh, right, his full name is Benvenuto?" he asked, holding Ben in his large arms like a little football.

Ben's cries slowed to a stop to my surprise. Even Laura said she couldn't get him to stop crying yesterday morning until she gave him a bottle. Usually, he only stopped crying once *I* picked him up or he was fed.

"Y-yeah," I said, sitting down beside Drew, baffled by how my son wasn't crying for me.

"Hi Benvy," Drew said, holding onto Ben's finger.

Ben smiled up at him and it felt like someone hugged my heart. I don't know why I felt so moved by Drew holding my son. Actually, that was a lie. I do know why, but I didn't like how I could be so sappy as to wish I could have a normal family—with a husband who was around to be with me and our baby. Thinking back, I felt the same feeling when I looked at Jordan, Haley and Aylin together, too. There was a longing inside me to have a whole family. Even when things were okay with Danny, something was missing. I thought it was as simple as a baby, but maybe there was a feeling missing, too. I longed for unconditional love, to have someone to come home to that looked at me like I was his world and I would be theirs. In a way, that's what I had with my mother. I was alone in all other aspects of my life, but my mother was always a constant. With the craziness of the industry all my friends and I are in, there are no constants.

Now, I had a son who would be my constant, though. I was holding onto that.

I knew Danny was going to be a good father. I just wonder if one day, when he remarries, because he will—he can't be alone—and has other children, would he be there for Ben as much? I already knew he would never be there for me again. I also knew I wouldn't get married again, that's for sure. I don't know if I'll ever date seriously again, actually. Ben would offer me that unconditional love I so desperately craved—as long as I don't screw up his life too much.

Friends with benefits should be my shtick. Guys love being friends with me because I'm not too emotional—until recently anyway, and my guy friends love to flirt with me, so it's perfect! I'll just get through this disturbing, woe is me phase, and then become fiercer than ever. Drew will help me on my road to recovery! We want the same things from each other—a good time.

I was snapped out of my thoughts by Ben's cries. Drew handed him over to me.

"My poor baby is hungry," I said, making sure his diaper was still dry.

I had changed him before I left Matt's. I pulled a bottle out from the diaper bag and Drew looked at me surprised.

"I thought you breastfed?"

I sighed, "I tried to at first, but I guess between stress and Ben coming a little early, I didn't produce enough milk."

Drew just looked on as I fed Ben the bottle. It made me self-conscious. I was pretty sure Drew had never been with a mother before. For a moment, I wondered if I was part of some unlived fantasy, like those guys who like pregnant women or to be disciplined like a child. So far, he hadn't shown any signs of anything too kinky, thankfully.

"What?" I finally asked him.

He shrugged, "I don't know. I'm kinda fascinated by boobs."

I laughed, "You're a grown man and you're still fascinated?"

"Well, yeah. I don't have them and it's strange that stuff can come out of them. They're pretty amazing."

I shook my head, slightly amused, "Well, I don't have a penis and I'm not all that fascinated with them, even when stuff comes out of them."

Drew chuckled, "Are you sure about that? You seemed to be fascinated a little bit yesterday."

I smirked, "It wasn't that little."

Drew grinned proudly and I looked down at Ben.

"So, was yesterday a one-time thing?" he asked.

I looked over at him and his brown eyes looked so sweet—just like how a little boy would ask for a new bike.

"I don't know..." I said. "Do you want it to happen again?"

"Stupid question, Cami..." he said standing up.

I looked down at Ben to make sure he was still drinking before looking up at Drew as he played with the zipper on his hoodie.

"I don't think it's that stupid. You said you couldn't stop thinking about us together since the idea was put in your head. We were together, so...maybe you're satisfied," I said, still not believing I was even having this conversation with him.

If anyone would have told me years ago that I would have amazing sex with Andrew Ashton, I would have laughed and thought they got the wrong brother!

"I am definitely not satisfied," Drew said, staring at me.

I just stared at him, not sure if that was a compliment or an insult.

"Wait, that came out wrong. I mean, yes, yesterday was very satisfying, but I want more."

I smirked, "I do, too. I just..." I looked down at Ben.

Drew sat down again.

"I didn't mean right now," he said, touching Ben's head lightly.

"Good," I said.

"Let's eat," he said, standing up.

I was glad he suggested food because my stomach was starting to growl. After Ben was finished with his bottle, I placed him in his carrier and we put it on the kitchen table as we ate.

"You want to come to the game tonight?" Drew asked.

"Um, of course," I smiled as I took a spoonful of oatmeal.

It was a simple bowl of rolled oats, but Drew mixed agave nectar, brown sugar, nuts and fresh fruit with it. I figured he'd be a simple cereal kind of guy like his brother was. Maybe it was the rich kid in him.

"Bring Matt and his girl."

"One problem, who's going to watch Ben?" I motioned to my baby who was fascinated by his own fingers at the moment.

"He's invited too," Drew said. "Tomorrow I have an away game, so I'll be leaving in the morning."

"Aw, does that mean no workout for us?" I pouted seductively.

He leaned closer, "You can use my guest pass if you want. I asked Kelsey."

I pulled back and scoffed, "Kelsey at the gym? She said yes to you, but she'll say no to me."

"She told me she'd let you work out."

"Drew, that girl doesn't like me."

"What are you talking about?" Drew asked.

"She's jealous," I shrugged, not bothering to let him know that I felt the same way.

"Oh well."

"How come you never made a move on her?" I wondered.

He laughed, "She's the one who's jealous? Or is it you?"

"A little tip about me...I'm always jealous," I admitted.

"Danny and Jordan have said that about you."

I frowned and stared at my oatmeal. Drew got quiet too. It was awkward to mention my jealousy in previous relationships with him.

"Sorry," he said. "So you were asking about Kelsey?"

"Yeah. She's beautiful and perfect. Why would you pass that up?" I asked.

Drew shrugged, "She's pretty, but she's not perfect. I don't know. She makes it really easy, and maybe that's part of it."

I raised an eyebrow, "I made it easy, too."

Drew held his finger up, "Not really. You made me wait like eighteen years."

I scowled, "You were ten when we met. You weren't even in my line of sight."

"Ouch, that hurts," he chuckled. "I used to check you and Haley out all the time."

"You were such a horny kid," I rolled my eyes.

He shrugged, "I was going through a lot of changes. The girls in school just didn't cut it for me. My cool older brother knew real women."

I laughed, "How did Jordan feel about you drooling over his woman? I know he didn't care about me, but Haley..."

Drew shrugged, "He used to get annoyed with me a lot. Thankfully my crush on Haley faded, especially once she had Aylin. At that point, she was family and girls my age started maturing enough," he laughed.

"You're such a punk," I shook my head at him.

"Come on, you never thought I was cute?" he asked.

"I thought you were cute, of course, but in that little boy way. I knew you'd be a heartbreaker some day," I said, standing up to clear our bowls.

On my way back from the sink, Drew grabbed me and pulled me into his lap.

"You never found me attractive?" he asked, his voice dropping.

I swallowed as he stared into my eyes.

"Well, when you visited on tour that time...you were on spring break from college..." I said remembering back.

Drew ran a finger over my lips.

"You and Sebastian were playing basketball."

"Uh huh," Drew said, running the same finger down my throat before kissing behind my ear.

"You took off your shirt and..."

Drew's hand went to my breast and I found myself pushing it toward him as his kisses went to my neck.

"And what?"

"I thought you looked hot..."

Drew looked at me and kissed me. I pulled away to look back at Ben before I stood up, pushing his hands away.

"You're sick, you know that?"

Drew laughed incredulously, "Why am I sick?"

"Because you want me to admit I was slobbering over you when I was married!"

He shrugged, "Come on, you can't admire someone's looks when you're married?"

"Have you no loyalty to Danny?" I asked.

"Wow," Drew said. "You want me to have loyalty to Danny? Fine. Then we can just stop whatever it is we've started. All I know is I've been loyal before and all it got me was a broken heart. How about you? How's loyalty working for you, Cami?" he asked, frustration in his voice.

He walked upstairs, leaving me there with Ben who was dozing off. I felt tears coming to my eyes and I wiped them away. How could such a stupid conversation, that was getting me hot, turn into a serious argument about my estranged husband?

I was projecting my own issues with loyalty onto Drew. I felt so much disloyalty to

Danny by still feeling something for Jordan. On top of that, I felt disloyal to Haley for it as well.

I took Ben's carrier off the table and walked upstairs with him. I set him down right outside Drew's bedroom. I walked into the room and Drew was lying down with his eyes closed. I crawled onto the bed as quietly as possible. Without saying a word, I pulled his shorts down. Drew's hands ran through my hair as I used my mouth on him. His moans drove me to please him further.

His fingers tightened around my hair, pulling slightly, telling me he was close. Hearing him call my name out as he exploded was incredibly sexy. I looked up at his face and crawled next to him. He looked at me with a silly smile. I felt so small next to him. His large hand caressed my cheek.

"Screw loyalty," I smiled.

He smiled in return, "What they don't know won't hurt them."

"Katie really hurt you, huh?" I asked.

Drew groaned, "I don't want to talk about Katie."

I nodded as he began kissing me. Why did I keep trying to get personal? I used to do it with Jordan. I did it with Danny when we first got together, but he was a blunt kind of guy—he kind of laid his cards on the table with what appeared to be no emotional scars. Now I realize, Danny's baggage will be me. I was his only serious relationship and I will be the one to blame in all future relationships, I'm sure.

As Drew began taking my pants off, I realized it was going to be harder for me to have a purely physical relationship than I thought. How do girls do it? Do girls actually turn their emotions off or are they pretending? How the hell do guys do it?

I finally shut my mind off as Drew's tongue made contact with my thighs. I cried out, wanting him closer to my center. He didn't disappoint. It didn't take long for me to have another mind-blowing orgasm. By that time, Drew was ready to be inside me. His fingers went to the bottom of my tank top and began to lift it.

I pushed his hands away.

"No, leave it on," I pleaded.

Drew looked at me confused and I just pressed my lips on his. It took some maneuvering, but I got the thick straps of my tank top down past my breasts. I took my sports bra off. Drew forgot about trying to remove the protective covering of my flabby belly as he made out with my breasts, pushing himself into me as he did.

Afterward, we lay there in silence for a moment with my head on his chest and his hand on my butt.

"Where's Ben?"

"Sleeping," I said, yawning.

"I have to get in the shower and get going to the field."

"Oh okay," I said, slowly sitting up.

"You can stay here and sleep if you want."

He slid out from underneath me and I curled back up with his pillow. Before I knew it, I was waking up to Ben giggling. My eyes opened and Drew was sitting on the edge of the bed, fully dressed and blowing raspberries on Ben's belly. I watched for a moment before speaking up.

"I wish all your fans could see this."

Drew turned to see me.

"I miss Aylin at this age," he said.

"I'm sure she misses you as a teenager, too."

Drew shrugged, "I still act like a kid around her."

I crawled over to him in just my tank top.
I raised an eyebrow, "Just around her?"

We kissed softly and he wiggled his eyebrows.

"I hope I'm more skilled than some kid."

"Mmm," I said in a relaxed state. "Definitely."

Ben smiled up at me and he reached his hands out to me.

"Aw, someone loves his Mommy," Drew said handing my son to me.

I cuddled Ben close and he was making the cutest sounds, as if he were happy to be in my arms. I was happy to have him there. Drew stared at us for a moment before standing up.

"So, I'll see you tonight?"

As I got ready for the game, I debated on wearing Yankees gear or dressing up a little. Drew had only really seen me in workout clothes, but since Matt and Laura would be at the game, dressing down would probably be wise. Besides, keeping things casual was a frame of mind. If I went and got all decked out, tonight might as well be a date instead of a casual night seeing my favorite baseball team play.

Laura walked into my room in a Yankees t-shirt stretched across her belly.

"Hey, how are you feeling?" I asked, since she was having morning sickness earlier.

"So much better. I don't think little Maddie likes spicy food. She must take after her daddy," Laura said, rubbing her belly.

"I thought you weren't sure on the name?"

Just the day before, Laura said she didn't like Madeline anymore and was leaning toward Emmaline. I didn't really like either, but I kept my mouth shut, knowing most people probably didn't like Benvenuto as a first name.

"Well, I'm not, but Matt suggested Madison last night, which I like so much better," Laura said with a smile. "Then we can still call her Maddie after her daddy."

"Aw. I like Madison too," I agreed in all honesty.

"So how are things with you and Drew? You've been spending a whole lot of time with him the past few days," she said, with a goofy smile.

"Things are good. We're friends."

"Just friends, huh?"

I sighed. It wasn't that I didn't want to confide in someone. It was that I feared if I told Matt and Laura too much, it would get out somehow.

"Laura, I think you can figure it out."

"Oh, okay. I'm sorry to pry. I just thought...well, you two would make one beautiful couple."

I smiled at her widely, "He is gorgeous, isn't he?"

Laura nodded with huge eyes.

"Gosh, yes! But you're just as gorgeous as he is!"

I laughed at her, "Right."

"You seriously are," Laura said. "To be honest, when Matt asked if you could stay with us, I was intimidated by it all."

"Wait, by me?" I asked.

"Yeah. Matt told me how he used to have a crush on you, but how much he appreciated your friendship. He said you were real and didn't kiss his ass like everyone else he knew. He was hurt when you lost touch," Laura explained.

I felt bad. Talk about disloyalty. I was the epitome of it, wasn't I? In order for me to be loyal to one person, I was disloyal to others.

"It hurt me, too," I sighed. "Thank you for trusting me enough to have me here," I smiled.

"Oh, I didn't trust you enough," Laura laughed. "I barely know you."

I looked at her, not knowing how to respond.

"I trust Matt completely though," she smiled before walking out.

It hit me then that I don't understand that kind of trust. I never trusted Danny when I actually thought about it. My jealousy proved how little I had trust in people. With how little my faith was, it was astonishing to me that I let my pain cut so deeply. Shouldn't I have expected how my life ended up?

My cell phone began to ring and I frowned at seeing Danny's number. I realized I never texted him back. I wasn't in the mood to argue. I sent the call to voicemail. Laura walked back into the room and I looked at her expectantly.

"I'm sorry," she sighed. "That came out so bitchy."

I laughed, "Wow, is this what nice people do? Apologize? Laura, I would have done a lot worse to any girl friends of my husband's."

She smiled, "So we're still friends?"

"Yes. I need some of those lately," I nodded.

Twenty minutes later, we were all getting into the Mercedes truck. Matt was laughing at how much he had to adjust the seat since I was the last one to drive it.

"Are you sure you're tall enough to legally drive?"

"I'm not that short," I huffed.

I was of average height for a woman, but to Matt, everyone was short. Ben squealed from his seat and I looked over at him. He was smiling with his tongue poking out of his mouth.

"Are you making fun of Mommy?" I asked him and he smiled bigger.

His smile had the same effect on me as Drew's did. I smiled back at him and it felt good. After being so down for so long, it felt like a miracle to be smiling again.

We got to Steinbrenner Field with a bit of time to spare, which was good. I hated to be late to anything. Working with hot shot celebrities who enjoy being late to events drove me insane. Danny always made me late. He would procrastinate getting ready until the last minute. Darren was even worse. Luckily, Jordan and Sebastian were the reliable ones when it came to punctuality, but even they slacked once in a while. It made me so angry. I am the type of person who likes to get to a movie before the previews start. If I missed one preview, I would complain the rest of the night to whoever was responsible for our tardiness.

I was surprised Matt got us to the game so early, but I realized it was because he was eager. Drew was arranging for us to come into the clubhouse before the game, mostly for Matt's sake, but I was pretty excited as well, even though I had met and hung out with the team already. We arrived a half an hour earlier than the time Drew asked us to.

After we parked, I sent Drew a text to let him know we were there. I grabbed the diaper bag and put it on my shoulder before taking Ben out of his seat and resting him on my hip. He was dressed in a white onesie with a baseball design on it and khaki shorts. I wish I had brought some of his Yankees clothing with me to Florida.

We made our way inside the stadium. Greg Riccardi met us outside the clubhouse. He shook Matt's hand first, recognizing him.

"We're glad to have ya," Riccardi smiled.

I knew what Riccardi's greeting meant. He was going to use Matt Porter's presence in the Yankees' clubhouse as a publicity tool. I knew that behind the doors leading to the locker room, there would be a ton of photographers. I was sure Matt wouldn't mind; it would be great publicity for him as well.

I wasn't sure how I felt, though. If I were just another girl, it wouldn't matter. Photographers would pay me no mind. Even though I wasn't a traditional celebrity, I was still the wife of the bad boy of alternative rock. I was also on several business publications' most successful entrepreneurs list. Cami Woods wasn't exactly a name that the media will ignore—especially the tabloids.

Riccardi led the way into the clubhouse. A few flashes from cameras went off immediately. I looked down at Ben, who was looking around at all of the people curiously. I could already see the headline: Danny D's estranged wife recovers in Tampa with new baby while he parties on tour with new girlfriend.

Just like I told any of my clients when they received bad press or paparazzi nosing into their personal lives, it was part of the job and you just have to choose to ignore it. It was easier said than done, that's for sure. It wasn't like I looked like the bad guy in the headlines. The blame was thrown on Danny mostly, but it still upset me—to be the victim and to see negative press go toward Tortured. I never wanted to be a victim and I never tried to act like one. I hated the way people looked at me, with those sympathetic smiles and soothing voices. What's really weird was that I didn't want the negativity to hurt Danny. Why wouldn't I? Didn't he deserve to be publicized as a dirty cheater?

"Hey Cami," the deep voice of Will Nostri, the third baseman called out to me.

"Hi Will," I smiled with a wave.

Nostri was the youngest player on the team. It was his first year playing professionally. He was a sweet kid and it was obvious he looked up to Drew.

"Cami!" Francisco "Cisco" Rodriguez called out.

He came over and kissed my cheek.

"Is this your little guy?"

"Yup. This is Benvenuto."

"Ben-va-who?"

I laughed, "It's Italian."

Matt nudged my arm and I introduced them. Matt was enthralled with speaking to Cisco as I waved to a couple of the other guys walking around. Laura excused herself to the bathroom. Nostri offered to lead the way.

The photographers were snapping photos like crazy by this point, even asking Matt, Nostri, Cisco and me to pose for one. I was wondering where Drew's locker was when someone tapped my shoulder. I turned around and Drew stood there with a tiny Yankees cap on his head.

"Your hat shrunk!" I laughed.

He grinned, "It's for Benvy."

Drew placed the hat on Ben's head. It was a little big, but he would grow into it.

"Thank you. I was thinking he wasn't dressed up enough for his first baseball game."

"I'm honored I get to play his first game."

"I think Matt wants to live back here," I whispered, nodding over to him getting a ball signed from several players.

Drew laughed, "You think he'll hook me up with backstage passes for a Sound Wave show in return?"

"He'd give you passes to every show," I rolled my eyes. "I still can't believe you like Sound Wave. I don't even know if I like Sound Wave," I laughed.

"Come on, they're a classic pop group now."

"I'm more of a rock chick," I shrugged.

He smirked, "You sound like my brother. Even Jordan is starting to admit to liking some pop music. Besides, Tortured is pretty mainstream for rock. Who are you guys kidding?"

"Ugh," I gasped. "Mainstream? What an insult."

We were both teasing each other so much that we forgot all about the photographers and Matt. It wasn't until Riccardi was yelling at Drew to get in the group photo with Matt that we came back to the rest of the world.

Laura and I stood watching. Matt then insisted Laura get in the photo.

"Cami, you get in here too," Cisco called out.

"Oh, no, I'm fine," I waved him off.

Drew walked over and grabbed Ben out of my arms before taking my hand. I scowled at him, but followed him over to the team. The photo was snapped and I figured there wasn't much drama the paparazzi could create from it. It wasn't like I was making out with Drew or anything in the photo. The connection between Drew and I was easily identifiable to the outside eye. He is the brother of one of my clients/friends. End of story.

That connection led me to believe hugging Drew in front of the photographers was perfectly acceptable as well.

"Have a good game," I smiled, kissing his cheek.

His brown eyes stared into mine and I wanted to give him a much bigger kiss. He got a sideways smile on his face as he winked.

"I'll miss you tomorrow morning," he said.

A stupid smile came across my face and I blushed.

"Working out won't be the same."

"It's no fun playing by yourself," he said.

I laughed loudly, drawing attention to myself. To cover up our hushed conversation, Drew grabbed Ben out of my arms and kissed his cheek. He handed Ben back to me.

The team was flying to Philadelphia right after the game tonight. Originally Drew thought they wouldn't be leaving until tomorrow, which means I won't get to see him tonight.

"See you when you get back," I waved before Matt and Laura said their goodbyes.

You can bet your butt I didn't get up before six-am the next morning. There was no motivation to. I woke up to Ben crying. After changing him and feeding him, I walked downstairs. Matt and Laura weren't up yet. They had gone out after dropping me and Ben off to celebrate the Yankees win.

I searched the cabinets for breakfast and found some sugary cereal. It made me crave the home cooked breakfast Drew made me the other day. I smiled thinking about Drew. He is quite a person. Not only did he have the body of a god and the face of a devious angel, but he was sweet, quick-witted, talented, and honest. At first, I didn't know how it made me feel for Drew to tell me he had crushes on Haley and me, but now it was flattering.

I'm sure had Haley not married his brother, it might be her fooling around with him instead of me. That thought upset me and I didn't know why. It was probably due to the fact that I'm already jealous of Haley for having what I want—to know she could have Drew if she wanted to, if Jordan wasn't in the picture, frustrated me.

I guess I wanted something—or someone—that was all mine. I wanted to be special. I never felt special before—especially to a man. Yes, Danny told me he loved me, but it didn't feel like it most of the time. Even when I thought about my love for Danny, I don't think of it like my love for Jordan. I love and loathe Danny all at once—kind of like a brother. That sounds sick, I guess. If I had a brother, I would have never had a child with him—I know that, but I almost feel about Danny the same way I feel about Darren and Sebastian. They're family to me. I love them, but it's different.

I never had that all-consuming feeling that people talk about in books and movies. Though I hurt over my relationship with Danny, it wasn't necessarily because my heart was breaking; it was because I felt betrayed or like I had lost. Or maybe it was because I was frustrated to know deep down Danny and I didn't love each other the way people *in love* loved one another.

My phone made a noise and I jumped, snapping out of my thoughts realizing I hadn't touched my cereal. I let go of my spoon and looked at my phone. There was a text message from Drew or "Hot Ass" rather. I had changed his name to something more discreet, in case anyone broke into my phone.

Cisco doesn't fill out a tank top like you do ;-)

I smiled to myself before replying.

Soggy cereal doesn't compare to your breakfasts.

A moment later, a new message came in.

I think we have a problem…

My heart pounded wondering what he was going to say as I sent my response.

We do?

I'm addicted to you.

I read the message three times. I couldn't help the smile on my face, but I was freaking out at the same time. What did he mean? Was he just being cute and flirty? Yes, of course he was. I decided to flirt back.

I'm looking forward to your next hit ;-)

I was waiting for a text back about my drug/baseball pun when my phone rang instead, causing me to jump again. It was Danny. I sighed and looked at Ben.

"Your daddy sure can ruin the mood," I mumbled before answering. "Hey."

"What the hell, Cami? I've texted. I've called. I'm in another part of the world away from my son and you don't respond to me? You had me fucking worried!" he yelled.

I groaned, "I'm sorry. I've been busy."

"Doing what?" he snarled, like I had no right. "Don't tell me you're doing work in Florida."

"I'm not. I've been taking some me time, like you wanted."

"Right. You time. Is that why I saw a photo of you and that jackass Matt Porter with our baby?"

I groaned, "That jackass is my friend. I'm staying with Matt and—"

"You're what?" Danny screamed. "Funny how you failed to mention that! I can't believe you took our son to stay with your boyfriend after you lectured me—"

I was surprised Jordan didn't tell Danny where I was staying. He knew I was at Matt's. I was still skeptical Jordan somehow enlisted Matt to help get me out of my funk. The thought frustrated me, but it also made me happy knowing Jordan cared so much.

"Danny, shut the hell up! Matt is not my boyfriend. I'm staying with him and his fiancée. And I don't have to explain anything to you! You broke up our marriage, remember?"

"Right, keep telling yourself it was all me," he said.

I heard something in his voice and I didn't know what. Remorse, maybe? Pain?

"What's wrong?" I asked, in spite of me wanting to hang up.

"I just really miss home right now."

"You love touring," I reminded him.

"Yeah, but usually I have you there for a good part of it, and now, I miss Ben."

I actually felt bad for the son of a bitch.

"Anastasia is not coming to visit you?"

It killed me just saying her name.

"She said she would in a few weeks, but...I miss you."

I squeezed my eyes shut, feeling tears come to them. I miss the tour. I miss the band. I missed work, but not as much as I thought. However, did I actually miss Danny? Not as my husband. As my friend, yes.

"I miss you too," I said, trying to steady my voice.

"Why don't you bring Ben to see me? I bet he's grown so much..."

"Danny, I don't know..."

"Please Cami..." he said, sounding as if he were crying. "I just want to see you and my baby. Do it for him."

I looked over at Ben who was sucking on his finger. He smiled as soon as I looked at him. I thought about how hard it must have been for Danny to be away from Ben. I couldn't stand being away from him for longer than several hours, let alone days, weeks or months.

"Okay," I agreed. "I'll look at the tour itinerary and find a good week to come see you."

"Thank you, Cami. This means so much."

"I have to go," I said quickly before hanging up.

Tears rolled down my face and I looked over at Ben. I knew the trip would be good for Ben and Danny, but for me, it might be an emotional rollercoaster.

CHAPTER THIRTEEN

I had been in Florida for a little over three weeks and already I was feeling better than I had in months—maybe even years. It could have been the warm, sunny weather, or change of environment. Maybe it was nice to be around Matt and Laura instead of the usual friends who were connected to Danny. Ben was also coming into an age where I could play with him. He responded to sounds and images much more, and it was enjoyable to see the world through his eyes.

I definitely knew my depression beginning to diminish had a good deal to do with working out and eating better. I no longer felt like some blob stuffed into a 5'4" body. Even my boobs didn't feel as heavy, though they still weren't back to their normal size.

I can't discount Drew for being responsible for the change in me either. He made me smile on a daily basis, even if he was at an away game. If he wasn't making me smile or laugh, he was making me moan. He may be addicted to my body, for whatever reason, but I was addicted to everything about him. From his gorgeous face, with his big brown eyes and even bigger smile, to his in shape body that wasn't overly muscled down. I even found the birthmark on his left big toe adorable. There were also Drew's modest culinary skills to enjoy. In spite of eating great homemade food, Drew was really good about keeping things portion-controlled. There were never any leftovers. As an Italian-American, I knew nothing about moderation. Mama was always trying to feed me. Not finishing my food was considered an insult to her.

Even though I was learning to eat in moderation, in other areas I was a glutton. Sex and shopping were the things I overindulged in. I guess since I never indulged in those things frivolously in my youth, I was overdue for it now. Even still, I only indulged in sex with Drew. It wasn't like I was out on the Ybor City strip prowling for men every night. I didn't know if I was the only one sleeping with Drew, but when he was in Tampa, I didn't see how he had much time to squeeze in any other girls. We pretty much spent every morning working out, playing with Ben, eating, and going at it like animals. Then Drew would go to practice, press interviews or a game, or all of the above. More often than not, I would go to the games with Matt and Laura or by myself, and go out with the team after.

I suppose Drew could have easily been hooking up with girls when he was out of town, but I didn't care to think about it. That was his business, not mine. Even though I was infatuated with Drew Ashton, I still knew that our fling would end in less than a week. I was very much aware of that fact. I just wanted to live for the moment and cherish it while it lasted. I had to accept that everything was temporary in this world, just like my short-lived relationship with Jordan or my ongoing saga with Danny. I could either dwell on it ending or enjoy the time I had. It was better it ended now, before I wound up hating Drew—or more likely, him hating me.

As for my many recent shopping excursions—that was Laura's fault—so I told myself. She invited me to come with her to pick up a dress for some event she and Matt had to go to. Before I knew it, I was trying on a handful of dresses as well. I still had kept my style fairly simple. I wasn't one of those girls who could shop for hours and had a closet full of "nothing to wear". In my marriage, Danny was the spend thrift, blowing hundreds on a collection of sneakers and thousands on cars he rarely got to drive.

Since I had Ben, my wardrobe left a lot to be desired. It was a mix of maternity clothes and things that didn't fit me right anymore. I only had t-shirts and a few pairs of pants that fit me okay. It was time I treated myself to a new wardrobe. Laura kept pointing things out for me to try on—one being a bikini. I refused the bikini and settled on a one-piece bathing suit. I don't think my stomach will ever be what it once was. The stretch marks weren't going anywhere and I still thought it looked flabby.

Drew and I decided to skip a workout today and go swimming instead. He had the entire day off and Laura was bringing Ben for another play date with her nephew. Drew picked me up in the late morning and we went back to his place.

"Did you eat anything?" he asked as I walked into his kitchen, eyeing the pool where we were first together.

"I had a banana. I didn't know if you were planning something food wise."

He laughed, "You just expect me to cook all the time, don't you?"

Drew leaned against the refrigerator with his arms crossed and I shrugged.

"You've spoiled me."

"When are you going to cook for me, huh?"

"I can't cook," I laughed. "I can't do much of anything really."

"Oh stop," he rolled his eyes. "Don't throw yourself a pity party because you can't scramble an egg."

I sighed, "Sorry. It's just...I'm nervous about next week."

"So don't go to Europe."

"I promised Danny I would."

"And he promised you he would be faithful," Drew shot back.

I was quiet for a moment.

"Let's go swimming," I said, smiling.

Drew walked over to me and caught my hand.

"Cami, you can talk to me."

I shook my head, "No. It wouldn't be right."

He laughed, "Since when are we about doing the right thing?"

Drew was so easygoing about everything and I was the opposite. The only thing I was laid back about was him. He never stressed me out. I wasn't guarded or forcing anything with Drew. I was just me—not that girl who felt she had to show she was boss, but I could be sweet or sassy or sexy or sensitive, and I didn't feel weak or judged for it. I suppose that comfort Drew gave me caused me to say something I probably shouldn't have.

"I had feelings for someone else the entire time I was with Danny," I blurted out.

Drew looked surprised.

"Did you ever act on those feelings?" he asked.

"No, never."

"Cami, you're not a bad person."

"Danny's no worse than me."

Drew shook his head, "You never actually cheated on him."

"I was emotionally attached to someone else, Drew. Don't you think that's worse?"

He wrapped his arms around me.

"If you cared about this other guy, why did you stay with Danny for so long?"

I felt tears come to my eyes and I just wanted to disappear into Drew's chest where my face was pressed.

"He didn't love me back."

Drew's arms tightened around me. He just held me as I cried, trying not to, but not being able to help myself. I felt so much pain, so much frustration, so much self-loathing, and I let it all out on poor Drew Ashton.

"I'm sorry," I sniffled, trying to pull away, but he wouldn't let me go.

"For what?"

I looked up at him, "For being such a mess. I don't let people see me like this."

He smiled at me and began to wipe my tears.

"I like seeing you like this."

My look turned angry quite quickly and he laughed.

"That came out wrong. I didn't mean I like to see you upset. I just like seeing you have feelings."

I wanted to punch him! I pushed him away and he pulled me back to him quickly.

"I didn't mean it that way, either!"

"How did you mean it then?"

"I don't know," he sighed. "The past month I've seen a lot of different sides of you. I used to only know you as the tough, bossy Cami."

"I miss her," I frowned. "She was in control of things."

"To be honest," Drew said, pulling me closer. "I like this Cami more. She's sensitive and caring and a great mother. She's way hotter, too," he winked.

I blushed and he leaned down to kiss me.

"There is one thing I don't like about her, though."

"What's that?" I wondered, running my hands up the back of his shirt.

"She's pretty down on herself."

I snickered, "Well, can you blame me? I lost my husband. The guy I had feelings for never loved me back. I have stretch marks now and..."

I stopped myself from going further, stuck on a thought.

Did I just say I *had* feelings for Jordan? As in past tense? It hit me then. I didn't love Jordan anymore. Yes, I loved him, but I didn't feel that longing for him! It hit me so suddenly, just as suddenly as my love for him began.

Drew didn't notice my epiphany. He was too busy kissing my neck as he ran a hand over my belly.

"I think every," he said kissing my earlobe. "Single," he said, kissing the side of my neck. "Part of you," he kissed my lips. "...is beautiful."

I snapped out of my thoughts to smile at him. He smiled in return and I wrapped my arms around his neck.

"Thank you," I whispered before kissing him with so much force, he almost fell backward. "Do you want to see my new bathing suit?" I asked, nipping his bottom lip.

"Please," he said as I pulled away from him.

I lifted my shirt over my head. The baby blue suit looked vibrant against my tan skin. It was a halter style that provided a ton of cleavage, with a peek-a-boo hole in the middle. I only intended Drew to see me in this suit, so I didn't care how revealing it was.

Drew's eyes stared at me like a kid about to unwrap a gift. I unsnapped the buttons on my denim shorts, slowly and seductively, before unzipping them and sliding them down my legs.

"How can you think you're not gorgeous?" he asked.

I smiled, "You're the gorgeous one. Take your shirt off."

He shook his head. "Turn around first."

I rolled my eyes and turned. I heard him groan before his hands were on my backside. He ran a finger up my spine and I shivered. The suit exposed my entire back practically. Drew's arms wrapped around my waist as he pressed himself against my butt. He began kissing my neck again as his hands slid up to grab my breasts.

"I want to take you out to dinner tonight."

"Mmm, okay..." I said, turning around and inching his shirt upward.

I wasn't thinking about dinner at that point. He helped me take his shirt off and I sucked on each of his nipples before leading him out to the pool. I dove into the water first. Drew followed suit, swimming over to me just as I surfaced. I stood in the shallow end and Drew's eyes stared at my breasts as the suit left little to the imagination once it was wet.

I untied the halter and let the material fall down. Drew began lavishing my body with his tongue. He helped me out of the suit completely. Before I could protest, he lifted me out of the water and onto the side of the pool. I immediately covered my midsection.

It usually was too dark in the room or I kept some kind of covering around my belly—like the water, my shirt or a blanket. I knew once he got a good look at my stomach, Drew would wonder why he wasn't fooling around with some young, hot celebrity like Topaz anymore.

Drew pushed my legs apart and looked up at me as I tried to cover up. He grabbed both my hands and I squealed as he pulled my arms away from my stomach.

"Drew, stop!" I yelled, desperately wanting to jump back into the water.

"No, you stop!" he yelled back.

His mouth immediately went to my stomach. He kissed around my belly button and I stopped fighting him since it was useless. He practically made out with my stomach as I just let tears fall. I was lying down, not looking at him.

Drew placed a finger at my entrance and pushed it inside me. I moaned.

"Look at me, Cami," he said.

I propped myself up, feeling the pavement dig into my elbows as I did. Drew ran his free hand down my thigh as he stared into my eyes.

"Every part of you is beautiful. Don't be ashamed of these," he said, running his hand over a group of stretch marks on my stomach. "They just remind me of how amazing and strong you are."

The tears were running down my cheeks full force now and I smiled at him. I wanted to say something to him, but I didn't know what. I just lay back down on the smooth, warm tiles surrounding the pool as he pleasured me, first with his fingers and then his tongue. It was such an erotic and emotional experience. I didn't expect Drew and me to have a bond like we did.

I called his name out as an orgasm washed over me. I sat up and he kissed up my body. We were both breathing hard as he pulled me back into the pool. Without any warning, Drew slid himself into me.

We both groaned. Drew was moving slowly. He was being gentler than usual. We stared into each other's eyes with our arms wrapped around one another.

"I'm close," he whispered. "Are you?"

I smiled, "Take me home, Drew."

He chuckled at that before picking up the pace. We climaxed together, which was something we often did together. I never had that with anyone before.

Drew didn't pull out of me right away. We stayed wrapped together. He kissed me before looking into my eyes, so deeply that I felt he could see into my soul.

"I love you."

He what? Did he…? No. I blinked a couple of times wondering if I simply imagined those words leaving Andrew Ashton's lips out of some sort of misplaced need to be loved. So what if he did say what I think he said, though? I mean, I love him too, in that I've known him so long and he's awesome kind of way. I figured he offered those words to me simply because he thought I needed to hear them. I should have never told him about my feelings for Jordan—even if he didn't know who I had unrequited love for.

I hugged Drew instead of responding.

"Thank you," I said.

We swam around a bit, going back to playful mode. By the time we got out of the pool, I was starved. Drew offered up his shower for me to use while he made lunch. As I washed the chlorine from my hair and skin, I couldn't help but think about Drew saying those three little words. For a few moments, I allowed myself to imagine Drew and I in love. Would sex still be so incredible? Would we play around in the pool? Would I still cheer him on at games or wear his jersey? Would I still be infatuated with him the way I was now? Would he care when I was upset or just walk away mad?

I felt myself lingering on these thoughts and the feeling that came along with them. It was euphoric, but I knew it was just a fantasy. In real life, I had come to realize that love is in fact a fantasy—a tease. If you love someone, they don't love you the same. If they love you, you don't love them enough. And you can pretend you both feel the same way and force something to work until it breaks into a million pieces that you don't know how to put back together. That's the reality I have been living in and my eyes were finally wide open to it.

I wouldn't allow myself to be fooled again. I always thought I was smart staying with Danny—he was important to me, but our puppy love phase wasn't blinding. It was short-lived and we both kept each other in check. Now I wonder if it was really love at all. I couldn't go through those emotions again.

Things were better this way—just having a good time with someone who makes you feel good. Who knows? Maybe Drew and I could still have secret rendezvous once I leave Florida. We would just have to be really careful.

I put my t-shirt and jean shorts back on while my bathing suit dried. I walked downstairs and smelled something delicious. When I walked into the kitchen, it was empty. There was a Panini press that was dirty and a spatula in the sink.

"Drew?" I called out.

"In the dining room!"

We usually ate in the kitchen. I walked into the dining room. The one large window had the curtain covering it, so it was dim. There were candles lit—uncoordinated ones, but that made it even more adorable to me for some reason. The tablecloth had Yankees logos all over it, and it made me laugh.

Drew was smiling at me as I stared at the table. He was still shirtless, with a pair of shorts loosely hanging on his hips.

"Is this dressy-casual?" I asked.

"Me or the table?" he joked.

"Both!"

"I was trying to be romantic, but I'm lacking some tools," he shrugged.

I walked over to him and wrapped my arms around his neck.

"You have all the tools," I smiled.

He kissed me before pulling out a chair for me. On the plate in front of me was a Panini sandwich with pesto sauce, which Drew made himself on top of turkey and Swiss cheese. It was amazing! On the side was baked barbeque chips—my favorite, along with beets—Drew's favorite.

"I love this," I said, picking at a chip. "Somehow you make simple so elegant."

"Thank you," he smiled. "That's a compliment, right?"

"Yes. A big one," I nodded. "Any girl would be lucky to be wined and dined by you."

He winked before taking a sip of his sweet tea. After we ate, I looked at the time.

"I should be getting back for Ben," I said.

Drew nodded. We blew out the candles and headed to his jeep. On the ride to Matt's, there was an odd silence. I can't really explain it, but it felt like there was something we wanted to say to one another, but didn't know how to say it.

"I'll see you tomorrow?" I asked as he pulled into the driveway.

"Yup. Back to the gym," he grinned.

I made a face, "Oh joy."

"You don't have to go to the gym," Drew shrugged. "We can always hang out after."

I noticed the concern on his face. I placed my hand on his cheek, knowing he was worried I was taking the "Drew Boot Camp" ethic to mean he thought I needed to workout.

"I like going to the gym—with you anyway," I smiled.

He got the cutest, biggest, dimply grin on his face. I kissed him softly before getting out of the jeep.

CHAPTER FOURTEEN

When I got inside the house, I could hear Matt on the phone.

"JT, I'll talk to her soon…" he said. "She's on vacation, man. We still have time before the next album comes out. We'll be able to get a new manager by then."

JT is another member of Sound Wave, the boy band Matt is in. He hadn't really spoken to me about problems with their management company, though I had heard they were looking for a new record label. I knew their label had been mistreating them for years, but the band was loyal to them since they had been with them since they first hit it big.

Matt saw me walk into the living room. Ben was lying on an activity blanket, playing with the toys above his head. He started to whine as soon as he saw me. Matt rushed JT off the phone as I picked Ben up.

"How are you baby boy?" I asked, kissing his cheeks, making him giggle. "Did you have fun on your play date?"

Matt smiled at me, "Did you have fun on your play date?"

I rolled my eyes and sat down on the couch.

"You only have a few more days left of being a Yankees ball girl," he winked.

"Ugh, if I weren't holding my son, I'd smack you!" I hissed at him.

He laughed, "Seriously. Are you and Drew going to be able to end this?"

I shrugged, "We can probably hook up here and there... We do both live in New York technically."

Matt's mouth dropped.

"You're delusional."

"Why?"

"You think you'll be able to carry on a no strings attached relationship indefinitely and not have anyone else find out?"

I sighed and went to speak, but he kept talking.

"...And you think you can keep it up without developing feelings?"

"Y—" I tried to speak again, but once more, Matt kept talking.

"Or is it too late for that? You two are practically inseparable. Tell me you're not attached..."

He finally gave me an opening to speak.

"We're not inseparable. He's out of town like every other day, Matt."

Matt scoffed and went to speak, but this time I shut him up.

"So, ask me what JT wants you to ask me," I said, raising an eyebrow.

His mouth closed and he sat down beside me.

"I know you're on vacation, so I didn't want to talk business."

"But?"

"Sound Wave needs a new management firm. I had brought you up to the group a couple of times. We all threw names on the table, but have agreed that you would represent us fairly and with renewed vigor that Mega Music and our label have been failing to do," Matt explained.

I understood what he meant. Sound Wave has been one of the only surviving boy bands of their era. They never broke up. They never stopped recording or touring, but sometimes, the industry forgets that. A countless number of times, the press called a new album or tour date, a "reunion" or states the group is "back together".

I could only guess how frustrating that has been. They needed to rid the image of a returning fad and be known as pop music icons that are still doing their thing. That would mean big TV appearances, gracing covers of top magazines, and not looking like aging men hanging onto their youth. It would be tough. It would be a challenge. And I'm all about tough challenges, especially when it gives me a chance to steal one of Mega Music Management's clients. I considered the firm I used to intern for my biggest rivals. I bet the president is kicking himself for letting me go all those years ago.

Even though I knew my answer, I decided to make Matt sweat it out a bit.

"So, this is why you invited me to Florida?" I accused. "This was all about business and not our friendship."

Matt shook his head, "No. Cami, you're my friend first and foremost. I invited you before we came to the decision."

I smiled, "Good, then you've got yourself a manager."

"Seriously?" Matt asked, his face breaking out into a grin.

"Yes," I smiled widely. "Let's get a meeting together and I'll have our lawyers draw up a contract."

Matt put his arm around me and hugged me, careful not to squish Ben.

"Oh, and one more thing..." Matt said. "We want to work with you directly. I know you have a good team of people, and you can't be with us all the time now, since you have Ben. But for the most part, we want you—someone who believes in us."

I smiled, touched for a moment before deciding to chide him.

"Who says I believe in you?"

He cocked his head to the side, "Underneath that hardcore punk-rock chick is a teenage girl who loved us..."

I laughed, "Um, no, I never had your poster on my wall or even owned a CD."

Matt's smile fell.

"But I do believe in Sound Wave," I assured him. "I will admit to liking some songs," I sighed, hating to admit that. "I even like a few more that Drew's been playing in his car," I shook my head, finding it ridiculous how much he likes Sound Wave.

Matt grinned, "I love that guy."

I smiled, "I believe in good music and potential. Pop music or not, Sound Wave has both those things and more, so I will directly oversee your business and make sure you get the best record deal possible."

Matt hugged me again before grabbing his phone to call the rest of the group. As I looked down at Ben and listened to Matt talk, I thought about the next phase of my life. It was a good thing I loved challenges. Now I was going to have to balance raising a child and work. The important thing I learned from my time off, though, is that I can take breaks.

Sound Wave wouldn't need me on tour all the time. They wouldn't need me to hold their hand through everything either. I knew Lisa Ann would be a perfect fit as my partner working with them. She is genuine and is a fan of theirs. They'll love her and she'll go the extra mile because she loves them.

Matt got off the phone and kissed my forehead.

"The guys are so excited," he grinned.

"Me too," I nodded.

"We're going to celebrate tonight."

"We are?"

"Yes. You, me, Laura, Drew, JT, Mikie, and their women."

Matt, JT, Mike or Mikie, as Matt called him, along with Ryan and John made up Sound Wave. Ryan and John are brothers; I heard Matt say something about them being out of town for a family event.

"Drew?" I asked, wondering how his name got into the mix. Maybe I was forgetting a member of the group?

"Well, yeah...you don't want to be the seventh wheel. You need a date," he winked.

"Ben can be my date," I smiled, waving him off.

"He can come too, but he doesn't add to the conversation. Invite Drew."

I felt weird about the idea for some reason. It was one thing when I went out with Drew's teammates. Not everyone was paired off. Tonight, it *would* feel like a date, wouldn't it?

As if on cue, I looked down at my phone. I had a text from Hot Ass.

I forgot about something. Are we on for dinner tonight?

I vaguely remember Drew mentioning taking me to dinner while he was making out with my neck earlier.

"Fine," I said, looking at Matt. "Do not embarrass me, though."

The rest of the afternoon, I spent on the phone with lawyers and various employees of mine. When I got Colin, J.J. and Lisa Ann on a conference call, I think they were in shock.

"Cami, we miss you," Colin said.

"Right, I'm so sure," I laughed.

"Seriously. Walking in your shoes has been rough," Colin said. "When are you coming back to work?"

I laughed harder, "Oh, now you're begging me to come back?"

"Not begging," Colin snickered. "Hoping."

"We thought we'd hear more from you," Lisa Ann spoke up. "You must really be loving that Florida weather. You sound good."

"Thank you," I said.

"You sound much more relaxed and happy," J.J. said.

"I get the feeling you don't want me back, J."

"I do, I do. I just..."

"He screwed Rad Trick out of a sponsorship deal," Colin blurted.

"Thanks asshole," J.J. sighed. "Look Cami, I thought I could get more money out of the deal, but they backed out and went with that other pop star, Bex something or other..."

"Bex Moore?" I asked, smacking my forehead. "J.J., Bex Moore is riding Rad's coattails. Have you been paying attention?"

"Yeah, I know," J.J. said, which meant he was hoping I've been too busy with my personal drama to not know who Bex Moore was.

"Rad is flipping out," Colin said.

"He's being ridiculous," J.J. sighed. "I've done so much for him and because of one little mess up, he's thinking of firing us…"

I closed my eyes and I felt everyone on the line hold their breath. I wanted to curse J.J. out. I wanted to fire him on the spot. If this was a month ago, I would have. Something inside me told me not to. J.J. despite his overly cocky, "I don't care" attitude was just a kid in the industry. He still had a ton to learn and he showed promise as a marketing and branding genius. I didn't want to lose that. He had good enough qualities that I couldn't afford to lose. His sometimes bad qualities, like his greed and cutthroat ways, were qualities I couldn't afford to face against if he was at another firm.

"Don't panic," I said. "Rad is just mad and he has every right to be. I'll give him a call and see what I can smooth over."

"Thank you, Cami," J.J. said.

He sounded like a stranger without the overinflated ego. From the way they spoke to me, I must have sounded like a stranger to them as well. I was way too laid back and way too understanding. I couldn't help it to be that way. Maybe it was Florida. Or maybe it was spending time with Ben in a positive environment rather than my apartment with all the old, broken memories. Or maybe it was how good it felt to be having a ton of sex with a gorgeous guy. I don't know. Maybe I was actually changing, realizing the life I was leading wasn't what I thought it was.

I told the team about Sound Wave becoming our new client. Lisa Ann tried to hide her excitement, but I could tell. Colin had some concerns, but I convinced him it would be a smart move for everyone involved. J.J. was agreeable, but he wasn't in a position not to be.

After that phone call, I patched things up with Rad. I let him vent, which was a lot of bitching and moaning like a five-year-old who didn't get his way. I promised him a bigger, better sponsorship, and that we'd take less commission for it. Delivering this sponsorship wasn't a challenge for me. I just called up the competing soda company who got Bex as their spokesperson, and offered them Rad Trick. Upon finding out the inside scoop on Bex, they happily offered whatever we wanted to get Rad on their campaign. It felt good to be working again, but at the same time, it was nice to only step in when I was needed. I will remind myself of that when I get back to New York.

That night, I put on one of my new dresses. It was a pale yellow dress with spaghetti straps that stopped above my knees. There was a mesh overlay and it had a satin band under my breasts. The dress made me feel soft and dainty. My mother used to always tell me I looked best in yellow because of my tan skin.

I put my hair up, but curled a bunch of loose strands to fall down over the clip. I put on a little more make-up than I normally do, and looked myself over in the full length mirror. For the first time in a long time, I liked the way I looked. My skin was clear. My boobs didn't look too big or too small, and my waist was back to normal for the most part.

My phone went off just as I was slipping into the heels I knew I would regret wearing later. There was a text message from Danny, and I sighed to myself. He had been calling and texting more frequently the past week or so. It wasn't just to check up on Ben, either. Half the time, I had to ignore him. He would call when I was with Drew, or text in the middle of the night.

The messages varied from a casual "how are you?" to a random "remember that time…". The past few texts have gotten remorseful—more so than usual. Danny would apologize for cheating on me and for not being a better husband.

It wasn't like I hadn't seen this pattern before with him. When we were dating, we'd break-up only to make-up. Danny would apologize and two minutes later, he would yell and point a finger at me. I wish I didn't care about him. I wish I could just keep him out of my life like any other poison, but it was impossible. Danny DeSano was entwined with every aspect of my life—from my career, to my friends, to our son. Aside from all of those things, I did still care about him. To what extent did that caring go to? That was the confusing part.

A half an hour later, I was getting out of the car. Ben was already getting sleepy, which meant I would actually be able to eat dinner. We walked inside the restaurant. The place was pretty packed for a Thursday night. I didn't know much about Tampa hotspots, but I presumed this place was one of them.

The hostess practically tripped over her own two feet to greet us; not because she was frazzled over how busy the place was either. It was obvious she was a little star struck.

Sometimes, it was easy to forget almost everyone I knew was famous in some sort of way.

I sometimes forgot I was a little famous as well. To me, the guys in Tortured, or Sound Wave, or even Drew, the famous Yankee, were normal. Maybe some of them were quite beautiful, that part I understand. It wasn't until I saw how befuddled people, especially girls, got around the company I kept that I remembered all eyes were on us. The thought freaked me out, especially after being the subject of one too many tabloid exposés.

"Mr. Porter, some of your party is already here," the hostess grinned.

We followed her to a table outside by a beautiful waterfall. Mike Bailey, also known as the boy band stereotypical "sweet one" was sitting down with his wife, Kelly. I was introduced to Kelly for the first time and reintroduced to Mike, whom I met a couple of times throughout the years.

"JT's running late," Mike said. "Big surprise, right?"

Mike was an adorable Hispanic man that I could tell would be my most reliable go-to-guy in Sound Wave. I'm sure the other guys would be pretty easy to work with, though. Sound Wave were pretty well-rounded, down-to-earth guys who knew how the business worked by now. I could only imagine at this point in their careers, Sound Wave were professionals and not a group of boys I had to wrangle. Matt himself has gone from hot shot heartthrob to mature man in what magically seemed overnight! I could just tell from speaking with Mike, however, that he had the business sense in the group.

"I guess Drew is running late, too," I said, about to sit down.

"Oh, he's in the bathroom," Mike explained.

I was pleasantly surprised. Being how much I hate lateness, to know that my "date" was on time, made me happy. As if on cue, I saw Drew walking toward our table. I didn't sit down, waiting for him to approach me. He looked incredible in the army green dress shirt he was wearing. He grinned at me as his eyes scanned up and down my body appreciatively.

For a moment, I thought he was going to pull me into a kiss in front of everyone. For that moment, I wished he did. Instead, he pulled me close to kiss my cheek and whisper in my ear.

"You look amazing."

I smiled at him somewhat bashfully. I never met a guy who made me blush as much as Drew Ashton did. Every compliment felt more flattering coming from him for some reason.

"Thank you," I said, my voice coming out in a whisper.

We sat down, except for Drew, who first greeted a half asleep Ben, who's carrier was on a chair next to mine. JT and his wife, Anna, arrived a few minutes later. By that time, everyone had a drink and conversation flowed freely. The boy band members wanted to talk about baseball to Drew and he wanted to talk about their upcoming album with them. It was amusing to me.

I cleared my throat and raised a glass.

"I believe the reason we're all here is to celebrate me being your manager," I teased.

Everyone laughed and raised their glasses.

"To Cami!" JT yelled.

"That's more like it," I said with a flirtatious smile toward him.

His wife didn't seem to mind, which was good. I was naturally a flirt and loved attention—sometimes it didn't matter if it was positive or negative. I was working on it, but I still had certain tendencies. Drew's hand was on my thigh and as soon as I smiled at JT, it moved down to my knee and squeezed. Of course, my reflexes kicked in and I jumped. I don't know how he always manages to hit that weird spot in my knee, but he did, and I always wanted to get revenge. Unfortunately, I hadn't found any sensitive spots on his body...yet.

"You okay?" Mike asked with a laugh.

"Fine," I said.

As soon as no one was looking, I glanced over at Drew. He smiled innocently. Just then, Ben began to cry—more like wail! I picked him up and grabbed his diaper bag. I took him into the bathroom to change him, which was awkward considering they didn't have a changing table. I'm sure not many people brought babies to this swanky restaurant. I found a couch that I could lay him on instead.

Ben quieted down once he was changed and laying on my shoulder. I walked out of the bathroom and Drew was standing there, leaning against the wall.

"Are you stalking the ladies' room?" I smirked.

"Hopefully no one noticed," he winked before kissing my lips softly.

I pushed him away lightly as Ben lifted his head to look at Drew sleepily. Drew kissed Ben's forehead before looking at me like he was going to kiss me again.

"We're playing a really dangerous game," I sighed.

He trapped me against the wall with an arm on each side of my head.

"I don't want to play games," he said, his voice deeper.

He kissed me and I didn't want him to stop, but I didn't want to risk being caught. I pushed away from him and hurried back to the table. The rest of dinner was spent chatting. I felt at ease with everyone at the table. It felt kind of like how I vibed with Tortured, which was weird for me.

Was I replacing my family with a new one? Lately I have felt a million miles away from the guys—not just physically, but emotionally. I knew if they were forced to choose between Danny and me—they would choose him. I knew that managing Sound Wave was a business move, for both me and Matt, but I know we're friends that go pretty far back, too. That was a comfort.

After dinner, there were talks of going somewhere after. Drew looked over at me as if wondering what I wanted to do.

"I should get Ben to bed," I announced, even though he was back to sleep already.

"Oh," Laura said. "Of course. We can take you home..."

I looked over at Drew and he was already about to butt in.

"No, I can take Cami and Ben home."

"Are you sure?" Matt asked, with a stupid smirk on his face.

"Yeah. I am beat anyway. I have a busy day of traveling tomorrow."

We all walked out of the restaurant and headed to the cars. Drew retrieved the base of the car seat and met me at his jeep. After getting Ben settled in the back, we got in the front and looked at each other.

"That didn't seem suspicious," I laughed.

Drew shrugged, "It's not like Mike and JT are going to call up the newspapers."

About ten minutes later, Drew pulled into the driveway. He followed me inside Matt's condo. I brought Ben to bed before heading downstairs now barefoot, of course, and with the baby monitor in hand.

"You look so much shorter," Drew laughed.

"Oh well. My feet hurt."

"I guess you're not up for a walk on the beach then?"

"We can walk a little. I don't want to go too far since Ben's all alone in the house."

The condo was only about thirty feet from the water. There was no public access to the house or the beach, which eased my mind that Ben was completely safe. There were four other condos on the strip that had use of the beach, but they were pretty spread out. I loved the seclusion. It was such a change from New York.

Drew took his shoes and socks off before we walked outside. It was pretty warm, with little to no wind, even close to the shore. Drew reached his hand out to me halfway to the water. Once the water licked at my toes, I let out a contented sigh. My sore feet felt soothed by the salt water. I placed the baby monitor in the dry part of the sand. My right hand was still being held by Drew.

"The water feels so good on my sore little feet."

Drew frowned, "Poor baby."

He rubbed my knuckles before pulling me against him. We kissed as the water splashed our ankles. It was cold, but neither of us cared.

"Your eyes really do glow out here," he smiled, staring into them as he often did.

I blinked and smiled. I loved how when he complimented my eyes, he actually stared into them. Drew was a breast man and an ass man, but he stared at my face just as much as he looked at any other part of me. I don't remember the last time someone looked into my eyes the way Drew does.

"Tonight's our last night together..." I said softly.

He sighed. I couldn't tell if it was out of frustration or sadness or maybe contentment? Drew pulled away from me. He pushed some wet sand around with his toes.

"I want to sleep in your arms," I said, stepping closer to him and pressing my forehead against his bicep.

Drew looked down at me and kissed me. Not before long were we walking back to the condo. We wiped our feet off at the door. I took Drew's hand and led him upstairs. Drew pushed one strap on my dress down as I looked in on Ben.

"I can't do this with him in here," I whispered.

Drew nodded. We wheeled the portable crib into the next guest room. As soon as we were back in the room I was staying in, Drew lifted me up and threw me on the bed, causing me to squeal. He unbuttoned his shirt and I whistled. He smirked before tossing his shirt to the side as he made it to the foot of the bed. I sat up and began kissing his stomach. Oh, how

I loved every inch of his body! I undid his belt before working on his pants. I pushed the garment past his wonderful butt and he pushed me back onto the bed, playfully and teasingly.

He lifted my left leg and ran his hand from my thigh to my foot. He began to massage the arch, which felt amazing. His hands are incredibly strong, but had a gentleness about them. He repeated the process with my right foot before kissing down both my legs to my inner thighs.

I moaned as his fingers hooked into my thong. He pulled it down my legs and tossed it over his shoulder. He got on the bed and hovered over me, kissing my cleavage then my neck. When his lips hovered over mine, I was eager to get my tongue back in his mouth, but he wouldn't give me the satisfaction—the tease!

"Tell me you're not going to miss this," he said, staring into my eyes.

"Of course I'm going to miss this," I laughed, running a hand through his hair and kissing him longingly.

I tried my hardest to flip him over and he obliged. I got on top of him with my back facing him. I yanked his boxer shorts down to his knees and heard him groan when I began to play with his erection. His hands squeezed my butt and I turned around to face him, hiking my dress up enough, so I wouldn't rip it. My center rubbed against him and I bit my lip. Drew's eyes closed for a moment as he started to lift my dress.

"I want to see you," he hissed.

"You have to unzip it," I said, laying my chest down against his.

He reached his hands around my back and pulled the zipper down for me. I pulled the dress over my head before unhooking my strapless bra. It was amazing how I no longer cared about him seeing my not so perfect belly or its stretch marks. We teased each other by rubbing against one another before we couldn't take it any longer. Drew entered me and I had an orgasm instantly.

"You're so sexy," he said, starting to thrust up into me.

I just about collapsed against him and he flipped us over again. I studied his face as he lay on top of me, his eyes closed, near his own release. I kissed his throat and ran my nails down his back. He lost it and exploded into me. His eyes opened and we stared at each other before meeting in an amazing kiss.

We were both exhausted as we lay in each other's arms. I got up reluctantly to go to the bathroom and changed into shorts and a tank top. I got back into bed with Drew. He was already falling asleep, but managed to wrap his arms around me. I woke up a couple of hours later to bring Ben's portable crib back into the bedroom. Drew woke up as I closed the bedroom door. He pulled his boxer shorts on and reached for his pants.

I sat down on the bed next to him and kissed his shoulder, right above his tattoo.

"You can stay," I said, hoping that didn't sound too needy.

"I don't know how Matt and Laura would feel..." he said. "Besides, I still have to pack."

I nodded and he smiled at me. I kissed him.

"I guess I'll see you when you're back in New York," I said, forcing a smile.

"Or you can come and visit?" he asked.

I sighed, "I don't think we can hide this if I plan trips to see you on the road."

"What if I didn't want to hide it?"

I stared at him, wishing I could see his eyes clearer in the dim lighting.

"Drew, you don't mean that. No one would be happy we're sex buddies..." I chuckled.

"Oh right," he said, standing up.

He sounded grouchy and I could only guess it was the same reason I was upset. I would miss Drew. I walked over to him just as he finished getting dressed.

"So, be careful in Europe," he said, sitting down just as I went to touch his arm, moving just out of my reach.

He started putting his socks and shoes on.

"I've been there before," I laughed.

"I mean with Danny."

"What?"

"From what I've heard and from what I've seen, you spent months trying to get over what that marriage did to you... Do you really want to go through that again?" Drew asked.

I was grateful for the dark now. I felt tears come to my eyes.

"I'm not going to get back with Danny."

"Right, and we're just sex buddies," Drew said, walking out the door.

I went to follow him, but Ben began crying.

"Drew!" I hissed trying not to wake anyone, but he was already heading down the stairs.

Ben started crying louder and I picked him up before he woke everyone up. I heard

Drew's jeep start up and I sighed. I didn't quite understand what happened. All I knew is that I cried along with my son. Once he stopped crying, I kept going until we both fell back asleep.

CHAPTER FIFTEEN

Traveling to another country with an infant is not exactly easy. Chivalry was obviously dead as most men watched me struggle with bags and Ben through the airport.

I barely slept the entire flight to Paris, and neither did Ben. I know it wasn't simply because I was uncomfortable, but more likely because I had a ton on my mind. My soon-to-be ex-husband was one of those things, but my now ex-lover was also taking up many thoughts. It was quite early in the morning. Danny told me he would be awake when we arrived. I called him five times and each time, the call went straight to voicemail.

By the time I got to the hotel, I was ready to spit nails—preferably into Danny's forehead. I had to jump through hoops to find out what hotel the band was staying in. Danny told me, but it was some French name that he couldn't pronounce properly. I wound up calling my office to find out.

This was just like Danny to oversleep; to let the ball drop where it concerned me. I may have been a bitchy, nag of a wife to him, but he was forgetful and insensitive when it came to me.

The taxi driver didn't speak any English and he had terrible road rage. He was making me nervous since Ben was in the car. I practically jumped out of the taxi once it stopped. The driver didn't get out to help with my things, which made me feel justified in not tipping him. The bell hop rushed out to help me and I just waved the driver off, since he was lingering and recounting the fare I had given him, hoping for some compensation.

"Bonjour, Madame, I am François," the bellhop said, taking several of my bags and loading them onto a cart.

"Merci, François," I forced a smile.

I was not feeling in the mood to talk, or smile, or even frown. I just wanted to sleep. Once all my things were on the cart, I placed Ben in his stroller and walked up to the front desk. I gave the concierge my name and he typed it into the computer.

"Sorry Madame," he said, his thin mustache twitching as he spoke. "There is no reservation under Cami Woods."

His accent was thick and each word, especially reservation, seemed overdramatized.

I sighed, "I guess he put it under his name. Do you have a Danny DeSano staying here?"

"Madame, we're not allowed to reveal our guests," he said.

I groaned and blurted, "I'm his wife."

For the first time, those words coming out of my mouth sounded foreign just like the country I was in. I didn't feel like Danny DeSano's wife anymore, but I felt like there was no other way to get into a bed where I could sleep the day away. The concierge held his finger up to me as he picked up the phone.

"Monsieur, sorry to wake you. There is a woman down here saying she is your wife..." he gave me a dirty look as he paused. "Yes, she has a bébé with her."

He apologized and hung up before calling out to François.

"Please escort Madame DeSano to her room."

I was never Mrs. DeSano. I always kept my maiden name for business purposes. I didn't like the idea of taking my husband's last name, afraid I would lose sight of my own identity. I suppose with marriage that happens whether you give your last name or not. At this point in my life, I am reevaluating everything about myself, before and after Danny.

As I approached the room, the door opened and Danny stood there, half asleep smiling stupidly at me. I wanted to smack him.

"Sorry, I overslept."

He looked down at Ben and rushed to pick him up. I squeezed past him, dropped my purse, diaper bag and kicked my shoes off before throwing myself down on the bed.

François came in with the rest of my luggage and looked at Danny expectantly who was still wrapped up in his son.

"Danny, can you tip François, please?" I asked, curling up under the blanket and closing my eyes.

After François left, I felt the bed shift. I opened my eyes and Danny was stretched across the bed holding Ben.

"You could have at least booked me a separate room," I huffed.

Danny shrugged, "What for?"

"So you don't have to sleep on the couch," I smirked, with my eyes still closed.

"Cami, we're married. We can manage to sleep in the same bed without arguing, can't we?"

"Doubtful," I said, yawning.

"Take a nap. Ben and I will get some father-son time and then we'll get something to eat before the show," he said.

I was drifting off into a deep sleep as I nodded. I felt Danny's lips press against my forehead before the bed shifted again.

It felt like mere minutes that my eyes were closed. I jumped up when I heard Benvenuto crying his little lungs out. I panicked and glanced around the room. Danny was sitting on the floor with Ben trying to quiet him down. I got out of bed and looked down at him.

"He won't stop crying," Danny looked up at me frustrated. "I took him for a walk. I gave him a bottle. Changed his diaper. What's wrong with him?"

I picked Ben up and cradled him against my hip. He began to quiet down.

"Nothing is wrong with him. He wants his mommy, that's all."

As if he was helping me emphasize this point, Ben put his head down on my chest. Danny sighed and stood up. He rubbed Ben's back with a pout. I didn't bother to mention that Ben was also teething.

"Does he ever want his daddy?"

Immediately, I felt bad for Danny.

"Sure, he does. He just isn't used to being away from me, especially in new surroundings."

"Well, how was he in Florida?"

"He got used to it," I smiled. "He definitely recognizes you," I offered as Ben stared over at him before he placed his head back down.

"He probably thinks asshole Porter is his dad."

I rolled my eyes, "No, he doesn't. Why are you so jealous of Matt?"

"He practically drooled over you every time he saw you."

"And you knew I wasn't interested in him," I sighed. "Yet you still made me give up a friendship with him."

"Why would you need a friendship with another guy when you had me?" he asked, anger hitting the tone of his voice.

"Danny, I don't have a lot of people in my life. I don't have family. Matt knew me before I was anyone. He's like a brother to me just as Sebastian, Darren and Jordan are."

"I don't think you ever thought of Jordan like a brother," he snarled.

"You want to blame Jordan for our marriage going sour? Why not blame Anastasia?" I asked, stepping away from him.

"I'm not blaming Jordan. I'm blaming you."

I whirled around, wanting to punch him. I might have this time, if I weren't holding our son.

"Me? What are you blaming me for exactly? I never cheated on you!"

"Not physically. Admit you love Jordan. Admit you wish you were married to him instead of me!"

"Danny, right now, I wish I was married to anyone but you!"

I placed Ben down in the stroller. Danny rushed toward me and for a moment, I thought he was going to hit me. Just as I let out a gasp, he grabbed me and kissed me. For a minute, I got lost in the moment and kissed him back. I came to my senses when his hands moved down to my butt. I shoved him away from me.

"What the hell are you doing?"

"Kissing my wife?" he asked, with a cocky smirk.

"I may be your wife on paper, but that's about to change. I can have my lawyer fax the divorce papers today and we can be done with this exhausting marriage."

The papers were drawn up a month ago. I told my lawyer I would sign them when I got back into town. I could have had them sent to Florida, signed them and faxed them to Danny to sign, but I didn't for some reason. I guess part of me felt like we weren't over. As much as I knew we should be over, it was hard letting go of the only serious relationship I have ever had. Danny was my shot at a real family, and I was afraid that would vanish after the divorce. It took me time away from him and everything else that was normal to me, that Danny may be part of some kind of family to me, but he wasn't a husband to me.

I wasn't afraid any more. I finally realized Danny and I might be better off divorced. Maybe then we could still be friends and raise Ben together without such hostility.

"Cami, come on," he said, pulling me toward him again. "I still love you."

"And I love you, Danny," I said looking into his big, sad blue eyes.

"This time away from you, it made me appreciate us. I want to make it work."

It was weird to think while my time away from Danny made me reevaluate the misplaced love I had for him, but for him, it made him want to hold onto me. I knew Danny was just afraid of being alone. He was afraid of failure and change. He liked familiarity, and as dysfunctional as our marriage was, it has been all we have known for so long.

I swallowed, "What about Anastasia?"

"We're over. Maybe I was just going through a mid-life crisis or something," he laughed with a shrug.

I didn't laugh, though. Part of me wanted to tell him I was willing to try again, but I just wasn't. I didn't want to try. I was not in love with Danny. Maybe I never was in love with him.

He stared into my eyes and I don't know what came over him, but he released his hold on me.

"There's someone else, isn't there?"

"No," I said, choking on the word.

I don't know if you can consider Drew someone else. What we had was an affair and it was over. I found my heart tightening and I wanted to cry. What was I mourning exactly? The end of my marriage or the end of my affair? I couldn't tell. I just knew I needed to cry. As if he were feeling my emotions, Ben began crying. Neither Danny or I moved.

"Is this really happening?" Danny asked, his voice a bit choked up.

I nodded, "Danny, we don't love each other the way we're supposed to. You see Jordan and Haley...they're in love. We're not."

Danny hung his head down and nodded. He walked over to Ben and picked him up. The two of them cried together on the bed. I walked over and wrapped my arms around both of them. I allowed my tears to fall. The first thing we ever did together as a family was cry. I guess that was something!

It would have been so easy to take Danny back, but I knew we both deserved better than each other.

A few hours later, I was watching Sebastian play with Ben in the dressing room. I felt Jordan's eyes on me.

"Why are you staring at me?" I asked. "I'm okay!"

Jordan smiled, "I can see that. You look great."

I grinned, "Thank you. Florida has been good to us."

"It's impossible to be down when my brother's around," Jordan said, grabbing a bottle of water.

For a moment, I thought Jordan knew about the affair. I stared at him and realized he was talking from his own experience.

"Even when I was a brooding teenager, that kid could make me laugh or smile," he said. "I knew spending time with him would be good for you."

I smiled, "I appreciate you assigning people to babysit me during this difficult time, but I can handle myself."

Jordan laughed, "Assigning people? I didn't assign anyone to you. You wanted to hang out with Drew!"

I rolled my eyes, "Did you call Matt and let him know I wasn't doing well?"

He got quiet.

"I thought so," I shook my head.

I wasn't really mad. I was actually flattered that people cared so much.

"It was Haley's idea," Jordan said. "She was in Florida for a shoot with Sound Wave...and she thought it was a shame you two lost touch."

I couldn't help but smile. Haley really is my best friend, isn't she?

"Don't tell Danny it was Haley's idea," Sebastian laughed. "He was going nuts when he found out."

"Matt is engaged with a baby on the way," I waved Sebastian off.

"So you didn't get biz-zay with anyone in Florida?"

"Seb," I laughed, hoping I wasn't blushing.

"How would she have time?" Jordan asked, taking Ben out of Sebastian's arms. "She had to watch out for this little guy."

"Oh, there's always time," Sebastian winked.

"Speaking of time, we go on in fifteen minutes. Where are Danny and Darren?" Jordan asked.

"Some things never change," I sighed.

Danny and Darren had a tendency to wander off. I would find them playing videogames, running through the line of people outside, or mingling with the opening act. They had no concept of time. I knew it was probably worse that I wasn't here. Apparently, Colin tags along with them instead of reprimanding them. Being a manager was a lot like being a parent. As much as you were frustrated with a client, you'd always have a place in your heart for them.

I could tell Jordan was fed up with his band mates' behavior, and even Colin's.

"We do miss you, Cam," Sebastian said.

"I miss you guys too. I'll have a talk with Colin."

"No. You're not here as our manager," Jordan said. "You're here as our friend," he put his arm around me.

I hugged him, squeezing him. He had no idea how much that meant to me. For the first time since I had known Jordan, I was happy to be just his friend. I was also grateful he had someone like Haley, who made him happy and a person who lets people in. I don't think I could have brought that out in him, like she did.

The rest of the time I was in Europe with the band, it was pretty nice. Danny and I were fairly civil. We still argued, but just our normal banter. I didn't sleep much though. Between Ben's teething, the jet lag, and my brain not being able to turn off, I was a zombie.

I found myself wondering about Drew. Where was he? What was he doing? Who was he with? Did he think about me? I hadn't heard from him. I didn't expect to, but I guess I was hoping for it. I thought about contacting him, but I knew it was too risky.

If Jordan finds out I slept with his little brother, I'll lose him. If I lose Jordan, I lose Haley. It goes without saying that I'll lose

Danny, and I wouldn't be surprised if Sebastian and Darren followed.

We were in Berlin when Danny and I signed the divorce papers. We both hugged afterward. It was a weird experience. It was practically official that we were single. I was actually a divorcee, something no one ever wants to be. I know there are tons of divorced people in this world, but you still never think it'll actually happen to you. I don't think I ever thought I would get married in the first place. I certainly don't think I'll get married ever again or even love again. Was I even really in love with Danny or Jordan to begin with? Sadly, I lean more toward no. I truly believed my heart was broken—not because someone broke it, but because it was never whole to begin with. I never felt right inside. The only time I have felt true love is when I hold Ben in my arms. Other than that, I didn't trust any fleeting feeling of love with a man I have ever had. Those feelings always turn to pain, for me and for that person.

On the plane ride back to the states, I saw someone reading some British tabloid. I didn't want to look, but I couldn't help it. On the cover was Topaz. She was an even bigger superstar in Europe. She was just now starting to be a success in America. Her appearances on Drew Ashton's arm have helped her, from what Matt tells me.

I never did ask Drew about his relationship with her. For all I know, he could have been cheating on her with me. To be honest, I didn't care to know. Our affair was over. Drew and I could go back to being acquaintances.

It wasn't like I didn't fantasize about more with Drew. Of course, I fell into the stupid, infatuated girl routine and imagined something much more than what we actually had. The cynical, hard-ass Cami knows better though. I reminded myself of the damaged heart I had, the one incapable of giving and receiving true love. Besides, I am too old for him. I am at an age where I'm settling down. I'm a mother. Drew is still a bachelor who travels a lot and parties with the team after games. I'm sure I was just one of the many girls he wines and dines during spring training.

Then there is the whole Jordan/Danny interference. Drew would choose his relationship with his brother over me. Hell, I would choose my friendship with Jordan over Drew, too. I wasn't going throw away a nineteen year friendship for a four-week romp. Though, I have to admit, it was enticing. I was tempted to risk everything to be in Drew's arms again, and that scared me that I would allow myself to get burned like that. Just when I think I'm getting my life straightened out, my stupid hormones get in the way.

CHAPTER SIXTEEN

It felt weird to be back in New York. There was a comfort in being home, but a loneliness there as well. The remodeling of the apartment looked great. It didn't quite hurt as much to be there now. I busied myself the first week back home by rearranging the apartment to make it feel more like mine, and not mine and Danny's. I had even ordered a new bed. Ben's tooth finally came through, which was a relief. I hated seeing him suffer.

Once everything was organized, I had Haley over for dinner. She and Aylin would be visiting Jordan on tour in a couple of days and it felt like forever since I had seen her. Haley was full of compliments on the apartment as well as me.

"Florida was good for you, huh?" she asked, taking a sip of her wine.

I finished pressing the Panini and slid it onto a plate. I had bought the same Panini press Drew had. I couldn't help to allow my mind to drift to that day Drew made that sandwich with his homemade pesto. I smiled remembering the way he had set the table and how he had gotten a little bit of pesto on his lips as we ate. I didn't expect to miss him like this. Watching the Yankee games only made it worse. I would just stare at him on the TV screen, and think of us in bed, or in the pool or anywhere around Tampa.

"Cami?"

I turned to look at Haley and I shook my head at her.

"I know it was your idea."

Haley played dumb.

"What was my idea?"

"Me going to Florida. Jordan told me you talked to Matt."

"I could kill him," she shook her head and I laughed. "Matt and I were talking after a photo shoot. He asked how you were. I told him you could use a friend and a vacation..."

I walked around the island and hugged her.

"Thank you."

She squeezed me.

"I know you don't think of us as close, Cami," Haley began. "But you are family to Jordan and me..."

I smiled at her, "You're my best friend. I know you have other best friends, but just know you're my best friend, Haley. I'm sorry for every time I was a bitch to you. I was just jealous."

Haley rolled her eyes, "Cami, you are a gorgeous, headstrong, courageous person. I wouldn't mind being like that," she shrugged.

I laughed, "You're just being nice."

"Drew said you were a lot of fun. He said the rest of the team loved you, even Billy Lotto. Billy doesn't like anyone!"

At first I tensed at the mention of Drew, but then frowned with disgust.

"Lotto is gross inside and out. I thought there was like a Yankee rule that you had to be good-looking?"

Haley laughed hysterically, "Well, I guess they couldn't discriminate!"

I chuckled, "It was a lot of fun to hang out with the guys."

"We all know you're one of the boys more than the girls," Haley nodded.

It was true. I could charm a room of men just as fast I could make a bunch of girls hate me with one look.

"So, are you bringing a date to Aylin's sweet sixteen party?"

"Who am I going to bring? Billy Lotto?" I rolled my eyes.

Haley shrugged, "I don't know...one of your hot, young clients maybe? Danny would flip out!"

I laughed, "Is he bringing someone?"

"Who knows...he originally RSVP'd when he was still with Anastasia."

I didn't care quite as much if Danny was bringing a date as I thought I would. I was more curious if Drew was bringing someone.

"Hey, is Drew bringing Topaz?"

"I don't even know if they're actually dating," she shrugged. "Drew doesn't talk much about anyone he dates. He hasn't been serious about anyone since college."

I nodded.

"Katie was that girl's name, right?"

I was trying to act like I didn't know much about Drew's personal life, even though I even met Katie once or twice back in the day.

Haley sighed, "She was sweet and Drew was crazy about her. She just couldn't handle him traveling so much."

I shrugged, "I guess not every girl can be as supportive as us Tortured wives. Get it?"

I was amused by my own pun. Though "tortured" was a fitting adjective for my marriage with Danny and not Haley's with Jordan.

Haley chuckled, "Yeah. I mean it isn't easy, but you learn to make it work."

I nodded, "At least that wasn't why Danny and I split."

Haley took a bite out of her sandwich. She's a vegetarian so I swapped the turkey Drew had paired with the pesto for zucchini. Of course, my pesto was also store-bought. Maybe it wouldn't hurt if I sent Drew a text asking for the recipe. Or maybe I was just looking for excuses to contact him.

"You make a hell of a Panini," she said, surprised.

"Thanks," I took the compliment.

I wasn't exactly known for my domestic skills. Aside from a good pot of tomato sauce once in a while, I didn't know my way around a kitchen. I wish I had paid more attention to my mother when she cooked. Just as I bit into my sandwich, my cell phone rang. I practically choked when I saw it was Drew calling. I panicked and rejected the call.

"You could take that if you want," Haley said.

"No. We're eating dinner; that would be rude."

I wanted to at least text Drew back, but I was too nervous to do it with Haley around.

Nervous wasn't something I felt often. I wasn't good at hiding it. Haley kept asking if I was okay. If I didn't feel so guilty, I could have easily told her Drew was calling and made something up as to why. It wasn't like Drew and I couldn't be friends. We never called each other prior to the affair, but everyone knew we spent some time together in Tampa. It wouldn't be so odd, but my guilt ruined any inability to be clever and quick. It made me wonder how Danny could lie to me so easily about his affairs.

"Cami, what is going on with you?" Haley asked.

"Nothing!" I laughed. "Why do you keep asking that?"

"Because you're different."

I rolled my eyes, "Is anyone ever happy with me? When I was a bitch, no one liked it. When I was depressed, everyone was frustrated. Now, I'm moving on with my life, and still, it's no good?"

Haley sucked her teeth and shook her head.

"I didn't say it was no good. I said different. Aside from you being jumpy, I kind of like this woman who invites me over for a girls' night and makes jokes. You seem carefree," she smiled.

I was taking a sip of wine, hoping to calm my nerves. I returned Haley's smile.

"Thank you. I feel carefree actually. I guess I'm just nervous about returning to work. You know, balancing being a mom and a music mogul," I chuckled.

"You'll do great," she waved me off.

We finished dinner and cleared the table. I checked on Ben before we took our wine into the living room. Haley's phone rang.

"It's Drew," she said and I choked, yet again, on my wine.

I waved my hand to let her know I didn't mind her taking the call.

"How is my favorite brother-in-law?" Haley answered the phone.

My nerves returned full-force.

"Oh, I'm sorry," Haley spoke as I tried to pretend I wasn't listening. "A. and I will be visiting Jordan. What about your dad?" She asked Drew and paused. "Oh. I wish we could be there. We miss you. Jordan hates missing your home games, you know that."

She suddenly glanced over at me and her eyes lit up.

"Hey Drew, I'm sure Cami would love to come out to represent."

My eyes widened.

"What are you talking about?" I whispered.

Haley ignored my question to answer Drew's.

"She's right here actually. Hold on," she said before handing me the phone.

I reluctantly took the phone from Haley and put it to my ear.

"Hey," I tried to say casually.

"Hi. Are you avoiding me?"

I loved the sound of his voice. It was so deep, but weightless.

"No."

"You ignored my call," he laughed. "I guess you didn't want to talk in front of Haley?"

"Nope," I said, also laughing. "But here I am."

Drew laughed even louder. I'm sure Haley could hear it.

"Sorry. Anyway, I wanted to know if you would want to come to see the opening day game?"

I couldn't help but to smile.

"Seriously? Yes!"

Haley laughed at my excitement, but I guess Drew couldn't tell on his end.

"Don't feel like you have to."

"Drew, I want to. Regardless if you were playing or not."

I realized that sounded terrible.

"Right. Big Yankee fan, how could I forget?" he asked, sounding less playful.

"That came out wrong. Of course I'll be there to support you."

"All right, see you then."

Before I could even respond, the line was dead. I handed Haley back her phone.

"You know," Haley said, almost slurring the words.

I guess the wine was starting to affect us both.

"I think Drew had something to do with the change in you."

I laughed loudly and shook my head vehemently.

"Drew? What?"

Haley smacked my knee and for a moment I thought she was going to squeeze the sensitive spot that Drew always managed to find.

"Seriously. Drew is so easygoing and fun. He rubs off on people."

I realized I was off the hook and calmed down as she continued.

"It's impossible to be depressed with Dew around."

I looked at her funny. Did she just say Dew?

"Who?"

Haley covered her mouth and laughed hysterically.

"I mean Drew!"

We now laughed together and it was obvious Haley was a tad tipsier than I was. Since I was not playing it cool when it came to the topic of Drew, at all, that was a blessing!

After Haley left, I checked on Ben once more. He was out cold. He definitely got his good sleeping habits from Danny. That man could fall asleep anytime, anywhere and it was difficult to wake him.

My phone was sitting on the kitchen table. I stared at the missed call from Drew. Before I could over think what I was doing, I called him and voicemail picked up immediately. It was after midnight. He might be traveling or sleeping. I decided to leave a message.

"Hey Drew. Um, I just wanted to make sure we're okay. I feel like you're mad at me. I am really happy to see you and to cheer you on. I would like us to be friends. Um...yeah, so I'll see you in a couple of days. It's Cami, by the way."

I hung up the phone and didn't understand why I had such an unsettled feeling in my stomach. It didn't feel like nerves from people finding out about my affair with Drew Ashton. It didn't feel like guilt for lying about the affair to the people I love, either. It kind of felt like something was missing. That feeling wasn't new to me, but this time, I am more confused than I had ever been in my life about what I wanted, or maybe whom I wanted.

I finally was released from the love/hate emotions I had for Danny. I even feel released from the longing feelings of wanting to be with Jordan. Maybe that is what's missing... an inner conflict of wanting the wrong person. That had to be it. My heart wasn't used to being free. I felt relief at that thought as I got into bed that night.

I just lay there for hours not being able to sleep. If my heart was so free, why did it feel so heavy still?

CHAPTER SEVENTEEN

I fussed over what to wear all day. Ben was easy. I put him in a complete Yankee uniform. He looked adorable in pinstripes. I took a million pictures of him and sent them to every person I knew, except for Drew. I figured I would see him at some point today. He would at least glance over, I would hope. He never called me back. I didn't even get a text.

Matt was the first person to respond to Ben's photo.

> ***Are you going to opening day?***
> ***Yup!***
> ***Jealous... So... You and Drew still?***
> ***Nope. Just friends.***

I sent that last text hoping it was true.

> ***Lame. I like you two together. Your last man hated me. This one is even a fan of my music!***

I laughed to myself at Matt's reply and sent him one last text before focusing on what to wear. I wound up going simple with a white t-shirt, pink Yankee hoodie and a matching baseball cap. I took the Subway to the Bronx. The train was packed, which of course made me nervous with Ben. I figured it was safer for him in the long-run. I hated how taxi drivers stopped short all the time. Plus, it was a pain to lug the car seat around.

I loved being at Yankee Stadium. There was nothing like seeing a game there. As a little girl, I rarely went to games. We couldn't afford them. For my twelfth birthday, Mama surprised me with tickets to my first game. Of course, back then it was a different stadium, but still on the same grounds the new one is on now. Every time I am in this stadium, I felt like Mama was with me, cursing in Italian when the umpires would make an unfair call.

Now, I was bringing my little boy to Yankee Stadium for the first time. I could afford to take him to plenty of games, but thanks to Drew, I didn't have to pay. That seemed to be how the world worked. When you can afford things, you get them for free and when you can't, somehow you get charged extra.

Ben looked at every single person that passed us as I picked up the tickets at will call. I think he was starting to recognize baseball. Lately, when I watched it, he would clap his hands with the crowd on TV. If Drew was on the screen, he would point. I couldn't tell if he already loved the sport or if he just missed Drew.

When we got to our seats right near the dugout, I recognized some of the players' wives and girlfriends. Cisco's wife, Ava was the only one who greeted me. I guess I wasn't surprised.

The last time the other women saw me, I was drunk and inappropriately flirting with the entire team.

I suddenly felt bad about that. I treated women I didn't know, and even some I did know, coldly. I would alienate them from conversations. I know now it was my insecurities that made me that way. I had such a need for male attention. I grew up without a father and without friends. I just saw other women as competition.

I needed to learn to put the claws away. I tried to do that as I began to chat idly with some of the women, making small talk. Ben helped give me a warmer presence and I was grateful for that. The women spoke like I was one of them, a player's girl. I kind of felt like one for a moment.

Things were going well until Sabrina, the second baseman's fiancée, asked how long I had been dating Drew.

"It's about time he settled down," Sabrina said.

"Well, actually we're not..."

"You're not?"

"We're just friends," I shrugged.

"Friends, right," Ava laughed. "You two certainly don't look at each other that way."

"Wait, so this isn't Drew's kid?" Sabrina asked.

I laughed and so did everyone else.

"No!"

"Girl, don't you pay attention to the gossip?" Kyla, the right-fielder's girlfriend, asked. "She's married to Danny D. from Tortured."

The girls seemed to buzz over that and I wanted to hide.

"The hot drummer is your husband?" Sabrina asked.

"Well, ex-husband now, yes."

"Oh, right. I'm sorry," Ava put her hand on mine.

She looked over at Sabrina and Kyla. I couldn't really see, but I could tell Kyla was mouthing something to them. I could only guess it was something about Danny's affair. I heard a simultaneous "aw".

"We're sorry, sweetie," Sabrina said. "I was cheated on once..."

Maybe this was why I didn't warm up to women. They didn't get that I didn't want to talk about it. I tried to shrink away from them and luckily, the team was now being announced.

The roar of the stadium was insane. Ben was startled and I hoped it wasn't too loud for him. Drew was announced to the field and he definitely received the biggest response. He jogged into view and naturally my eyes followed his butt. He stopped in front of our section and waved to the crowd with his hat off. He winked in my direction, and just as I waved, I heard someone yell as they approached the seat next to me.

"Go Drew!"

I looked to the left and to my disgust Topaz was standing there cheering Drew on! How dare he invite us both to the game! Unlike me and just about everyone else, who was dressed in casual attire, Topaz looked like she was walking the red carpet. She had on a white halter-top romper and four-inch red heels. Her blue hair had a matching red bow. She sat right next to me and my mouth must have hung open.

"Aw, if you want me to take a picture with you and your baby, can it wait until after the game?" She asked, pursing her fire engine red lips at me.

"I don't want a picture with you," I scoffed.

"I'm sorry. You just looked so shocked to see me, I figured you were a fan."

"I prefer rock music."

My instinct was to tell her I actually thought she couldn't sing. All of Topaz's appeal was in her outrageous style, sex appeal and a really good producer, not to mention a ton of money. The word in the industry is Topaz is the granddaughter of some billionaire.

"Wait, I've seen you somewhere. Oh, you're Tami something, right? I saw you in some magazine my assistant was reading..."

At first, I thought she purposely screwed up my name. That was definitely something I would do, like call her Turquoise instead of Topaz, but it actually seemed like she didn't know any better. Great, no talent and no brains!

I prepared myself to hear about Danny's affair in some tabloid for the hundredth time. I had to remember to send him an unpleasant text to once again thank him for humiliating me.

"*Forbes Magazine* or something like that? You're like in the top one-hundred successful women in entertainment..."

Oh, thank God! I smiled confidently.

"That's me."

"Maybe I should get a picture with *you*," Topaz laughed. "I'm always seen as an airhead when it comes to business."

I was trying not to hate her, but I did. I just couldn't put the claws away with this one. Not only was she self-absorbed, but she was flirting with the hot dog guy when he came around. How would Drew feel about that? Or maybe they had an open relationship? I was too infuriated to ask her about Drew. I was too humiliated, too.

Ava tapped my shoulder.

"Sorry you got stuck sitting next to the attention whore," she whispered before laughing.

I just shrugged and tried to focus on the game. It was hard though. I wanted to go home. I didn't get why Drew would put me in such an awkward position.

When he got up to bat, Topaz began screaming her head off.

"Come on, baby!"

That was it. I was out of there. I pretended like I was just going to the bathroom, but I headed straight out of the stadium. I could hear the chanting of "Take us home!" as I left. I kissed Ben's forehead and wished I could snap my fingers and we'd be home.

Thanks to the game going on, the subway was much emptier on the way back. I put Ben down for a nap and I didn't know what to do with myself. Part of me wanted to watch the game, as a fan of baseball, but I knew I would just get upset especially when they flash to Topaz. The camera crew always showed celebrities in the crowd and with her cheering on her favorite player; it will just put more attention on her.

I don't know what Drew was thinking! Was he playing games? Did he want me to be jealous? Or maybe this was his way of saying we are just friends now. Well, good, that's what I want. Why do I feel like shit then?

I threw my hat and hoodie off, kicked off my sneakers, and flung myself on the couch. I passed out for maybe twenty minutes before Ben started crying. I was amazed I fell asleep at all. My mind just wouldn't turn off. I saw I had a text from Drew.

Why'd you leave?

I laughed aloud to myself and threw my phone onto the couch before going to retrieve Ben. I opened a jar of sweet potatoes, which seemed to be Ben's favorite of all the foods I've been introducing him to the past month. He always spit out the strained peas and beef, but I couldn't blame him. I'd choose the sweet potatoes too!

I had no appetite myself, so I just focused on Ben. After I fed him, I bathed him before putting him on his play mat to see if he would actually crawl. He's been getting on his hands and knees since Europe, but no real movement yet. My phone began ringing while I was coaxing

Ben to me. I ignored it, not in the mood to speak to anyone.

After I put Ben down for the night, the phone for the building's front desk rang. It was after eight, so it couldn't be a package. I answered the phone wondering if they dialed me by mistake.

"Ms. Woods, Andrew Ashton is here to see you."

I could hear the excitement in the doorman's voice as he said something about a great play Drew made.

I sighed, "Send him up."

I doubt the doorman listened to my response. He would allow Drew Ashton to come up to my apartment regardless of what I responded with! I probably looked frumpy by now. I was in a tank top and gym shorts with my hair thrown up. I wondered if Topaz even played dress up at home. I bet her real name is Jennifer or Tiffany—something simple.

There was a light rapping at the door and I opened it to see Drew, with his big brown eyes and that easygoing smile. Hell, if I were the doorman, I wouldn't have even called the apartment. I would have given him a key!

"Are you planning to ignore me forever?" he asked and I walked away from the door, allowing him to shut it behind him.

"You ignored me the other day," I shrugged.

"Why did you leave the game today? Is Ben okay?"

"He's fine," I said, kind of coldly. "He's asleep. I should have left after the players' women began to discuss my cheating ex-husband as if it happened on some soap opera and not to me."

"What?" Drew asked, putting his hands on his hips.

"I should be used to it by now, but it still hurts."

"I'm sorry..."

I put my hand up to stop him, "I left because your pop princess with the stripper name showed up."

Drew laughed, "I didn't know Topaz was going to be there..."

"I'm glad you think it's funny. Was it some kind of joke to seat us next to each other?" I asked.

He was still laughing and he tried to stop, making his dimples more prominent.

"I swear I didn't know she was coming to the game. Do you really think I am dating her?"

"From what all the tabloids say, you are," I said, crossing my arms over my chest.

He gave me a look.

"You're going to trust tabloids?"

"Well, they were right about Danny's affair, so why not?"

He shook his head, "You know this business better than most, Cami. Can't you spot a publicity stunt from a mile away?"

"A publicity stunt?"

"Not only does little Miss Blue Hair have the same agent as me, but her Daddy is someone very big in the Yankee headquarters," he said, putting his hands on his hips again.

He looked tough and like he was mocking me in that stance. I had to admit, he looked sexy.

"So you and Topaz never...?" I asked, dropping my arms from my chest.

"We never even kissed," Drew said and I raised an eyebrow. "Well, we did a couple of times, but just pecks on the lips when a few reporters were present."

I sighed, "And you're okay with them using your name and image to make her a star?"

Drew shrugged, "I kind of have to be okay with it. At least Topaz can act better than she sings. She had you fooled."

I laughed and then frowned.

"So I missed opening day for nothing?"

"Yup," he nodded. "But it's nice to know I can make you jealous," he winked.

"That's not hard to do. I'm jealous of any girl. Haley could tell you stories," I sighed.

Drew groaned, "Okay. So I guess I'll see you then."

Gone was the teasing and mocking expression in his posture and face. He turned to leave abruptly, and I grabbed his arm to stop him.

"What's your problem?"

"My problem is I'm done playing games, Cami. Aren't you?"

I stared at him confused.

"I got your message the other day. I was hoping you'd forget this whole just friends bullshit. That's why I ignored you. It's not going to work!"

I looked at him surprised. He was so annoyed with me and I was trying to figure out why. Maybe I just had that affect on men. They all think I'm cool in the beginning and then it wears off.

"So, you don't want to be friends?" I asked, hearing the hurt in my voice. "We'll just avoid each other?"

"No, Cami. I don't want to be friends," Drew said before grabbing me.

Before I knew it, he was kissing me and damn it, I missed this too much to even think of pushing him away. I wrapped my arms around him. He pulled away from me and I went to kiss him again, but he held me back. His hand was on my chest. My heart was racing under him.

"I want you to admit to me that you feel something," he said, staring into my eyes.

"Drew," I sighed.

"Don't give me excuses. I don't care what Jordan will say or Danny. Don't we deserve to see what this is between us?"

He looked so beautiful and I couldn't turn him away. I fought so hard against feeling something for Andrew Ashton, but it was becoming painfully obvious that I craved him in every way. The sex is great, but this amazing guy wants more. I know there are a million reasons I could think of to turn him away. Our age difference, my cynical heart that gave up on love, Drew's lack of relationship experience, and the already mentioned Jordan and Danny.

"Cami, it feels right. Doesn't it?" he asked.

I felt tears fill my eyes incredibly quickly. I guess Drew took that as a negative response. His hand dropped from my chest and he turned away from me. I saw him reach for the doorknob and I willed myself to speak. I wasn't sure what words were going to come out.

"I love you!"

CHAPTER EIGHTEEN

Wow. Was that too much? Too soon? It felt like Drew turned around in slow motion.

"Oh my God," I panicked.

"Did you...?" he asked, just as surprised as I was.

I nodded before rushing toward him, knowing the words weren't a lie. I didn't have to think about it anymore. With Drew, there was no complicated formula and time put in to be the equivalent of love. With him, it was spontaneous, raw, and the most natural feeling I have ever felt. Now, that I have admitted it to myself—I didn't even have to think if I loved Drew. I never felt the way I feel for him about anyone else.

That whole revelation about me being incapable of feeling true love was a lie. Nothing felt truer than the love I felt for Drew. There was need, passion, lust, respect, comfort—every possibly amazing emotion in the world was alive when I was with him.

"I love you," I reaffirmed, pressing my lips to his.

I didn't even care if Drew said it back at that point. I just wanted him to help christen my new bed. It didn't take us long to make it to the bedroom. We started out ravenous, but then went slowly, savoring each other.

"I'm starving," I said, after an hour later, as we lay in bed.

Drew laughed, "Worked up an appetite, huh?"

I smirked, "Actually, I didn't eat dinner. I was too upset over you and the blue haired Smurf."

Drew sat up as I slid out of bed.

"Poor baby," he said, pulling me back down for a kiss. "You're the only girl I've been thinking about."

His voice sounded so sexy.

"I'm not a girl anymore," I bit my bottom lip innocently and climbed into his lap.

I rubbed against him and he ran a hand over my butt.

"I'm all woman," I said, kissing him deeply.

Another hour later, I was finally getting myself something to eat. Drew came up behind me as I was making a sandwich.

"I see you got yourself a Panini maker," he laughed, wrapping his arms around my waist.

"Yeah, I was inspired when I got back from Florida. This guy I was sleeping with made the best breakfast foods and sandwiches. He got me hooked," I teased.

"Huh, I just thought you liked me for my body," Drew said, sitting at the table.

I smiled over my shoulder, "Do you want one? I'm getting pretty good at this."

"Sure," he yawned.

I began to prepare another sandwich.

"So this guy you're sleeping with?"

"Yeah?" I asked placing the first sandwich on a plate and placing the other one on the griddle.

"Does he love you?"

I shrugged, "I'm not sure. I vaguely remember him telling me once, but we were in bed…"

I tried hard to put those words that Drew had said months ago out of my mind. Guys did stupid stuff like throw around feelings when their penis was involved.

I didn't look at Drew, afraid of what he was about to say. Drew pulled me away from the counter and looked into my eyes.

"I love you, Cami. I knew I loved you back in Florida," he smiled. "I just needed you to admit there was more for us."

I kissed him until we smelled the sandwich burning.

We sat in the kitchen, eating and talking. Drew didn't have to be up early, thankfully. We finished our sandwiches and Drew washed the dishes for me. He sat back down and took my hand.

"Look, I know you're worried about a lot. We don't have to tell anyone about us just yet."

I nodded, "I'm really scared. Not just about telling everyone, but I'm just getting out of a divorce..."

"I know. We don't have to rush anything."

I smiled, "So, are you going to continue being the Yankee playboy? I really will be crazy jealous...even if a girl interviews you on Yes!"

Drew laughed, "I can handle your craziness if you can handle my crazy work schedule."

"That's nothing. My work schedule can get pretty crazy, too. And now I'm a mom, can you handle that?"

"I love kids, especially Benvy. You know that."

I chuckled, "That nickname only sounds good coming from your lips."

He smirked before leaning in and giving me a peck.

"Wait, you didn't answer me," I pulled away.

"What did you ask me?" he wondered.

"That whole playboy thing. You have quite the reputation with the ladies," I raised an eyebrow.

He shook his head, "I'm done with that crap. I would have been done with that stuff years ago if I found the right girl."

I grinned.

"I'm not sure how much you know, but I didn't grow up with the best family environment."

"I know your dad wasn't the best...and you told me you don't really talk to your mom..."

"I didn't grow up with much parental attention. They pretty much ignored me," Drew sighed.

I squeezed his hand and rubbed his thigh with my free one.

"My dad was abusive and drank too much. Yeah, we were rich, but Jordan and I didn't care about that. Dad drove Jordan away. My brother was the only person who treated me like I mattered," Drew sighed. "Mom was even worse than Dad at times. She checks in a couple of times a year—if that."

I put my hand on his cheek.

"I'm sorry."

"It's fine," he shrugged. "I still have Jordan and Haley and Aylin... I have some great friends. Cisco is a good guy, even if his wife gossips too much," he said apologetically.

I chuckled and slipped my hand into his.

"I just always longed for a family. I swore to myself I wouldn't take after my parents. I would be good to my kids and my woman. After Katie broke up with me, I thought I might never find someone who loved me for me, and not for my uniform."

"Well, I do love your uniform," I smiled. "But you know I'm not fazed by celebrities."

He nodded, "And I'm not intimidated by a successful woman."

I laughed before turning serious.

"Who would have thought we want the same things?" I said, in disbelief.

Drew stared at me, wanting me to elaborate.

"I don't even remember my dad. He left my mom when I was a baby. It was just Mama and me, and no money. After Mama passed away when I was a teenager, I was all alone...until I met the band," I said, taking a deep breath.

I didn't tell many people my life story. I opened up a little to Drew once before about my mother, but not about the loneliness.

He stroked my jaw, "You never have to worry about being alone again."

I smiled, "I'm not always good at allowing myself to be vulnerable. I wasn't very good at emotions in general. I tried to force love with the wrong guys. The truth is, I don't know if I was ever in love before."

Drew was staring into my eyes and he ran his fingers through my hair.

"How did I marry someone I wasn't in love with?"

He smiled sympathetically.

"Danny was family to you; it's understandable to confuse feelings."

I sighed, "Yeah."

There was more I wanted to tell him, but I knew I couldn't. It was too soon to tell him I feel different inside with him, that maybe I could fall in love with him. I didn't dare mention my brief romance with Jordan. It was better not to remind him I dated his brother, or to admit I thought I was in love with him for the past eighteen years.

We finally decided to go to bed around four-am. I'm sure he was just as beat as I was. I may have lost a whole night's sleep and gone through a slew of emotions, but Drew had just gotten back into town, had a two-hour press conference, played a game, and had a team dinner before even getting to my apartment. I fell asleep in Drew's arms, happy to know neither of us had to rush off anywhere in the morning.

I must have been conked out. I woke up to the smell of eggs and a bunch of baby talk going on in the kitchen. I threw my robe on and headed to the bathroom to freshen up. Despite my lack of sleep, I looked surprisingly okay for the morning. Or maybe I just looked happy. Was it still morning? What kind of mother am I to sleep through my son's cries? I peeked at the alarm clock and it was just after eight-am.

I stepped into the kitchen. Drew's back was to me as he stood over the stove in just his boxers. Ben was sitting in his high chair and started clapping and smiling as soon as he saw me.

"Good morning, Ben," I rushed over to him and kissed both his cheeks. "Good morning, Drew," I said turning and kissing his bare back.

Drew turned and gave me a proper kiss.

"How long have you been up?" I wondered, feeling bad that he had to take care of Ben.

"Less than an hour."

"Oh, I'm so sorry..." I sighed. "You should have woken me. I can't believe I slept so soundly."

Drew waved me off.

"It's fine. You needed the sleep," he winked. "You're very organized by the way."

I laughed, "What?"

"I found everything just fine. Bottles, diapers..."

I smiled. He was too cute.

"Drew, where did you come from?"

"What?"

"If it were any other guy, my son would be naked, peeing on the floor and drinking soda."

He laughed, "I babysat Aylin a lot when she was little."

"Still, it's been a while since she was in diapers," I shrugged, amazed.

"It feels like yesterday. Can you believe she's turning sixteen?"

"No," I shook my head. "I remember when you turned sixteen," I grimaced.

Drew rolled his eyes, "So you're a cougar, get over it."

I laughed, "The age difference doesn't bother you?"

He shrugged, "No. I don't think about it much. Does it bother you?"

I thought about it for a second.

"Not really. Just when I think about knowing you as a kid."

Drew's dimples showed as he tried not to laugh at my slight hang up.

"Well, don't think of me when I was a kid."

I laughed and he reached down to squeeze my knee. I smacked his hand away, afraid I would fall on the floor if he succeeded in his attempt while I was standing up.

"Speaking of your niece turning sixteen," I changed the subject. "The party is a little over a month away. Will you be in town?"

"Of course," he grinned. "Aylin personally checked in with my schedule before planning it."

"Aww, she loves her uncle very much," I wrapped my arms around his neck and kissed him.

"Just think how happy she'll be when she finds out I'm bringing a date," he wiggled his eyebrows.

I made a face.

"I wouldn't count on anyone being happy about it."

He laughed, "You worry too much. So Danny will definitely not be happy, but Aylin loves you. Haley will be happy and I bet Jordan will be too."

I just patted his chest. Drew really was easygoing, huh? Jordan was too, but not like this! On a day-to-day basis, Jordan was laid back. When it concerned his music or his family, though, his temper came out.

"I don't think Aylin's Sweet Sixteen is the time to tell anyone about us," I said.

"Have I told you how beautiful your eyes are?" he asked, knowing that compliment usually made me smile stupidly.

Pushing him away, I huffed.

"Can you be serious?"

"No," he said, leaning against the stove.

He yelled and moved away from the hot pan.

"Shit, are you okay?" I asked, turning him around to inspect his back.

There was a small burn mark.

"It's fine," he laughed, before serving up two omelets and turkey sausage.

He sat down and I followed him. I knew I better eat while Ben was content to stay in his high chair.

"We won't tell everyone at the party, in case of any arguments breaking out. I don't want to ruin Aylin's day," Drew said, after taking a bite of his food.

"Good," I smiled.

"We'll just have to tell everyone sooner," he smirked.

I bit my tongue on my first bite of food as I looked over at him. I knew this would be an ongoing debate. Luckily, by mid afternoon, once we were showered and ready to say goodbye for a few days, I convinced Drew we needed time to ourselves to allow our relationship to grow without any interference.

I knew that the truth had to come out sooner rather than later though. Lying was not my strong suit and discretion was not Drew's.

CHAPTER NINETEEN

Sneaking around was both exciting and frustrating. Obviously Drew was high profile and I was semi-recognizable thanks to the millions of Tortured fans who knew exactly who I was, and the constant tabloid attention that's been tracking my ex-husband's sexual escapes. It wasn't like we could just go to any restaurant or walk down the street holding hands.

With us showing up at each other's apartments whenever he was in town, the secret was bound to come out. The doormen to my building would give me these knowing smiles. One of these guys could easily tip off reporters.

I started to increase my workload for the rest of the month. It worked out perfectly since I would only get to see Drew for a total of three days! At least I had work to keep me busy. Not that Ben didn't keep me occupied, especially now that he was crawling. My mind had time to wander when I was home, though.

I was going to hire a nanny, even though I really didn't like the idea of a stranger being with my son every day. It would only be for five hours Monday to Friday. Then it would just be

Ben and me. Danny kept asking me to let him take Ben on the road, but I thought it was a bad idea. The road was no place for a baby, especially without his mother. I know Danny felt helpless and missed Ben, but it just wouldn't work. He suggested his mother become Ben's nanny since she was semi-retired. I liked the idea of that!

Since I had no relatives to gush over Ben, I was happy he would be close to Danny's family. The DeSanos were nice people; Danny's mother especially. I couldn't have asked for a better mother-in-law. Unlike her son, I never argued with Leslie DeSano.

When I walked into work, I made sure to smile and converse with all of my employees. I wanted to turn over a new leaf, though I knew if I was going to be friendly, I needed to remain tough as well. There was a reason I kept a cold front with people—as soon as they think you're their friend, they think they can take advantage.

"Cami, you look amazing," Lisa Ann gushed.

"Thank you," I smiled.

"You look more in shape now than before you were pregnant!" She laughed.

I *am* more fit than before my pregnancy actually. I now exercised regularly. Drew turned me on to him and working out. They both became part of my daily life.

I couldn't wait for the first weekend in May when Drew would be home. He was off Saturday and Sunday, but then a double header on Monday. Still, for two whole days I had him to myself!

I arranged for Leslie to take Ben to her home in Staten Island for that weekend. I felt bad lying to her about what I was doing. She was happy to have her grandson in her own home and to bring him around the rest of the family, so I didn't feel too guilty. I kept busy until that weekend, planning to do nothing but immerse myself in Drew once he was in town.

That Friday, I packed up Ben's things for the weekend and kissed him goodbye a million times. I handed him off to Leslie and felt myself having a hard time letting him go. It was the first time I would be away from him overnight. Leslie assured me it was natural for me to have a little separation anxiety, and it would be good for Ben and me.

I went to work and the entire day, focusing was slightly difficult. I felt like a kid waiting for Santa Claus to arrive. Still, I made sure I got as much work done as I possibly could, which included looking over endorsement deals for Rad Trick and Tortured, a new record deal for Sound Wave, and listening to a new potential client's demo.

After work, I headed to the grocery store. I was planning to make a big Italian dinner for Drew—my one culinary specialty. My phone rang while I was in the pasta aisle. I smiled, seeing Drew's gorgeous face. I had a few pictures of him and us on my phone, but I kept them locked in case anyone tried to look through it. Yes, I was paranoid.

"Camilla, buon giorno!"

I rolled my eyes and laughed.

"I should have never told you my real name, Andy," I teased, knowing he hated being called that.

"Okay, we're even."

"I'm surprised to hear from you. Don't you have a game?"

"About to head to the dugout. I just wanted to tell you I booked us a place to stay."

"You got a hotel room?" I asked, confused. "Why?"

"Because I want to take you out."

"What?" I laughed. "A hotel is not taking me out. That's keeping me in bed," I whispered since some little old lady was trying to listen to my conversation as she pretended to look at a box of rigatoni.

"I'll be doing plenty of that, too. But I rented us a house," Drew said.

What a romantic, was my first thought. My second thought was, the Hamptons was a high profile place where Danny knew many people. We have a house there. Well, had. I let Danny keep it in the divorce since he had friends there and I could care less about it.

"Drew, we can't go to the Hamptons—"

"I didn't say it was in the Hamptons," he said. "It's in the Catskills and fairly secluded."

"Oh," I smiled, falling back into the "what a romantic" thought.

"Is that okay?"

I looked at my cart full of food and figured I could always cook for him at the rental house.

"Of course. It sounds great."

"I can't wait to see your face," he said.

"Drew, I can't wait to see you."

I must have gotten the cheesiest smile on my face because the little old lady gave me a toothless grin.

After I hung up the phone, the lady patted my arm.

"Now, that's the look of love."

I just laughed. I finished my shopping as quickly as possible and headed home. I packed up everything I would need for the weekend before plopping myself in front of the TV to watch the Yankees game. They were going against the Boston Red Sox for the third straight night.

The team had lost the first two games and the crowd was extra rowdy. I sat on the edge of my seat, hoping they could catch a break. By the bottom of the seventh inning, the Yanks were down by two runs. Both teams were playing extremely hard.

The eighth was a 1-2-3 inning with no one getting on base. By the top of the ninth, it was not looking good for the Yankees. Lotto was the first out. Cisco was up next and got a single. Messina struck out. Nostri, the rookie of the team, got a double and Cisco scored. The Yankees were on their feet cheering, hoping to at least tie the score. I would hate the game to have to go into extra innings, but if it meant beating the Red Sox, then so be it!

Drew was up at bat, and it was no surprise that the Sox pitcher walked him, trying to avoid another run. Drew's record of homeruns with a player on base was one of the highest in the league.

Dwyer was up next. He racked up two strikes quickly. I held my breath on the third pitch, thinking the game was over, but saying a prayer it wasn't. My prayer was answered. Dwyer's bat connected with the ball in a loud way. It was a line drive down the first base line. Nostri reached third base then headed home, tying the score. Drew made it to third and Dwyer to second.

If I wasn't on the edge of my seat before, I definitely was now, literally. My butt was barely on the couch as I watched. Lou Briggs was up to bat next and I worried he would strike out. He hasn't gotten a hit yet this season.

Briggs hit the ball finally, and it looked like a homerun for a moment, but it was foul, heading just outside the third base line. The next pitch was a strike. On the third pitch, the bat made contact, and Drew ran as fast as he could toward home plate. The ball was a grounder that made its way directly to the first baseman, who let it slip through his glove, and scrambled for it. He was able to get Briggs out at first before tossing it to the catcher. It was too late; Drew had already slid into home before Briggs was out. The Yankees took the lead! I jumped up, clapping, as if the team could hear me.

I had always been a rowdy spectator, but it was worse now that my boyfriend was on the team. I was the same way at award shows for my clients. I am highly competitive and have pride in things and people I love.

The bottom of the ninth inning was a bit of a nail biter. Tommy Baines was sent in as the Yankees' closing pitcher after two players got on base. Baines was another rookie on the team and looked like he was twelve! I didn't quite get why the coach would send him in now when it was so critical. The kid had only played one other game before! Drew said Baines had a ton of potential, but he was still a nervous kid.

When Boston's star hitter, Suarez, stepped up to the plate I knew why Baines was sent in to pitch. Suarez had a powerful swing, but he had a history of striking out to lefty pitchers. Baines was a lefty, of course. Sure enough, Suarez struck out rather quickly. Baines must have gained some confidence before he struck out two more hitters and the game was over!

I was excited the Yankees won this particular game, aside from the obvious reasons. I didn't want Drew to be down in any way this weekend. Knowing Drew, though, he probably would have turned upbeat quickly. It was weird to see someone, especially a guy, who didn't brood for most of the day. Sure, Drew got mad from time to time, like when I wondered if he were on steroids or when he was frustrated I was holding back feelings for him. He even warned me of a temper, but still, it was nothing compared to Danny's or mine even. Drew got mad, let off some steam, and it was over. I liked that a lot, correction, I loved that.

I keep waiting for the euphoria to wear off with Drew. It's been almost three months since our one-night stand started. We jokingly refer to our relationship as a one-night stand, since neither of us predicted any of this would happen. I can't remember when puppy love fades. With Danny, we didn't have much of a puppy love stage. We were on the verge of breaking up every other week.

Like with my month long fling with Drew, I'm enjoying our relationship while I can. Who knows what will happen once everyone knows? Who knows if Drew will still want me after a few months? I only know how I feel, and right now, I am falling in love with Andrew Ashton. Or at least, I think I am. I couldn't tell what was real and what was an illusion anymore. I spent so many years with Danny, thinking that was love when it wasn't. What if I'm wrong again?

I can't predict if I'll always feel this way, or if Drew will always want me. Maybe nothing does last forever. The only thing I can do is live in the moment.

I went to bed early that night, knowing Drew was coming over some time in the wee hours of the morning. He had a key to my apartment and the doorman knew to allow him up by now.

I must have been tired because I didn't even hear Drew come in. I woke up to his arms wrapping around me.

"Hi," he said, his smile visible even in the dark.

"I missed you," I said, running my fingers down the side of his face.

We kissed, but we were both tired. I don't remember which one of us passed out first, but before I knew it, the sun was shining through the blinds. Drew was still asleep. I got ready and made sure I didn't forget to pack anything once more before waking him.

Less than an hour later, we were on the road in Drew's red mustang convertible. It seemed he and Jordan had the same taste in cars as well. At least this one wasn't a fixer upper like Jordan had purchased with his first royalty check. Jordan Walsh is quite the enigma. If he were poor, he'd still be happy. I guess that's what happens when you grow up rich with messed up parents.

When you grow up poor with just one good parent, you'll do anything not to stay that way. Then again, I have enough money to have anything I want, but I still wasn't happy. So I guess the old saying goes, money doesn't buy happiness, or love.

I am finally starting to feel happiness creep into my life more and more.

My thoughts were interrupted by Drew squeezing my knee. I smacked him as I always do and he laughed.

"Why are you so quiet?"

"I'm just happy," I smiled.

"Me too," he winked.

"Why didn't we get together years ago?" I asked with a laugh, squeezing his hand in mine.

"Let's see," he pretended to think. "Well, you were married, and before that, I was jailbait."

"Oh, right," I shrugged.

The drive to the Catskills was not bad at all. Before we knew it, the chaos of Manhattan was behind us with all of its traffic and congested buildings. Clear highways and trees replaced it all.

Drew had made a playlist for the ride, which was cute. There was a nice mix of songs we both liked, plus some of my favorites and some of his. When a pop song came on, I turned to him and shook my head.

"Is this Sound Wave?"

He grinned innocently.

"This is a great song," he said turning it up.

"Wait, this isn't even released yet..." I shouted over the music.

"I know. Matt sent it to me," he yelled back.

He stopped it and started it over.

"Listen to the words," Drew insisted.

I'm not perfect
My heart's got, got a permanent defect
But your love, the one thing I can't reject
I know, like me, pain is what you expect
Time to let go, ohh

You made me dream, yeah
When I've given up on things
Please love me for who I am
In spite of everything
I've ever done

Because you, you are everything
I always wanted
And never thought I would find

Baby, you take me home
When I've got no place to turn
You pick me up
When I am dropped so far down
And on my own
Baby, you take me home
You're the safety net
That'll catch me when the day is done
I want to go home with you
Baby, take me

I stare at your face
And I know what I was missing
Hell baby, I've got scars
And you needed space
We both needed time, time, time
To find this magic place
Baby, you take me

You take me home
When I've got no place to turn
You pick me up
When I am dropped so far down
And on my own

Baby, you take me home
You're the safety net
That'll catch me when the day is done
I want to go home with you
Baby, take me

With you, I'm alive
With you, I see truth
Behind every lie I felt inside
I am home, home, home
With you, I am home[‡]

As I listened to the lyrics of the song, which I had heard a rough demo of last week, I found tears come to my eyes. I didn't think much about what the song was about when I heard it. I paid more attention to how the vocals sounded and the ability to market the song. I was listening to it with my head then, now I listened with my heart.

"I think this should be our song," he said, placing his hand on my thigh and caressing softly.

I placed my hand over his and squeezed.

"It's perfect," I smiled.

[‡] The lyrics to "Home" was also written and owned by Sandy Lo.

Before I knew it, we were driving up a blacktop driveway. The house was a modern day log cabin. It was three stories with all the amenities I had in New York City and more. There was an actual sauna and indoor swimming pool on the top floor!

After looking around, I jumped into Drew's arms, wrapping my legs around his waist.

"This is amazing," I said kissing him.

"I'm glad you like it," he smiled as I unwrapped myself from his body.

"How can I not?" I asked, glancing around and running my hand over a wooden pillar.

"It's not too rustic for you?"

I rolled my eyes, "Oh yeah. We're really roughing it in the sticks. Not that I would mind," I smiled coyly.

"So my body is enough to keep Cami Woods busy?" he asked, raising his eyebrows.

"Your body, your face," I said, walking closer to him. "Your voice..."

Drew pulled me in for another kiss.

"Good."

"The real question is if I'm enough to keep Andrew Ashton, number 12 for the Yankees busy," I smiled, pulling his pendant out of his shirt.

He smirked, "You're the first woman I've been serious about in five years. What does that tell you?"

"That all the other women you've been with have been lousy in bed," I joked.

Drew laughed, but ran his fingers through my hair and kissed me.

"There have been some good ones."

I smacked him and he held me so I couldn't back away.

"I'm trying to tell you that you're more than that to me."

I just kissed him, not knowing how else to respond. If he was going to keep staring at me with those big brown eyes, I might cry.

That night, Drew insisted on taking me out to dinner. The last time we went out somewhere together was in Florida, but we weren't alone then. I decided on a black mini-dress that fit like a glove. I had to admit, it looked good on me. My body was finally in a place I was comfortable with. I'm sure that had to do with my love for working out and for Drew more than anything else. For all I knew, my body was exactly the same as it was right after my pregnancy. I just felt really good about myself lately. The fact that I was a size smaller than I was before my pregnancy let me know, it wasn't purely self-confidence. I swept my hair off to the side with a rhinestone clip.

"Are you ready?" Drew asked, knocking lightly on the half open door.

I turned toward him and he grinned. He was wearing a grey dress shirt and black dress pants. His hair was tousled a bit.

"Wow," he said, as I posed.

"Wow yourself."

He wrapped his arms around me and moved his large hands down to my butt.

"Is this like our first date?" I asked.

He laughed, "Sure, why not?"

We headed to the Tuscan Grille half an hour later. Neither of us had ever vacationed in the Catskill Mountains before. Drew had been on a day trip to the game farm in the area with Aylin, when she was little. With us both being big city people, it was refreshing to see so much space, even inside the restaurant.

The Tuscan Grille wasn't anything overly fancy, which suited me just fine. As uppity I can come off on occasion, I still liked simple meals, got ready quickly, and dressed practically.

Drew and I talked, ate, laughed, and stole kisses. It was perfectly comfortable and simple—

just how I liked it. After dinner, we got lost finding an ice cream shop. We playfully argued on which way to go as we both yelled at the GPS misguiding us.

We were back to the house before midnight. The downfall of being out of the city? Things closed early! We snuggled on the couch for a movie. I noticed Drew rubbing his neck a few times.

"What's wrong?"

"My neck is cramped. I'm a little beat up from that last game."

"I saw," I frowned.

Drew's thigh had a large bruise on it from where he slid home.

"Let's go into the sauna," I said, standing up and taking Drew's hand.

His eyes trailed up my body as he took my hand. The sauna would be good for Drew's achy body, but it seemed both of us were always eager to get each other naked.

We walked up to the third floor and began to strip. I took off my jewelry and Drew took off his pendant. The steam felt amazing as we sat down in the sauna. I began to massage Drew's neck as he relaxed into my bare chest. His thumbs caressed my thighs as I kneaded his muscles. There was something so intimate about everything Drew and I did together. It wasn't just sexual energy. I felt like every part of me was connected to Drew. We could say nothing or say everything, and it felt completely natural.

After getting out of the sauna, I wrapped a towel around myself. Drew picked up his pendant and seemed to be contemplating something. He walked over to me.

"Will you wear my number?" he asked, holding up the pendant to me.

I smiled, "Isn't that your good luck charm?"

He laughed, "I'm not superstitious."

"Okay."

"It would make me happy knowing a part of me is with you all the time."

"That would make me happy, too, even though a part of you is always with me anyway," I said and he grinned before clasping the chain around my neck.

I fingered the pendant before kissing him.

The next morning, I was up early to make the tomato sauce. I would think I would be more exhausted. Drew and I made love three times before we passed out. I guess I was running on the euphoria of love and lust. I felt surprisingly rejuvenated.

Drew didn't wake up until after eleven-am, which gave me plenty of time to get ready, cook and clean everything up. The weekend went by way too quickly, but at least Drew didn't have to leave town until Wednesday morning. He had two home games against the Toronto Blue Jays.

As I was turning the sauce off, Drew emerged from the bedroom in nothing but his boxer-briefs. His chest looked especially naked to me without the pendant, but I was so flattered he wanted me to wear it, that it made me smile.

"What smells delicious?" he asked, kissing my cheek.

"My mom's sauce," I grinned at him.

"You've been holding out on me, haven't you?" he asked, peering into the pot.

"No, really, this is the only thing I can make. Mama says every Italian woman needs to know how to make a good pot of gravy."

"You think your mama would have approved of me?" he asked.

"Hmm," I said, tapping my chin and looking him up and down.

He posed with his arms folded behind his head.

"She would say you looked like an underwear model," I laughed, running my hands up and down his sides.

"Pretend I'm fully clothed," he said, standing with his hands folded in front of his crotch.

I laughed harder, "I can't do that, nor do I want to."

He pouted, "Your mama hates me."

I wrapped my arms around his waist.

"Mama loves you. You're a good guy. You treat me well. And it doesn't hurt that you're the star player for her favorite baseball team," I smiled.

Drew grinned before kissing me softly.

"Now, your mother on the other hand, she probably won't like me one bit."

Drew shrugged, "My mother doesn't even like me."

"You don't believe that, do you?"

He didn't answer. I squeezed him tighter.

"Your mother loves you, Drew. She just doesn't know how to show you. That's her problem, not yours."

He smiled, "I love you."

"And I love you," I said, hugging him fully.

While my head was on his chest, I chuckled.

"Your issues with your mother didn't have anything to do with you going for an older woman, right?"

Drew looked down at me.

"What? Are you Freuding me?"

I gave a small shrug.

"Cami, I don't think of you as an older woman. I never went for an older woman before, either. My attraction to you has nothing to do with my mother. It has to do with you."

"I was just teasing."

"Hmm, sure you were."

"Go get dressed," I smacked his butt.

An hour and a half later, like a true Italian, I served a filling lunch that would keep us full for a while.

"This is amazing," Drew said, shoveling a heap of pasta into his mouth.

"If you don't like it, you can tell me," I offered.

"Do you see me right now?" he asked, his mouth muffled by the food. "This isn't an act."

I smiled and went back to eating my food. After lunch, we allowed our food to digest by lounging on the couch. My head was on Drew's shoulder and I was playing with the pendant around my neck.

"It looks good on you," he said.

"You look good on me," I smiled before we both laughed. "Can we be any cheesier?"

"No one's around to judge us," he winked.

"I am going to miss this place," I said glancing around.

"Me too. This can be our spot; like our little love shack."

"Aww, so now we have a song and a romantic hideaway?" I asked, turning toward him.

"This is getting intense, huh?" he laughed.

We packed up the car a little while later and headed back to the city. We were sad to leave, but I did miss Ben. I had checked in with Leslie a couple of times over the weekend. She assured me everything was going great. Still, I found myself worrying about my little boy from time to time, even with Drew as a wonderful distraction.

CHAPTER TWENTY

"Let's go Uncle Drew!"

Aylin was cheering from her spot next to me at Yankee Stadium. I was at the game with her, Ben, Haley and Tasha. For the most part, we were having a good time in spite of my nerves over trying to cover up my relationship with Drew, and my normal dislike of Tasha. I was trying to lighten up on her since she's been really sweet to me ever since Danny and I separated.

Unfortunately, the Yankees lost the game by one run. We were all bummed. After the game, I invited everyone back to my place since no one except Haley, and Drew, had seen the renovations I had made.

"I love it!" Tasha said, running her hand over the new couch after I returned from putting Ben to sleep. "It's very modern, but homey."

"That's the effect I was going for—home," I smiled. "It just stopped feeling like a home to me."

Tasha nodded with understanding.

"What do you think, A?" I called out to the teenager, who wasn't in sight.

I walked into the dining room, knowing she would be there.

"The pictures are gone," she pouted.

I laughed, "Don't worry, they're in the office."

Her face brightened and there was a knock on the door.

"Uncle Drew's here," she grinned, hurrying out of the room.

Aylin was mature for her age, but there is still such an innocence about her. I hope she never loses that. I hope she never gets her heart broken or is too cool for her parents, or uncle, or me.

I didn't want to greet Drew right away. For one, I didn't know how to greet him. To me, it was now natural to make-out with him. I can't remember how I said hello before we began dating. A hug? Maybe a kiss on the cheek? Did I smile as big as I do now? I am so afraid my body language will give it all away in an instant.

Instead, I busied myself in the kitchen making a pot of coffee and setting up the tea kettle. We had stopped at Junior's Bakery on the way home and picked up some dessert. I set everything up in the dining room before going back into the living room. Haley was falling asleep as Aylin was talking about some art exhibit she had seen on a class trip.

"Hi Drew," I said, trying to sound casual.

He looked at me, and I could tell he wanted to laugh.

"Hey Cami. So you redid the apartment, huh?"

"Yup. Do you like it?"

"I love it. Where's Ben?"

"Asleep already," I said.

"Aw, I wanted to see the little guy. It's been a while."

He, of course, was lying. He just saw Ben that morning.

"Mom is still jet lagged from being on Dad's tour," Aylin said, with a chuckle as Haley's head kept falling forward.

Aylin shook her lightly and soon we were all in the dining room. Conversation was being made easily and kept light. I stuck to talking about work and Ben, since aside from Drew, those were the biggest parts of my life. It was hard not to slip about what I had done this past weekend, or how I missed Drew while he traveled.

As for Drew, he told stories about the team. I wasn't all that surprised when Haley asked him about girlfriends. I knew she hoped he would find love and probably suspected he was seeing someone. Her intuition was great, which worried me to no end.

"You're not dating Topaz, are you Uncle Drew?" Aylin asked.

Drew laughed, "What if I was?"

"She's pretty and all, but she seems very Hollywood for you," Aylin shrugged.

"I agree," Haley nodded.

"Me too," I said and Drew looked at me before laughing again.

"No, I'm not dating Topaz. I'm not allowed to comment on it to the media. It's a publicity thing," he shrugged.

Haley yawned, "Good. Well, I think we should be going. Aylin has school tomorrow and I'm ready to pass out."

Haley and Aylin said their goodbyes.

"I'll help you clean up," Tasha said, taking some dishes to the kitchen.

"You don't have to do that," I called as Drew winked at me before he, too, helped clean the table.

I dropped a fork and bent down to get it. I stood back up and Tasha looked at me funny. Drew walked back out of the kitchen.

"Hey, do you want to split a taxi with me?"

363

"Um," Drew said looking over at me. "I have my car. I drove to the stadium. I can give you a ride home, though."

"Oh no, it's okay," Tasha smiled, and she looked at both of us before going into the kitchen and starting to load the dishwasher.

I eyed Drew and he shrugged. I sighed before walking into the kitchen.

"You don't have to do that."

She laughed, "Why do you seem so weird?"

"I'm not being weird."

She raised an eyebrow.

"You did well the whole night, but I see through you."

I just froze, looking at her.

"You and Drew, huh?" she whispered.

I groaned, "Were we that obvious?"

"No, not really. Drew played it cool, but you... I didn't think much of your behavior until five minutes ago."

"This gave it away," she said, lightly lifting the chain of the pendant around my neck.

"Shit," I closed my eyes.

I had the pendent tucked into my shirt. It's long enough to go into my bra. When I bent down to pick up the fork, it must have fallen out.

"If you're trying to hide something, don't wear your boyfriend's team number around your neck!" She shook her head as she continued to do the dishes.

"Please don't tell anyone."

"You want me to lie to my best friend?" she asked, with a smirk.

"No. I just don't want you to *tell* Haley. We will tell her and everyone soon."

"Okay," she nodded. "You're scared, aren't you?"

"Shouldn't I be?"

Tasha shrugged, "Well, Drew is Jordan's little brother. Danny will flip, but when doesn't he?"

I laughed, "True."

"I think it'll blow over, especially when everyone realizes how happy you are. We can all see it on your face. Drew's too," Tasha smiled.

"Thanks Tasha," I returned her smile.

"See, I told you it'll be fine," Drew said, standing in the doorway smirking.

Tasha dried her hands on a dish towel, "Well, I'm very happy for you. I will leave you two alone."

She punched me in the shoulder, since we didn't really hug and this was actually the first time I wasn't cold to her. She hugged Drew before leaving. He walked over to me and kissed me.

"We're going to have to tell everyone soon. How long do you think it'll be before she slips up?" he laughed.

We both knew it was bound to happen. Tasha would either tell Sebastian or Haley at some point. She told them everything.

"I figure we have a week, tops," I sighed.

"I'm excited to tell everyone. It's been so hard keeping this a secret, especially from my brother."

"I know," I nodded. "I'm excited too, but really scared."

Drew just didn't understand my fears. He had faith Jordan would be happy for us, but I knew I would be the one to get the blame. I would be seen as some tempest who just wanted to get my claws in someone else involved in Jordan's life.

We spent the next hour, discussing when a good time would be. We didn't want to tell anyone over the phone. The next time we would all be in New York would in fact be for Aylin's sweet sixteen party.

"Maybe telling everyone at the party would prevent conflict," Drew reasoned.

"Hmm," I was skeptical. "I'll tell Danny separately; alone. His temper is way too short and he isn't always concerned who it will affect."

Drew nodded, "I don't want him yelling at you."

"I can handle it," I assured him.

The next day, Drew played a double header. I had an important meeting at work, so I couldn't even make it to the first game and missed most of the second one, but promised Drew I'd come anyway. I arrived at the stadium during the top of the ninth inning. The score was tied.

Before I knew it, the Blue Jays had three outs and the Yankees were up to bat. They racked up two outs quickly. Drew must have been keeping a lookout for me. I saw him glancing around as he was on deck. He saw me, sitting next to Ava Rodriguez, and nodded with a smile. He had told me earlier in the day that he was going to hit a homerun for me.

He pointed at me with the bat and then to the outfield before winking. I nodded and blew him a kiss, hoping no one saw. Ava was too busy watching Cisco at bat to notice, thankfully. Cisco Rodriguez got on first before Drew stepped up to the plate.

I cheered, along with the rest of the fans. A chant of "Take Me Home" immediately filled the stadium. Cisco started waving his arms in the air from first base, urging the crowd to continue the phrase he coined.

On the first pitch, Drew sent the ball flying back to centerfield. At first, it looked like it was going to hit the wall, but it went just above it. A little boy ran to pick up the ball excitedly as he was shown on the jumbo-tron. Everyone was on their feet since the game was over. The Yankees beat the Blue Jays four to two.

I watched the excitement on the field before heading to the clubhouse doors. I had a special badge that allowed me to wait there. I stood there with some of the players' wives and kids or parents. Will Nostri's parents were really sweet. They seemed very grateful to Drew, saying how welcoming he was to Nostri when he joined the team.

Drew was the opposite of me in many ways. Where he was warm and welcoming, I was cold and clannish. I felt like I was getting better, though. The ice was slowly melting from this queen's throne.

The clubhouse doors opened and some of the press stepped outside, finally leaving. Soon, a few of the players came out to greet their friends and family. Drew was taking an unusually long time.

Drew finally walked out and I ran to him. He picked me up in a tight hug. I kissed him forcefully, not caring that Cisco, Messina and Briggs were making cat calls. I figured the secret would be out soon, and these guys already knew something was going on between us.

Drew laughed, surprised by the scene I had made.

"I guess I should hit a run for you more often," he smirked.

"That was incredible."

"Well, I got you a souvenir," he said, opening his hand to reveal a baseball.

I looked at him funny, "What's this?"

"The ball I hit the run with."

"But that little boy got it," I said.

"Yeah, I know, but I got it back from him," Drew shrugged.

"You took the ball from a kid?" I gasped, feeling terrible. "He looked so excited!"

I smacked his chest and pushed his hand away.

"You don't want it?" he asked, like I was crazy.

"No, give that ball back to the kid. You better find him..."

Just then, the clubhouse doors opened. A little boy walked out with the biggest smile on his face. He had a baseball in his hand.

"Thanks again, Mr. Ashton," the kid said, looking at Drew as if he were in amazement.

"No problem, Zac. Thank you for swapping balls with me."

"This one's even better," the kid smiled, holding up the ball that was autographed.

After the kid walked over to his father, I looked back at Drew. He looked smug.

"I think you owe me an apology."

I sighed, "So, you tracked that kid down and swapped him this ball," I pointed to the one in Drew's hand. "For one autographed by the whole team?"

"Yes, and I let him spend a half an hour in the clubhouse. Does that mean you don't think I'm scum for stealing this ball from a little boy?"

"I guess," I scrunched my face before laughing.

"I mean, if you don't want this dedicated homerun ball," Drew said, tossing it lightly. "I'm sure I can find someone who does want it..."

He tossed the ball again and I snatched it.

"I want it," I smiled before looking at the ball, noticing something was drawn onto it.

I turned the ball to see a big heart drawn on in red crayon. I bit my bottom lip before looking up at Drew. He pointed to the heart and smiled.

"That run was a labor of love."

I stepped closer to him, just enough to be almost touching him, as I curled the baseball against my chest. I stared into his eyes.

"Has anyone told you how amazing your eyes look?"

Drew laughed, since that was the line he used on me so many times.

"Not fair. I at least mean it when I say it to you," he said, wrapping his arms around me.

"You don't think I mean it?" I asked, putting my hand on his jaw.

I kissed him softly. He smiled before kissing me deeper. We spent the next few minutes kissing goodbye. It would be a couple of weeks until I saw him again.

"Thank you," I said, fighting the tears in my eyes as I held up the ball.

Drew waved sadly before disappearing into the clubhouse.

CHAPTER TWENTY-ONE

The next month passed. We still managed to keep our relationship a secret, aside from Tasha and the team knowing. Since Tortured was on tour until Aylin's party, we thought we might as well wait until the party was over after all.

The morning of Aylin's party, I was in bed with Drew, who had gotten into town at three-am. I wanted to just sleep in his arms as long as I could. The phone for the front desk rang, startling me awake. Drew was still sound asleep.

I rolled over and picked up the receiver.
"Hello?"
"Ms. Woods, Mr. DeSano is here."

It took me a moment to register it all, but my eyes widened. Danny was at my apartment at seven-am while Drew was asleep in my bed!

"Uh, just woke up. Tell him he can come up in a few minutes," I said, trying not to panic.

I jumped out of the bed and threw my robe on. Drew was unaffected by the phone call and me jumping out of bed. It wasn't until I stubbed my toe on my way to the bathroom that he began to stir. Shit, that hurt. I had tears in my eyes.

"Cami?" I heard Drew mumble.

I peeked my head out from the bathroom as I tossed my hair up. He was propped up on his elbows looking around the room, completely out of it.

"Danny is here."

"Where?"

He asked the question as if I had asked my ex-husband into the bedroom for tea.

"He's on his way up," I sighed.

"Good, we can tell him," he smirked, rubbing sleep from his eyes.

I flashed him a dirty look.

"What? Are you really going to make me hide in your closet or something?"

"Just stay here, okay?" I pleaded.

Drew groaned.

"It would be kind of hard for him not to freak out if he finds you in my bed."

He huffed, "Well, it's his own damn fault. He let you go."

I smiled at him, walked over and kissed him. This is where I see Drew's immaturity. Or maybe it was pure nonchalance. He took everything lightly while I made a big deal out of everything. Somehow I don't think Drew will ever grow out of that quality, and I really don't think I wanted him to. He balanced me out.

We both jumped at the pounding on the door. Drew lay back down and hugged the pillow as I left the bedroom, shutting the door behind me. I hurried to the door and opened it.

"Hey," Danny said, standing there with a big smile.

He pulled me into a tight hug, which I felt awkward about since I didn't have anything on underneath the robe. As he released me, I adjusted the material to make sure I wasn't revealing anything.

"What are you doing here so early?" I asked. "This isn't like you."

"I'm excited to be home and to see Ben...and you," he winked. "I missed you guys."

"Aww, we missed you too," I assured him.

"So, where is he?" Danny asked; his hands on his hips.

My eyes widened, "Where is who?"

He laughed, "Still too early in the morning? Ben! I want to see my son."

"Oh, he's still asleep. Let me go check on him," I said, heading into the nursery.

Ben was sitting up in his crib, sticking a plush Yankees baseball Drew had gotten him into his mouth.

"Good morning, baby boy!"

Immediately, Ben smiled at me and started making sounds. I was about to take Ben out of the room, but instead Danny walked in.

"Benny," Danny smiled and I handed our son over.

"Do you want coffee or anything?" I asked.

"Sure, thanks," he smiled sitting down in the rocking chair.

He looked so happy. Ben seemed to recognize him even more, too, which was good.

"You should change his diaper while you're bonding," I said as I left the room.

I put on a pot of coffee before going into my bedroom. Drew was sound asleep. I was happy he could sleep in. I threw on a bra, t-shirt and some yoga pants.

Just as I walked out of the bedroom and shut the door, Danny stepped up behind me, holding Ben. I jumped a little.

"The apartment looks good," he said, peeking toward the dining room.

"Thanks. I needed it to feel like mine, you know?"

He nodded, but had that sad look in his eyes.

"You look really good. Have I told you that?"

I laughed, tapping the poufy hair piled on top of my head lightly.

"Right, I'm just a living doll right now."

He chuckled, "Seriously. Every time I see you, you look better than the last. What's your secret?"

I shrugged, "Working out and eating better?"

"Hmm, maybe it's this guy making you glow," Danny said looking at Ben who was trying to stick his fingers in his mouth as he spoke.

"Of course he makes me glow," I said pinching Ben's cheek.

I looked at Danny's face and he was almost gazing at me. I sighed.

"Danny, can you please stop looking at me like that?"

"Like what?"

"Like you want to kiss me!" I huffed.

He laughed, "I can't help it."

"Well, try," I rolled my eyes. "We're divorced now. That means broken up...completely," I warned, letting him know I was serious.

In the past when we would break up, separate, or whatever, we would always wind up in bed together. He needed to know that was never going to happen again.

Danny just smirked, "Okay."

I sighed, knowing he didn't believe me. I finally just admitted it to him.

"I'm dating someone."

His mouth kind of hung open. He looked taken back. I couldn't tell if he was upset or not.

"Oh. Is it serious?"

I swallowed and nodded. Danny looked at Ben and then at me.

"Has he met Ben?"

I nodded silently once more.

"I thought we would talk about introducing Ben to anyone we date," he said, trying to control whatever emotions that were building inside him.

"I know, but I wasn't actually dating the guy when I introduced Ben to him."

Danny's eyes narrowed, "Is it someone I know?"

"Yes," I said, kind of gruffly.

"Who?"

"I rather not say right now."

"Cami, what do you mean? Who is it? Not Colin?"

How the heck would Colin and I have an affair when we hadn't even been in the same country? Danny obviously wasn't in a rational state of mind.

"No," I shook my head. "No one from work."

"Why won't you tell me?"

"Because I don't want you to make a scene."

"Make a scene?" he asked, his anger rising. "Where? When?"

"Tonight."

Danny squinted his eyes, "Tonight?"

"At Aylin's party."

"This guy is going to be there?"

I nodded.

"He's not one of Aylin's friends, is he?" he asked, and I think he was actually being serious!

"No! Do you really think I'd date a sixteen-year-old?" I asked, offended.

"Just fucking tell me already so I can prepare myself," he said, clenching his teeth.

"It's Drew."

"Drew?" he asked, confused. "Andrew? Andrew Ashton?"

I nodded and really wanted to grab Ben from Danny afraid he would drop him out of shock.

"Jordan's little brother!?"

"At least he's not a sixteen-year-old," I shrugged, trying to make light of the situation.

No dice. I felt like that's something Drew would say if he were a part of the conversation.

"He might as well be sixteen! He's like ten years younger than you!"

"It's only eight," I sighed.

Danny was about to lose it. I could tell just by his expression. I grabbed Ben out of his arms and took him into the nursery. Danny followed me as I put Ben in his crib.

"Drew is fucking my wife!"

I whirled around and smacked Danny's chest.

"I am not your wife!"

"I bet you were when this shit started!"

I sighed, "Technically, yes. But we were already separated."

"Cami, how could you do this?"

"What do you mean? You had an affair, Danny! While we were together; while I was pregnant. Don't make me out to be wrong!" I yelled, knowing Drew could hear every word, even if we hadn't been screaming.

The baby monitor was picking up everything.

"It's disgusting. You knew Drew when he was a kid! You dated his fucking brother!"

I swallowed, "Like ten million years ago."

I changed the subject quickly, not wanting Danny to talk more about Jordan with Drew listening.

"How is it disgusting? It's not like I had a crush on Drew when he was a kid or even while I was with you! It just happened..." I explained.

"Oh, it just happened? You didn't like when I gave you that excuse!"

"I don't owe you any explanations," I said firmly.

"No? What about Drew, huh? There is a guy code, you know? Screw that, there is an ex-wife code, too!"

I practically laughed in his face.

"And what code is that?"

"Don't screw your ex-husband's friends!"

He was getting in my face now.

"All codes are null and void when you fucking cheated on that ex-wife!"

Ben began crying and I backed away from Danny, wishing we didn't fight in front of him. Even at his young age, he didn't like when we fought. I picked Ben up and looked at Danny, who was fuming still.

"Now, would you like to have coffee?" I asked.

He shook his head at me.

"You're unbelievable."

"Look, your pride, anger, and craziness aside," I said in a controlled tone. "Tonight is Aylin's night. Drew and I will both be there. No one else knows. Can you control yourself for your Goddaughter's sake?"

He practically laughed.

"When do you plan to tell Jordan?"

"Soon. Just not tonight, okay?"

"Fine, but only for Aylin's sake. You tell Jordan tomorrow. I won't be able to bite my tongue and he'll know something is up with me."

I nodded, "Thank you."

"Save it," Danny said, walking out of the room.

A moment later, I heard the door slam. I sighed, looking at Ben who was quieting down. I hugged my son, feeling myself shake slightly. My nerves were shot. Before I realized it, Drew's arms were wrapped around Ben and me.

"You okay?"

I nodded, "I did it."

"I'm proud of you," Drew said, pulling away to look into my eyes.

"You broke a guy code," I pouted.

"Ah, screw it. You're worth it," he winked. "I was ready to kick his ass, by the way. It took everything inside of me not to come out here."

"Thank you for restraining. It would have made things so much worse," I sighed.

Drew kissed Ben's head before kissing my lips.

"No matter what anyone thinks, you are worth every fight."

I smiled at him, "Even with your brother?"

He laughed, "Jordan will get over it. Like you said, you dated ten million years ago."

I chuckled and rested my head against his chest. I wish I had the faith Drew had. He was being unrealistic if he thought everything would blow over quickly. Then again, Drew didn't quite understand the history that I shared with Jordan and Danny. He didn't know the problems my relationships caused all of us. Now, here I was moving onto another member of the "family". It didn't look good on me, and it definitely didn't look good on Drew's part with the whole guy code thing and all.

Speaking of guy code, Danny broke that when he began dating me! Why was he allowed to make exceptions? Ugh, I wish I would have thought of that rebuttal when I was arguing with him earlier.

CHAPTER TWENTY-TWO

I didn't get to enjoy too much more time with Drew. He had a public appearance Midtown before Aylin's party. I got Ben ready for Leslie who was watching him for me. She arrived a bit early. I was only half ready. I decided to curl my hair, which was always a project. I was grateful for my thick, straight Filipino hair, but sometimes I wish I had some of my mother's curls. Ben was being fussy on top of it all. I think he was sprouting another tooth. I grabbed him up from his baby seat and headed for the door, once again, in my robe.

As soon as I opened the door, Leslie reached for Ben and I handed him over.

"Thank you so much for watching him. You're the best grandma."

Leslie smiled, "It's my pleasure. I was hoping I was going to see my son tonight. He blew me off about coming over here before the party."

I sighed, "I'm sorry. We had a fight."

"What else is new?" she laughed before patting my arm. "You know what a hot head he is. Sure, he can have a girlfriend while being married to you, but you can't move on. Didn't you know that?" she rolled her eyes.

I shook my head, "He had to tell someone, huh?"

"He was letting off some steam," she waved it off. "Hopefully he got it out of his system before the party."

I bit my bottom lip nervously.

"Did Danny tell you who I'm dating?"

"Drew Ashton," Leslie nodded grinning. "He grew up into quite the ladies' man."

"I love him," I admitted.

She looked at Ben and kissed his forehead.

"Look, Danny didn't do right by you. He's my son and I love him. But you deserve to be happy. Ben deserves to have a happy Mommy. This will blow over."

I hugged her along with Ben, taking her by surprise.

"You're the closest thing I've had to a mother in so long," I said, hoarsely, trying to hold back tears. "Thank you."

Leslie squeezed me, "Now, go finish getting ready."

Twenty minutes before the party, Drew texted me.

I could pick you up...oh wait, too conspicuous, right?

Just a little. But thanks, Babe.

I knew Drew was sick of keeping us a secret, but he only had to one more night. If we could just make it through this party without Danny or Tasha letting anything slip, I would be happy. The last thing I want for Aylin is to ruin this night, and the last thing I need is another public scene. Some discretion is called for after all the publicity my marriage, separation, and divorce have received.

After saying goodbye to Leslie and Ben, I grabbed my purse and Aylin's gift and headed downstairs. I didn't have any difficulty hailing a taxi, which surprised me since it was a Saturday night. Maybe it was my sparkly silver dress that grabbed the driver's attention. He even had a passenger already; a balding man in a suit and tie.

"Hi," I said awkwardly, as I slid into the car.

"I figured you'd have trouble getting a ride, so I don't mind sharing," the man smiled, looking me over.

"Thanks," I said, wondering if I should get out and wait for another taxi.

The driver already started heading down the street.

"Where to ma'am?" he asked in a Middle Eastern accent.

"Virtuality on West Forty-Seventh and Ninth."

From what I understood, Virtuality is a new upscale arcade. What that means, I'm not sure. I was told to dress up, but I fully expected to play videogames all night. Knowing Aylin Ashton, that sounds about right.

It was Haley's idea to give her the Ashton last name, which was technically really Jordan's last name. He chose Jordan Walsh, in honor of his mother, as his stage name. He didn't want to be associated with his dad much. Haley liked the alliteration of Aylin Ashton, and Jordan figured she could have a much more normal school life if she had a different last name than him. With Andrew Ashton becoming a famous baseball player, normal kind of went to hell for the kid.

Aylin manages just fine, though. She is confident in who she was and proud of her parents for who they are. She is anything but typical—and not just because her father was a famous rock star. Aylin is girly in the sense of fashion and boys. She was also a tomboy, loving sports, videogames, and slasher films. She was kind of like Drew in ways, except Aylin was great at music and art, and he was terrible at both things. Her artistic side is all Haley and Jordan, not surprisingly.

"What's Virtuality? Sounds like a sex club," the passenger next to me said, licking his lips.

I didn't try to hide my disgust of him. He was probably in his sixties and smelled kind of funky.

"Stop looking at me like you're going to rape me, please."

Maybe that was too much, but at least I said please. He shut up after that, though. The cab driver seemed to be snickering to himself. I took my phone out of my purse and texted Drew.

I should have taken you up on your offer. I hate taxis.

Poor baby. Should have gotten a private car service.

I forgot to call for one. I was distracted by you this morning ;-)

What a beautiful distraction. :-p

Conceited much?

Oops, I meant you were!

Suuurre, you did.

Just as I hit send on the text, the taxi came to a sudden stop and I almost fell forward. The perverted older man paid the driver and got out without another glance at me. About ten minutes later, I arrived at Virtuality. There were a couple of teenagers hanging around outside. They were semi-dressed up, but I felt kind of overdressed. I walked past them and into the venue. The first room was set up like a traditional arcade with pinball machines, ski ball, and videogames. There were a bunch of kids playing games. I saw Sebastian and Tasha playing *Dance, Dance Revolution*, not surprisingly. Tasha is a professional dancer and Sebastian was one of the only straight guys I have met who loves to dance. Danny would only dance after a few too many drinks. Darren and Jordan both hated it. Actually, come to think of it, Drew didn't mind dancing either. He wasn't one to head onto a dance floor if no one was on it, though. That's the type of couple Tasha and Sebie are.

I saw there was another room and I headed for it. I peeked inside to see tables set up with a dance floor and a DJ. I spotted Jordan and Haley, who were smothering Aylin into a family hug. Aylin was pretending to be disgusted before kissing her parents' cheeks and getting out of their embrace. She was dressed in a gorgeous pink, elegant dress that hit her knees. She made the dress look casual by pairing it with black leggings and Converse sneakers. The look was quite glam-punk.

"Aunt Cami, you look hot!" Aylin yelled when she saw me.

I laughed and walked over to hug her.

"So do you," I smiled. "Happy Birthday, A."

She hugged me and I handed her the gift. I gave her a copy of her favorite photo of her and her father that used to be in my dining room along with a gift card to her favorite clothing store. After she walked off, I wrapped Jordan into a hug, realizing how much I missed him and the guys while they've been gone.

"You look good," Jordan said.

"You really do, Cami," Haley smiled.

"Thank you. I'm not too dressed up, am I?"

Haley laughed and shook her head, "No. Aylin wanted it formal and informal at the same time."

"Our daughter likes being an oxymoron," Jordan laughed.

I smiled, "That's because she has the best of both of you."

"I love when you're nice," Jordan teased, pushing me playfully.

"Who said I was being nice? I meant you're a moron and Haley's an ox," I joked.

Haley shoved me now, harder than Jordan did. I stumbled in my heels. She laughed and quickly apologized.

Soon, the place was filling up with people. I kept checking my phone since I was wondering where Drew was. I was playing that game where you have to squirt water in the clown's mouth with Jordan and Sebastian, and I was actually winning until something distracted me.

"Sorry we're late," Danny's voice said.

I turned my head slightly and couldn't believe Danny brought Anastasia Milos! First, he said they broke up. Second, he was doing this out of spite.

"I win!" Sebastian yelled.

Jordan slammed his hand down on the table before turning around and seeing the "couple" in front of us. I felt Jordan's arm hang casually around my shoulder.

"Hey D. I didn't know you were bringing a date," Jordan said.

Danny laughed, "Sorry bro. It was kind of a last minute decision."

The entire time they spoke, Anastasia was staring me up and down. I didn't bother even looking at her. I kept my eyes on Danny, wishing he was able to handle things in a normal way. He couldn't just be upset about Drew and me, or the fact that it was really over. He wanted to try and hurt me.

"Sorry to crash Aslyn's party," Anastasia said with her Greek accent.

"My daughter's name is Aylin, Ana," Jordan said, not hiding the annoyance in his voice.

"Eylin?"

"A-lin," Danny corrected her once more.

"Cami, how about I offer you a rematch in ski ball?" Jordan asked.

"Sounds good," I said before walking off with him, not even looking at Danny and Anastasia as I did.

We headed over to the ski ball section. Aylin and her best friend were in front of us, so we waited our turn.

"Some things never change, huh?" Jordan sighed.

I smiled, "I'm fine. Danny is being spiteful because I actually went through with the divorce."

"I know. He kept thinking you'd get back together. I told him there was only so much you would take."

"Thank you."

"For what?"

"For still being my friend. I thought I might lose you and everyone else."

Jordan hugged me, "You're stuck with me."

We pulled apart and Aylin turned around to tell us our turn was up. Then she squealed.

"Uncle Drew!" She ran past us and jumped into his arms.

Drew's hair was cut short, making him look a little more sophisticated than usual. He was dressed in a full suit and tie. He held out a bouquet of flowers to Aylin.

He whispered something to her and Aylin reached into the flowers, pulling out car keys.

"Oh shit," Jordan hissed. "He bought her a car!?"

I laughed, "Surprised?"

Jordan gave me a look, "I told Aylin she'd get a car when she got a part-time job."

Haley looked over at Jordan and shrugged as Aylin and Drew headed outside to see the car. The whole party practically followed. It was some kind of new Hybrid that wasn't even out yet. Drew had a sponsorship with the company, so I wonder what kind of deal he got.

Drew looked over at me while everyone was focusing on the car. His eyes gave me the once over. He grinned and winked, showing his appreciation of my dress. I smiled and pointed to his hair before giving him a thumbs up.

Our gaze was interrupted by Jordan smacking Drew's chest.

"Why do you have to make me look bad?"

Drew laughed, "She's my niece. I can spoil her all I want."

"I'm trying to teach the kid the value of a dollar."

Haley walked over and wrapped her arms around Drew.

"Jordan, it was a nice gesture. At least it's good for the environment," she reasoned and I laughed.

"My wife and daughter are spoiled brats," Jordan teased.

Haley gasped, "And you're turning into a frugal old man!"

Drew laughed hysterically and looked over at me. It was so hard for us to be normal around one another. What was normal for us before we started dating? Did we talk much?

What did we talk about? I couldn't even remember!

"Can you reason with your client?" Drew asked, finding a way to bring me into the conversation.

"This is a family matter," I put my hands up defensively.

"You are family," Jordan argued, which made me smile. "Don't you think this car is a bit much for a sixteen-year-old who doesn't even have her license yet and lives in Manhattan?"

Drew was shaking his head "no" from behind Jordan's back while I mulled it over.

"I understand your concern," I told Jordan as I walked over. "But Aylin is Drew's only niece and she's a good kid. Don't you think she deserves it?"

Jordan sighed and just then Aylin hugged Drew.

"Thank you so much. I can't believe you did this. I promise I will be responsible when I get my license. I'll get a job to pay for my own insurance," Aylin said as she looked over at her parents.

"See?" I smacked Jordan's shoulder.

Drew laughed, "My niece deserves the best."

Jordan nodded, "Thanks bro. You outdid me on a gift as usual, but thank you."

Drew hugged Jordan, patting his back as he did. I looked up at Drew's face and he smiled at me. By this point, pretty much everyone was standing outside admiring the car. Tasha came over to me.

"Did you know about this?" She motioned to the car.

I rolled my eyes, "Why would I know?"

She laughed, "I noticed you're not wearing a certain piece of jewelry."

I decided against wearing the pendant since it would definitely show in my cleavage. I went to walk away from Tasha and she grabbed my arm.

"Okay, I'm sorry. I won't mention anything more about you and your mystery man."

"Mystery man?" Sebastian asked, overhearing, also grabbing Darren's attention.

In Tasha's defense, she thought she was whispering. Unfortunately for me, her whispers are raspy shouts.

"I knew you looked too happy," he laughed.

"I can only be happy if there's a man involved, Seb?"

Darren cut in, "No, I've seen you happy—and without a man. But there's happy and then there's bubbly. And you, Cam, have been bubbly, which is something I've never seen on you."

"Exactly my point," Sebastian agreed. "You weren't even bubbly on your wedding day."

I just laughed, knowing they were probably right. I didn't feel like the same person I used to be. Aside from going through a mid-life crisis, so to speak, I have rediscovered myself the past year. Even before Drew Ashton revitalized my life, I was already reevaluating who I was, who I want to be, and the mistakes I have made.

Marrying Danny was probably the biggest mistake I ever made. I'm sure he would agree marrying me wasn't smart on his end either. Our idea of love was not a healthy one. I don't hate him like I thought I did, but I don't love him like I thought I did either. However, I will forever be grateful to him for his friendship and for bringing Benvenuto into my life. I couldn't imagine my life without my little boy.

As if he knew I was thinking about him, Danny stepped outside without Anastasia.

"You see the sweet ride little A. got, bro?" Sebastian asked him.

Danny seemed to scowl at Drew, who's focus was on his niece, as he explained where the car will be kept until she can drive it.

"Isn't Andrew Ashton just the greatest guy in the world?" Danny smirked at me.

I sighed and walked closer to him.

"Don't," I warned.

I felt like my voice sounded more pleading than threatening though. He shrugged and walked away. I looked over at Drew and he was looking at me concerned. I offered a smile before walking back inside the party.

Haley's parents approached me.

"How are you, dear?" Mrs. Foster asked.

"I'm good," I smiled.

"How's your son doing?" Mr. Foster asked.

"He's great," I again smiled.

"It must be hard raising him alone," Mrs. Foster added.

"Well, with Danny on the road, yeah. But I've always been good at juggling things," I shrugged.

"Except your marriage," Chuck Ashton teased, approaching us from behind me.

Chuck Ashton is Drew and Jordan's bastard of a father. He and Jordan were estranged for years, and even now, have a rocky relationship at times. Drew's bond with their father isn't much stronger, but Chuck has made some effort to at least show love to his sons, something he lacked while they grew up. However, he was still an ass, and said ass-y things, especially when no one asked for his two cents.

"Chuck," Mrs. Foster scolded him.

"Sorry, it was a joke," he shrugged.

"My marriage isn't anyone's business. Yes, it's over, but I'm fine. You're not one to talk about juggling marriages, Mr. Ashton," I said. "Excuse me."

I headed to the bathroom, which was in a separate area. Someone grabbed me just as I went to open the door. I was relieved to see it was Drew.

"You okay?"

I nodded, looking around before pulling him into a kiss.

"What did my dad say to you?"

"He just made a bad joke at my expense," I blew it off.

Drew's jaw tightened, "I'm sorry."

"Don't be. I can handle your dad. And Danny. And loose lips Tasha..." I rolled my eyes.

He laughed, "We could solve a couple of those problems really easy."

"We will tell everyone tomorrow," I assured him. "It's not going to solve anything, though."

"It's going to be fine," Drew said, pressing his lips against mine.

"I love you," I said, kissing him again.

He smiled, "I like that you say that a lot. I love you, too."

I liked that Drew said those words plenty to me as well. What was even better, he showed me how he felt about me in some small way every day. I never had that before with anyone. It still surprises me that Drew has a lack of people telling him they love him, but I guess they tell him that for his celebrity or his good-looks.

His heart is what makes him so easy for me to love. I've been around hot, wealthy and talented guys my whole life, but not many of them can match Drew's personality.

After the party, I went home alone. Drew was meeting me there in an hour. I said goodnight to Leslie and checked on Ben after she left. He was knocked out, like the good sleeper he is. He certainly didn't start out that way. His sleep schedule was way off when he was first born, which was fine with me for a bit. At that time, I slept my days away and enjoyed spending time with him at night—when no one would check up on me in my depressed state.

As much as I hated what I was going through, I would never trade those first couple of months with Ben for anything. My love for him and need for him, especially at that time in my life has created such a strong bond that I will always cherish.

I got changed for bed and saw Drew's pendent lying on my dresser. I smiled and put it on, almost feeling naked without it tonight. There was a knock at the door and I opened it for Drew. We didn't say much. We went to bed after a little making-out. We would make it up to each other in the morning after we were well-rested.

After Drew's home game tomorrow night, we are telling Jordan and Haley about us. Part of me was still scared, but there was a growing part of me that was relieved that I wouldn't have to keep secrets. Drew and I could be seen in public holding hands, or kissing, or even just having dinner without any suspicions.

CHAPTER TWENTY-THREE

I watched Drew playing with Ben with a smile on my face. Ben was giggling loudly. Drew stood up and handed Ben to me. He kissed me and I didn't want him to leave. The phone rang and I groaned against Drew's lips. I answered it and it was the doorman telling me Danny was here. He was spending the day with Ben, but he was an hour early. I looked at Drew worriedly.

"He's early just to piss me off," I sighed. "He's always late."

Drew shook his head, "Well, I'm guessing he wants to run into me."

I looked horrified at the thought.

"Hide in my room!"

He just laughed and kissed my forehead.

"I have to face him, Cami. It's going to be okay. You worry more than Haley does."

There was a knock at the door and before I could rush to it, Drew made it over in a few short strides. He opened the door and Danny stood there, looking like he wanted to punch Drew in the face.

"Hey man," Drew said.

"You son-of-a-bitch," Danny seethed.

"Don't Danny," I warned, walking over with Ben.

"Don't what, Cami?"

"Not in front of Ben," I said.

Danny looked down at Drew. He was so much taller than him.

"Look D," Drew said, unfazed by the look in Danny's eyes. "I'm sorry if you feel betrayed. Cami and I didn't plan this. It happened and I don't regret it."

Danny narrowed his eyes at Drew.

"You fucked my wife."

I cringed at his choice of words. Danny always did have a foul mouth, not that I was much better, but he usually chose the worst way to say things.

Drew stood tall, as tall as he could in front of Danny. He looked him in the eye.

"I fell in *love* with your *ex*-wife."

I couldn't help but smile at that, especially the way Drew emphasized love and ex. While I relished in Drew's sentence, Danny didn't take to it well. He shoved Drew hard and I panicked. I was ready to throw myself in between them, but Drew stopped me.

"You want to hit me, D? Go ahead. Maybe you think I deserve it, but it's not going to change anything. You and Cami are over. We both love you and we hope one day you can accept us."

Danny laughed, "You're serious? Do you really think this shit is going to last?"

He got in Drew's face.

"You're still a cocky little kid, huh? Don't let her fool you with those pretty eyes," he said pointing at me. "She'll have you by the balls for the next twenty years of your life before you realize you can do better!"

Ouch. I am the first one to admit I wasn't the best wife and I am not the nicest person all the time. Am I that awful, though? Did I make Danny that miserable? Will I force Drew to cheat on me, too?

While I pondered these thoughts, I didn't even realize Drew had pulled back and punched Danny in the face!

"Drew," I hissed and quickly brought Ben into the nursery.

I rushed back to the foyer to see Danny and Drew shoving each other and swinging fists.

Drew's lip was bleeding and Danny's cheek was bright red from that first punch.

I immediately jumped in between them, not thinking much of it. I assumed once I got close enough, they would back off. That didn't happen, though. I wedged myself in between them just as a punch from Danny came flying right into my side.

I grunted and shouted some profanities as I fell to the ground. I was in so much pain that I could barely hear Drew yelling at Danny.

"Cami, are you okay?" Drew asked, crouching down next to me.

"I'm so sorry, Cam," Danny said. "Shit, why did you get in the way?"

I looked up at them, clenching my teeth as tears of pain came out of my eyes. I was furious now.

"Why?! Because you two were ready to kill each other!" I tried to get up, but whined in pain.

Drew and Danny both helped me up. I winced and lifted my t-shirt to reveal a bright red welt on my side right below my breast.

"Did I break anything?" Danny asked.

"I'm going to take you to the hospital," Drew offered.

"No, you're going to be late for practice."

I knew how hard the coach was on the team, especially Drew and Cisco for lateness, and I didn't want him to get in trouble.

"So I'll pay the fine."

"Drew, I'll be okay," I said, sucking in a breath of air.

It hurt to even breathe right now!

"I'll take her to the hospital," Danny offered.

"Oh great, so the tabloids will now see that you beat me," I rolled my eyes.

Danny sighed, "I'm sorry."

"Well, you should be!"

I cringed in pain as I yelled.

"I'm not leaving you."

Drew pulled me over to the couch. He walked into the kitchen. Danny stood back, not saying a word. Drew came back into the living room wiping blood off his lip with a paper towel, and with an ice pack for me.

"Just go, Drew. It's not like I'm dying," I said as he hovered over me and pressed the ice to my side, which made me jump from how cold it was.

"Cami, you're hurt..."

"I'll be fine," I said, staring into his eyes.

He leaned down and kissed me lightly before looking over at Danny.

"Take care of her," he warned.

Danny scoffed, "I've been doing that for a while now."

Drew just glared at him before he walked out the door. A little while later, I was sitting in the emergency room with Danny and Ben. We were silent on the way over.

"Is it feeling any better?" Danny asked.

"It's really sore," I shrugged, pretending I wasn't short of breath as I spoke.

"You know I didn't mean to hit you, right?"

I looked over at his worried blue eyes and I sighed.

"I know. You were aiming at my boyfriend."

"Please don't call Drew that."

"That's what he is, Danny. You need to accept that."

"Drew is like a brother to me. I remember when he started kindergarten."

I laughed, "Since when do you try to kick your brother's ass?"

"He started it," Danny said and I looked at him like a mother looked at a mischievous child.

Funny enough, Ben was staring up at him, too. I'm sure he disapproved of his father's behavior.

"You deserved to be punched for what you said."

Danny sighed, "You're right. I'm sorry. I didn't mean that."

"Yes, you did."

"No," he protested. "We both liked to aggravate each other over the years. That was our thing. Maybe with someone else you'll be different. Maybe I'll be different," he shrugged.

I raised an eyebrow, "Does that mean you're ready to admit we're better off as friends?"

Danny nodded, "It's hard to let go, but yes."

"Can you accept that the person I want to be with is Andrew Ashton?"

Danny shook his head, "Way too soon. I can promise I will try and refrain from punching him anymore, though. Or you."

I laughed, but immediately winced as it hurt.

"Cami Woods?" the nurse called and I stood up.

It seemed like a few people were staring at me. My name must have rung a few bells. Next thing I heard as I followed the nurse was someone asking Danny for an autograph. This would surely be in the tabloids tomorrow. Great, so now I'm a battered woman on top of being cheated on. I hate appearing weak!

I was in and out of the emergency room fairly quickly. It didn't take long at all to be diagnosed with two fractured ribs. The doctor prescribed me something for the pain and advised me on taking deep breaths and icing the area. I walked back out to the waiting room to see Danny playing with Ben. His cheek was now even more swollen than when we had gotten to the hospital. It was starting to turn purple. Great, now we really did look like an abusive ex-couple!

"You fractured two of my ribs," I scowled.

He cringed, "Can I buy you ice cream?"

I rolled my eyes, "You have a hard fist."

"So does your boyfriend," he said, pointing to his busted cheek.

"Good," I stuck my tongue out at him.

"You sure can take a punch for a girl."

Danny wrapped the arm that wasn't holding Ben around me, as I slowly walked toward the exit.

Well, at least I gained some kind of tough points today.

The rest of the afternoon, I lie in bed with an ice pack under me. The doctor recommended I lay on the side that was injured, which seems insane to me because it hurt like hell! Apparently, it helps with my breathing, though. Drew had called to check on me and insisted I stay home from the game. I argued with him, but in the end, he won.

"What about Haley and Jordan?" I asked. "We can wait until tomorrow..." I suggested, hopefully.

I don't know if I can take anymore fighting today.

"Nice try, but between you, Danny and me all bruised, I don't think we can keep this a secret until tomorrow."

I groaned before flinching, feeling pain in my ribs.

"I can't believe he hit you," Drew said hatefully.

"You know it was an accident."

"Yeah, he wanted to hurt me," he chuckled before changing the subject. "Call Jordan and Haley. Invite them over after the game."

"And why am I not going to the game?" I asked.

"Make something up. You have a meeting with a client or something," he said, knowing I wasn't looking forward to this night.

"Fine, I'll call them," I sighed, which again hurt like hell.

Making the phone call to Haley and suggesting she and Jordan come over was easy. Dealing with the rest of the day with my nerves and injury were the horrible part. Danny was keeping Ben overnight, so I didn't even have him to distract me. I turned the game on at five o'clock knowing in about three hours, I would be telling my best friends something they won't want to hear.

The first five innings went by quickly with a tied 2-2 score. By the ninth inning, the Yankees were down by one. I figured they could score in the bottom of the ninth. Before I knew it, the bases were loaded with two outs and Drew was up at bat. He shined in moments like these. The pitcher for the Baltimore Orioles shook off the catcher's signals three times. He was set against whatever the catcher wanted him to do.

I could only guess the catcher wanted to walk Drew since his odds were always good in these high-stress moments. The pitcher must have had a lot of guts because he wanted to try and strike him out, probably figuring a walked in run could start a rally for the Yankees.

The first pitch came down the plate as an obvious ball. The second one was a little low, but still in range. Though Drew didn't swing at it, it was called a strike. The third pitch was the same way, and this time, Drew tried to swing at it. He made contact with the ball, but it turned out to be a popup, not the kind of hit he usually got. The left-fielder caught the ball and the game was over.

As if this day couldn't be any more of a disaster. I'm sure Drew was upset that Jordan was finally able to make it to a game this season, and it was one he lost. I waited about twenty minutes after the game was over before texting Drew.

I'm sorry, baby.

You can't win every time, right?

It's what you do most of the time that matters. You're always a winner to me.

Thanks C;-) I'll see you in about an hour. Love you.

I smiled to myself. If I lost everyone else, at least I would have my son and Drew. As much as I would be devastated to lose Haley and Jordan, knowing I would have the one man who understood how I felt inside was comforting.

Almost two hours later, I received the call from the doorman that I had guests. It was almost ten-pm. Drew was heading out of town in the morning. I have to admit, even for me, his work schedule is more brutal than Danny's had been. At least with Danny I had some control over his schedule, considering I was his manager. I was able to travel with him a good amount of the time as well. With Drew, even when he's in town, he still has to work.

I played with the pendent around my neck nervously before tucking it into my shirt. I forgot all about the pain in my side until I got up to open the door. I hope they couldn't hear the whimper I let out from the other side of the door. I opened the door and smiled.

My eyes drifted to Drew's face, and the bruise on his lip was fairly noticeable. I'm assuming he covered with some story about getting injured during practice. Haley kissed my cheek and before I realized what was happening, Jordan was squeezing me in a hug.

I audibly cried out and almost buckled over. Drew moved forward and I shook my head at him.

"Are you okay?" Jordan asked, concerned.

"I just slept weird last night. My side is a little sensitive," I blew it off.

We walked inside and I offered to order food or make coffee. We decided to order from a nearby diner that delivered. As we waited for the food, small talk was made, but Drew kept looking at me, trying to get me to speak up. When I didn't after five times of him cueing me to, he got frustrated and interrupted the conversation about Haley's upcoming photo shoot for a celebrity wedding.

"I have to tell you guys something," Drew said, interrupting Haley mid-sentence. "Sorry."

He apologized to her and then looked over at me.

"Is it about your lip?" Jordan asked with a laugh. "I didn't really believe you didn't see a fly ball coming at your face."

"I was in a fight this morning," Drew shrugged.

"A fight? With who?" Haley asked, worriedly. "Are you okay?"

"I'm fine. Don't I look fine?" he laughed at her.

"How does the other guy look?" Jordan asked, obviously amused, and not quite as concerned as his wife.

"You'll see for yourself soon enough," Drew said.

"Oh no. It's going to be on the news, isn't it?" Are the Yankees pissed?"

Jordan still sounded amused. Brother like brother, they were so laid back about most things. Drew looked over at me and I reluctantly stood up. I lifted my shirt to reveal the large dark purple bruise.

Jordan and Haley's mouths dropped. They looked from me to Drew.

"Cami, what happened?" Haley asked.

"I was in the fight too," I shrugged innocently.

This was a bad way to explain everything, I realized, but maybe Drew was onto something with this starting the story backwards thing.

"What?" Jordan asked. "Wait, where was the fight? I didn't see anything at the party last night."

"It was here, this morning," I said.

"Wait, you two were in a fight?" Haley asked, confused. "With each other?"

I shook my head, "Danny came over..."

Haley gasped, "Danny hit you?"

"No!" I quickly said, not wanting to make Danny the villain. "Well, yes. I got in the way of his fist. He wasn't aiming at me," I said, glancing over at Drew.

"You were here this morning?" Jordan asked.

Drew nodded.

"Why was Danny trying to punch you, Drew?" he asked, the pieces slowly coming together.

I could tell he and Haley were still confused and a little shocked. Jordan was no longer laughing about the fight, not when it involved his brother and his best friend.

"Something happened between us in Florida," Drew said before getting up and standing beside me.

I could see Jordan and Haley's face turn from confused to shocked in an instant.

"We fell in love," Drew added for good measure.

"Oh my God..." Haley gasped.

"This is a joke, right?" Jordan laughed, as if the thought of Drew and I together were completely ridiculous. "You two...?"

"It just happened. I'm in love with him," I said, wrapping an arm around Drew.

"Whoa, love? What? Cami, you were married to my best friend and now...my brother? He's too young and..."

"Bro, it's eight years. It's not a big deal," Drew shrugged.

"It's not a big deal? Drew, you've known Cami forever. You've known her as Danny's girl and now you're just... How?"

"I couldn't help it," Drew said.

"You couldn't help it?" Jordan asked, appalled.

Haley was being quiet. Maybe this wasn't as bad as I thought it would be. Jordan is not even yelling too much; probably because he is in shock, but still, that's better than I could hope for.

"Look, we didn't know where this would lead. We don't even know how we got here, but here we are. I know it's going to take some time, but we hope you'll understand and we can have your support," I said, looking at Jordan and then Haley.

"Cami, you expect me to support you from moving on from me to my best friend to my brother?" Jordan laughed.

I swallowed and looked him in the eye. I didn't like these incredulous laughs Jordan kept making.

"We dated a really long time ago, Jordan, and not for very long. You didn't love me.

Danny didn't even truly love me. So why is this such a big deal?" I asked, frustrated.

Drew's arm tightened around me, which hurt a little, but I needed him holding me right now.

"Why is it a big deal?" Haley spoke up, causing us all to look over at her. "Cami, not too long ago you told me how you still love *my* husband! Since you can't have Jordan, what's the next best thing? His baby brother!" She said, with disgust in her voice.

A wave of embarrassment came over me. I couldn't believe Haley said all of that. I felt betrayed. Sure, maybe Jordan knew I carried a torch for him in some way. Maybe Haley had told him about my drunken confession months ago. Was she really that angry at the thought of Drew and me to spew all of that out right now though? Did she have to say it in front of Drew?

I felt Drew's arm slip away from me and I looked at him. He looked like he was surveying my expression.

"Haley, I don't..." I said, trying to steady my breath. "I don't love Jordan like that. I said that when I was drunk!" I hissed.

"And you meant every word of it!"

Jordan sighed and ran his hand through his hair, like he was bored of my previous feelings for him. I just wish everyone in my dining room could understand what I felt inside years ago and what I am feeling now.

"I..." I couldn't form a sentence or an explanation. "I am not in love with Jordan."

My throat was dry as I desperately wanted the situation to go away.

"It's different with Drew. He is..."

I looked over at him and he looked hurt, realizing what Haley said was the truth.

"I'm going to let you guys settle this, seeing how this really doesn't involve me, does it?"

"Drew, yes, it does," I said, grabbing onto his arm. "I love you."

"Now I know why you were afraid to tell them. They know all your secrets, and I don't. I won't be sucked into this. I won't live in Jordan's shadow."

He walked out of my apartment and I wanted to crumble into a ball. I looked at Haley and Jordan hatefully.

"Are you happy now?" I asked.

Haley looked at me blankly.

"Get out, please."

"Cami..." Haley sighed. "I'm just trying—

"

"I said get out, Haley. You said your peace and you got what you wanted. I'm sure Drew is out of my evil clutches now."

Jordan was already walking ahead of her out the door. Haley looked at me with this sad expression on before leaving as well. Between the ache in my ribs and in my heart, I wanted to pass out and hope it was all a nightmare.

CHAPTER TWENTY-FOUR

I didn't sleep at all that night. I must have called Drew ten times. He didn't answer his phone once. I sent him two texts and he didn't respond. I couldn't tell if this was a sign of immaturity in relationships or maturity.

I was used to Danny—who liked to fight. Even me, I rather scream and argue than ignore a situation or be ignored. Screaming matches were what I was familiar with. Danny's mother used to tell me ignoring him was the best way to get him to calm down. Of course, I never listened. We both had to have the last word.

I was definitely being ignored now by Drew. I told myself he needed time. I also felt I deserved a chance to explain. Around noon, Danny dropped Ben off. He took one look at me and groaned.

"You told Jordan, didn't you?"

I nodded, "And Haley."

After all, Haley was the key to things going the way they did. I lost Drew because of her. Now I know I was wise to never get close to women. They could backstab you better than anyone.

"They flipped out, huh?" Danny asked, amused as I hugged Ben close, needing his comfort.

I didn't respond. I sat down on the couch, groaning as I did so.

"Your ribs still hurt?"

"Does your face?"

"No. It's fine."

"Well, yes, my ribs still hurt," I said bitterly.

He sat down next to me.

"Cam, it's going to blow over," Danny sighed, patting my knee.

"I'm not worried about Haley and Jordan," I shook my head. "I'm worried about Drew."

"Come on, Jordan and Drew will not let this come between them."

"Drew thinks I'm still in love with Jordan," I said.

Danny sat up straight.

"Wow...well, aren't you?"

I groaned again.

"I'm being serious. In some way, don't you love him?"

"I love Jordan like I love Seb or Darren...or you," I said delicately. "I thought I loved Jordan differently for a long time, but..."

I looked at Danny and realized talking to him about my love life was a bad idea. I could tell he was just getting upset. I couldn't blame him. My strong feelings for Jordan had lasted through my relationship with him.

"I'm sorry. We don't need to be this divorced couple. We can wait on that whole comfort level thing, okay?" I asked.

He nodded, "Thank you."

We sat there for a few moments. Ben was the only source of noise as he played with Drew's pendent around my neck. I wanted to cry. I wanted to speak to Drew. I felt completely helpless, and I hated feeling that way.

My entire life I shielded myself from heartbreak and strong emotions. I was protecting myself from getting hurt. Now, here I was hurting, wondering if I would ever kiss Drew again. I don't regret my affair with Drew in Florida or the love we shared after. The only regret I have is not knowing what love is; for holding onto something for so long that I knew was a safe way out.

If I was in love with Jordan, who wasn't in love with me, I could settle for loveless relationships. I could use him as an excuse why I would never be happy with any man. Drew tore that excuse to shreds. I love Drew so much, and it feels like Danny's fist is pounding into my ribs over and over again at the thought of losing him.

After Danny left, I noticed I had missed calls on my phone. I checked my voicemail and to my dismay, the messages were about business. I completely blanked about two conference calls I was supposed to have.

In twenty years, I have never forgotten about a meeting, call or even responding to an e-mail. That's how organized and focused I was on business. I sent a few e-mails saying I was going out of town. I rescheduled the conference calls for later in the week.

Next, I booked a trip to St. Louis. I arranged for Ben to spend the next couple of days with Danny. I had to look Drew in the eyes and tell him the truth. In a matter of four hours, I was on a plane. I held onto the number 12 pendent as if I was praying to it.

As the plane landed, a torrential downpour had started. I didn't even bring a jacket or an umbrella. I grabbed my bag and headed to the taxi area. Luckily, I knew Drew's schedule for the rest of the month, which included hotel information.

By the time I stepped inside the lobby of the hotel, I was fairly drenched. I didn't know what Drew's room number was, which I didn't think much about until this very moment.

"Hi," I smiled at the concierge sweetly. "I was wondering if you could tell me which room Andrew Ashton is in."

"Ma'am, we can't do that. Is he expecting you?" He asked, looking at me skeptically.

I hated hotel protocols! They never worked in my favor.

"Not exactly," I sighed. "Could you call up to his room and tell him Cami is here?"

The concierge still looked at me suspiciously.

"Just please," I begged, hoping I looked pathetic enough, but not too pathetic to be a desperate groupie.

He sighed and picked up the desk phone. He hit a button before waiting.

"Hello sir," the concierge spoke. "There is a Cami here in the lobby." He paused. "Will do, sir."

He hung up the phone and smiled at me.

"You can go up to room 712."

I thanked him before grabbing my bag and heading into the elevator. I knocked on the door eagerly. Drew answered shirtless. He looked intimidating standing there with his muscular build, tattoo showing and the busted lip.

"What are you doing here?" he asked, as if he were annoyed by my presence.

"I had to see you. You wouldn't answer your phone," I said, going to touch him but he moved away.

Just then Topaz stepped out of the bathroom wearing a tiny bandeau top and miniskirt.

"Drew, I have to go, but..."

My eyes widened and I looked at Drew, who didn't even look apologetic for being in a hotel room with his tabloid girlfriend!

"Oh hey," Topaz smiled at me. "Cami, right? Drew's told me a lot about you. We should all get together sometime," she said, putting her hand on Drew's bare shoulder.

She kissed his cheek before squeezing between us and walking down the hall. I slapped Drew in the chest and he winced.

"Ow!"

"What kind of kinky crap are you into?" I snarled.

"Get in here," Drew rolled his eyes, pulling me by the arm into the room and closing the door quickly.

"You told me you weren't interested in that blue-haired tramp!"

Drew crossed his arms and leaned against the door.

"Yeah, well, you could have told me you're in love with my brother."

He sounded so cold; so emotionless. I could handle screaming and fighting better than him acting like he didn't care.

I sighed, "I'm not in love with Jordan."

"Why would Haley lie?"

I shuddered, feeling cold from the rain. The air conditioner was on in the room, not making things any better.

"I don't know why Haley said any of what she said last night. I guess she thinks you're too good for me. And I know she's right," I admitted. "And yes, I told her I had feelings for Jordan when I was drunk, but..."

"But you don't?" Drew asked.

"Definitely not now," I said pushing my wet hair behind my ears. "I thought I loved him for a long time."

"He was the guy..." Drew said, remembering what I told him a while ago, about cheating emotionally on Danny. "The guy who didn't love you back."

I swallowed and nodded, "I was misplacing feelings for him. Jordan was the first person to really care about me, even if it was just as a friend."

Drew looked at me, just like the concierge looked at me, skeptically.

"I won't be a substitute for my brother."

I walked closer to him, wanting to wrap my arms around him. He didn't seem open to that, so I resisted.

"You're not! Drew, you are the first person I ever truly loved. With you, I feel something so strong—it's more than lust, it's more than friendship or love..." I said with tears in my eyes. "With you, I'm home. Please, don't take that away from me."

My lips were trembling, giving into any vulnerability I ever felt. I let it all out. At first, Drew just stood there, watching me cry.

"I'm sorry..." Drew said.

I looked up at him and he wouldn't look me in the eye.

"You were right. This isn't going to work. We should have never told anyone. You shouldn't have bothered coming here," he said, walking past me and into the bathroom.

He slammed the door shut behind him.

My heart felt like it had been ripped from my chest. It took everything inside of me to move my feet and turn the handle on the door. I got onto the elevator and uncontrollable sobs escaped my lips. I haven't sobbed since I was a small child. I hurt everywhere—my chest, my ribs, and my head. I felt like my mother had passed away all over again. Even then I didn't sob like I was now; I was too numb from the shock of losing her. Now, I wasn't surprised I lost Drew. I knew it was bound to happen. Still, even knowing that it would most likely come to this, the pain was so unbearable. And I was going to have to face it alone—no Haley to comfort me or Jordan to check up on me.

CHAPTER TWENTY-FIVE

Stepping outside, protected by the awning, I watched the rain pour down.

"Ma'am, can I get you a taxi?"

I shook my head and began to walk down the steps of the hotel quickly. I didn't want to talk to anyone or look at anyone, not even a taxi driver. I wanted to hide and cry in private. I figured walking in the warm rain was my best option. At least my tears wouldn't be noticeable with all the precipitation coming down on my face. I had never felt pain like this. Sure, I was hurt that Danny cheated on me. I was hurt when Jordan didn't want something more with me. That pain was bearable, though. I could still pretend I was okay if I had to. Now, I don't think pretending was an option. I was audibly sobbing!

I began to walk down the street, not caring that I was soaked or that I hadn't eaten all day. My heart was broken so badly I barely noticed a car coming at me as I passed the crosswalk. I jumped back onto the sidewalk as the car honked its horn.

"Cami!" I heard yelled from behind me.

It sounded like Drew's voice. Maybe it was in my mind. I loved his voice—deep and smooth, but with the faintest rasp at the end of each word. It was sexy and playful. I missed the way he would whisper in my ear as we made love. Yesterday morning was the last time we were together like that; it already felt like a lifetime ago.

"Cami!" I heard once more.

I turned, expecting to see no one there. To my surprise, I saw someone running toward me. He had Drew's run. Watching so many baseball games, you pick up on certain mannerisms each player had. Drew was a fast runner with an easy, long stride. He always made running look effortless.

My damn clouded mind was playing tricks on me. The imaginary Drew came closer until he had grabbed my arms. That's when I realized he wasn't imaginary. I could feel his fingers squeezing my bare arms softly. His whole hand fit around the flesh of my arm.

I was still crying pretty badly. It wasn't difficult for Drew to tell, even with the rain pelting across our faces. His hair was matted down against his forehead; his white t-shirt soaked to his skin. He looked like someone out of a movie. The entire scene could have been a movie, except for the way I looked. I barely remember putting make-up on today and I'm sure it was all washed away now. I didn't have that pretty girl in the rain look either. I looked like a blubbering idiot who was probably going to grow old and alone with ten cats. I don't even like cats!

Drew looked at me for what felt like a long moment before pulling me into a kiss. Was I dreaming now? I wrapped my arms around him, not wanting to let him go. I didn't care if my injured side was pressing into him. That pain was dull compared to the ache I felt just moments ago.

"Come on," he said, wrapping his arm around me.

We walked back down the street to the hotel. There was no point in shielding ourselves or running—we were both sopping wet. Besides, I was pretty out of breath from crying and my injury. Running might just kill me at this point. As we stepped inside the hotel, we received stares from the staff and anyone walking by. Our shoes squeaked against the floor as we walked toward the elevator.

Once the doors closed, I hugged Drew. I didn't know what to say. I couldn't form words anyhow. My throat felt dry and I was still shook with emotion. We got into the room, and immediately, we both shivered.

"Take off your clothes," Drew said, going into the bathroom.

I heard the water running as I stripped. I was shivering so much as I stood in the room in nothing but Drew's pendent. Drew appeared a moment later in just his boxers. He waved me over and I followed him into the bathroom. He slid his boxers off and got in the shower, leaving the glass door open for me. Steam was filling the bathroom quickly.

I stepped inside the shower and Drew pulled me under the spray. The water was hot and it felt wonderful against my goose-bumped skin.

"Better?" Drew asked.

I nodded before pressing my head into his chest and crying.

"Cami, are you okay?" he asked, rubbing my back as he held me.

I took a sharp intake of breath, wincing from the pain in my ribs. All this sobbing was murdering my side.

"I thought…" I hiccupped. "I thought I lost you."

Drew picked my head up. I was so embarrassed. I was always a dignified person, never letting my emotions take over this much. Of course, anger and jealousy came out often enough, but sadness and heartbreak were things I rarely showed to anyone. Here I was, hysterically crying and naked in Drew's arms. I couldn't get more revealing, both emotionally and physically, than that!

Drew was staring into my eyes as his hands rested on either side of my face.

"You can't get rid of me that easily," he smiled. "I love you, Cami. I don't care about what's in the past. All I know is what I feel when I'm with you. Maybe you'll hurt me or maybe I'll hurt you, but I was never one to play a game safe," he said, with a smile.

"No, you're not," I laughed. "I don't want to play a game though."

He had said that to me the night we made things official. We both smiled at the memory.

"I retired from the game the first time I kissed you," Drew winked.

"You knew that long ago, huh?" I asked.

"Yes. I'll admit it's kind of nice seeing you crack," he smirked.

I smacked his arm; the slap sounding louder against his wet skin in the echoing bathroom.

"That's so mean! Is that why you turned me away? So you can see my heart breaking?"

Drew laughed before turning serious.

"It killed me to see that look on your face. I immediately regretted it."

I sighed and raised my arms, wrapping them around his neck before we kissed. It felt like forever since we kissed or made love, even though it was less than twenty-four hours ago. So much had happened since then. His lips were a little rougher than usual, with the bottom one healing from Danny's punch.

Drew squeezed me against him and I cried out. He pulled away and I motioned to the bruise on my ribs.

"Sorry," he said, grimacing as he looked down at the large bruise.

"I think they're worse now than yesterday," I pouted.

"Well, you haven't exactly been taking it easy. Jumping on a plane, walking in the pouring rain..."

I laughed, "Sounds like a pop song."

"Maybe we can suggest it to Matt. It would make a great Sound Wave song."

I shook my head before we were going to kiss again. I remembered something though.

"Wait, what was Topaz doing in your room?"

Drew chuckled, "She's secretly dating Nostri. I'm their cover."

"So, she wasn't in here comforting you while you were shirtless?" I asked, raising my eyebrow.

Drew shook his head, "No, but it fit perfectly with my plan to say goodbye to you, right?"

I gave him a mean look and he smirked.

"Luckily, my plan didn't coordinate with the rest of me."

The water was turning cold as we made out, making the shower pointless. We were both shivering as Drew turned the water off. He wrapped a warm, fuzzy towel around me before getting one for himself.

We didn't bother with clothes, even though we were cold. Instead, Drew turned the temperature down before joining me in bed. We made love for a while before falling asleep under the huge down comforter.

Some time in the middle of the night, I woke up shaking and achy. I slid out of bed and rummaged through Drew's things since I didn't bring anything to sleep in. I packed in such a hurry that I only had an outfit for the next day. I found some sweats of his and put them on. I loved the warmth of them and they smelled faintly of Drew.

I took some pain medication before getting back into bed and falling asleep. An hour later, I woke up with a stuffy nose. Drew was in the bathroom, getting ready for practice. I heard him sneeze as I approached. I felt lightheaded.

Drew looked at me with drowsy eyes.

"I think I'm getting sick," he pouted.

He looked like a little boy.

"Me too," I frowned.

"You should stay here and get rest."

I shook my head, leaning against the door frame.

"I want to be wherever you are."

He looked at me with a smirk before walking over to me. I pushed the long sleeves on the sweatshirt up my arms, in order to set my hands free. Drew was amused by this as I rubbed his arm.

"We don't have to hide us anymore," he smiled.

I laughed, "That's one problem solved. Now, to get your brother to accept us..."

"He'll get over it. I'm worried if you will get over being angry at Haley."

I looked up at him and shrugged, "Eventually. I like to hold grudges."

He laughed before sneezing, practically on me. I looked at him with disgust and he apologized.

We got breakfast, which consisted of toast and tea, before heading to Busch Stadium. By that time, it was clear Drew and I were fairly sick. I'm pretty sure we both had fevers. Drew toughed it out through the practice, an interview with ESPN, and the actual game. I didn't feel as tough. I just wanted to sleep in his arms, but instead, I hung around the team; careful not to get in the way.

By the time the game was over, which Drew managed to make two RBIs, even being sick as a dog, we were both shot. We went back to the hotel and fell asleep on each other for a few hours until it was time for Drew's flight.

"Take care of yourself, okay?" We hugged goodbye. "Get plenty of rest," he insisted.

"What about you? You need to take care of yourself, too."

"I'll be fine. I can walk off a cold," he winked.

"We might have the flu," I warned.

He shrugged, "Don't worry. I'll see you in about a week."

I nodded sadly. It kept getting harder seeing him leave. Our time together felt so restricted, partly due to our relationship being a secret, but also because of his schedule. I would not complain about it, though. I could handle it. Between my career and son, it wasn't exactly like I had all the free time in the world either. I will not make him feel guilty for living his dream.

He was usually gone every other week, which when I actually thought logically about it was better than Danny's schedule after all. There were too many surprise schedule changes in the music. With baseball, I was guaranteed Drew would be in town a couple of weeks a month. Still, when you're in love, days felt like weeks.

I forced the biggest smile I could at Drew.

"I'll be waiting."

"That's what I'm counting on," he said, wrapping his arms around me.

He sounded stuffy. It was kind of cute. He kissed me and stared into my eyes before leaving.

CHAPTER TWENTY-SIX

When I first got back to New York, I allowed myself to stay in bed, complete with tissues, flu medicine, and a VH1 *Behind The Music* marathon. It was either that or a Lifetime movie marathon, and that just wasn't my style. Danny and his mother were being great about helping me out while I was away and now that I am sick. They took Ben off my hands for another day. I missed my little boy terribly, but I didn't want to get him sick. Besides, I wasn't able to pick him up too much with my healing ribs.

"Up next on our *Behind The Music* Monday..." the TV said. "See Tortured's rise to fame."

I groaned, not really wanting to see myself or anyone else in the band at that moment. As much as I wanted to change the channel, I couldn't. The show started out with footage of Tortured performing at the Canal Room over seventeen years ago. I remembered that night well. That was the night that changed a lot of things. The band won the battle of the bands competition that night and I piggybacked that success by pushing harder to get them a record deal.

The story continued to show how Danny and Jordan met in junior high school. It followed with how they met Darren and Sebastian, and finally how they met me. I'll admit that I loved hearing the guys talk about me. It has become apparent to me that I had low self-esteem all these years. With me being confident in my looks for most of my life, I never thought it was possible that I could have self-esteem issues. I just figured I liked more attention than the normal person, since I didn't have a lot of people to give it to me growing up.

"Cami was this little waitress with an attitude and big balls," Jordan laughed on the television screen. "She was persistent and was all heart. That's what our band needed, someone who believed in us. Without Cami, I don't know if any of us would have pushed for more than being a local band," he said.

Danny's recap of meeting me was much more exaggerated. He made it sound like love at first sight for us, when everyone knew that wasn't the truth. The show continued to discuss Tortured's first single and then, their first number one hit, "Haley's Letter". Haley was blushing as she spoke about the first time she heard it.

Drew was on the screen next, and I had almost forgotten he was interviewed years ago for this. His hair was a little longer than usual, making him look even younger than he was at the time.

"As soon as Jordan told me about Haley, I knew she was it for him. Growing up, Jordan and I lacked stability and a sense of home," Drew explained. "The stage was always home for him, but once he met her... Haley became home for my brother. We should all be so lucky to have what they have."

The way Drew said that last part, made me ache for him. He smiled wide for the camera, to cover it all up, but I know now how much he yearned for that feeling. We both did, and now we have it with each other. I just hoped one day Jordan could be as supportive of us as Drew is of him and Haley. After the show was over, I turned the television off and texted Drew.

I love you.

Immediately, he responded.

I love you. You OK?

Sick as a dog, but so grateful for you.

Cami?

Yes?

Just checking ;-)

Jerk! I can be a sap if I want.

I'm not complaining. Just no one would expect it from you.

I know. It's your fault I'm like an M&M ;-p

Wait...are you saying you melt in my mouth not in my hand?

Haha! You said that! I meant I have a thin candy shell...

Hmm, I think you were making an innuendo.

Maybe :-p

Now, all I can think about is my mouth on you.

Same here. Soon, baby, soon.

Not soon enough.

After Drew and I were done "sexting", I fell asleep. I woke up hours later to hear noise in the kitchen. Leslie was cleaning up and I had almost forgotten she and Danny were staying at the apartment with Ben for the day. Ben had been getting fussy not being in his own home, and Leslie said he was missing me. I wanted to hold him so badly, but I wasn't in much of a condition to. Danny and Ben were nowhere in sight when I entered the kitchen.

"How are you feeling?"

"A little better," I said. "Where's Ben?"

"Danny's putting him to sleep. Are you hungry? I made homemade chicken noodle soup," Leslie said, drying her hands off on a dish towel.

"That would be great. Thank you," I smiled.

I sat down and Leslie heated a bowl of soup up for me. She also prepared two slices of toast. She sat down across from me and I thought about Mother's Day coming up. It would be my first. I always pretended the holiday didn't exist. When you no longer have a mother to celebrate, the day becomes pointless or even worse; it feels like something is missing.

I decided this year I was going to take Leslie out. She has been amazing during everything. I don't know any other mother-in-law who would be there for her son's ex-wife as much as she's been here for me. Danny and Leslie normally did something together for Mother's Day, but I figured it would be nice if we could all go out.

Danny walked out of the nursery and sat down. His cheek was turning a yellowish now, which was a good sign. I'm just glad the tabloids didn't post much on our hospital visit. There was some speculation, but we weren't front page news. Apparently, Topaz's alleged affair with Drew ending was bigger news. Thank God that mess would be over! The last thing I needed to be accused of was stealing Topaz's boyfriend.

"You look better," Danny smiled.

"You too," I motioned to his cheek.

He shrugged, "Have you spoke to Jordan or Haley?"

"No. I'm mad at Haley."

Danny laughed, "For what? How can you be mad at Haley?"

"She tried to sabotage Drew and me!"

"Oh-ho," Danny laughed. "How does it feel to have the tables turned?"

I rolled my eyes, "I never sabotaged Jordan and Haley."

"No, you were just a bitch to her."

"I hate you," I huffed.

He smiled, "Cami, just suck up your pride and give them a call."

I shook my head, "They don't want to talk to me. They think I corrupted innocent, young Andrew."

"Come on, we all know Drew was never that innocent," Danny shrugged. "He's a big boy, who can throw a good punch. I got over it and so will Jordan."

Leslie laughed, "You're not over it."

Danny shrugged, "I'm not happy about you finding love with a younger, almost as good-looking guy, but all I want is for you to be happy."

I think Leslie and I both stared at him in shock. I stood up and kissed Danny's cheek with a loud smack.

"As much as I hate you, I love you," I said.

Danny smiled, "Right back at you, kid."

The next day, I got an early start. I went for a walk in Central Park with Ben, got back to the apartment and then ready for work. Sound Wave was coming into the office today for a meeting with their new label. I was happy to see Matt, who was a nervous wreck since Laura was due to have the baby next week.

With my health returning to normal and being at work, I felt much better. It was hard to believe that just a couple of days ago, I was sobbing uncontrollably and now I was smiling uncontrollably. The rest of the week went well, but Friday made me a little uneasy.

Tortured was coming into the office to discuss the American leg of the tour, which was starting in another week. Darren, Danny and Sebastian were normal, as normal as those three could be anyway. But Jordan was distant and cold.

Colin ordered lunch for everyone and as we ate, I looked over at Jordan. I stood up with my food and sat next to him.

"So, Danny and I are planning to have a big Mother's Day brunch on Sunday. We were thinking Haley, you and Aylin should join us."

Jordan looked over at me.

"What makes you think my wife would want to spend Mother's Day with you?"

Ouch. Jordan could throw insults from time to time, but only when I did first. I wasn't used to him being plain rude.

"I just thought it would be nice..." I sighed. "You know, I always hated Mother's Day. I'm sure you haven't liked it much either," I said, looking at him. "Without a mom here to share it with..." I swallowed as I looked at him.

Jordan lost his mother just before Aylin was born. I knew he would understand the pain that day brought me. Jordan just stared at me; his green eyes looking at me wearily.

"This is my first Mother's Day where I have something to celebrate," I said. "I want my family there. Drew can't be there, but I would really like you to be."

Jordan didn't say anything as he stared down at his plate of food. I knew more needed to be said on my end.

"I know this is uncomfortable... My feelings for you..." I swallowed. "Jordan, you're my best friend, and I didn't know how to love a friend or anyone really. Ben showed me how to love again. And Drew taught me how to fall in love. I'm not with him because of some leftover crush on you. I promise you that. I'm with Drew because I am so far gone in love with him that I can't figure out how I lived without loving him."

Jordan still didn't say anything and I was about to ramble on, but finally he put his hand up to stop me.

"He's your home," Jordan sighed.

"Yes," I nodded; surprised he used those exact words.

Could it be pure coincidence? It described how I felt for Drew so perfectly. Drew had said in the VH1 interview that Jordan told him Haley was his home. There was also mine and Drew's song, "Home" by Sound Wave.

"Drew Skyped me yesterday," Jordan explained. "He told me he never felt like he had a home until he had you."

I smiled and looked down at my salad, smitten by Drew's words.

"Oh boy," Jordan chuckled. "If my brother can make you act like a school girl, you must be in love."

I looked up at Jordan and laughed. I stood up and hugged him.

"I know Drew deserves someone warm and good, but I promise I will love him the best I can."

Jordan squeezed me a little bit, "He already has someone warm and good."

"Thank you," I said, my voice getting caught in my throat.

I didn't receive many compliments like that. People made jokes about my personality flaws, hell, even I did, too. I never defended myself because I always felt everyone was right about me. Being a bitch was my defense mechanism, and I guess some people understood that, like Jordan and Haley.

I pulled out of the hug with Jordan and smiled.

"Tell Haley I'm still mad at her, but maybe she can make it up to me somehow."

Jordan laughed, "She feels bad. She knows she went too far. She's just protective of Drew, you know that."

"No one's protective of me," I rolled my eyes.

"Hey, I am!" Danny spoke up. "I took a punch for you."

"Ugh, you insulted me; that's how you got that punch."

Everyone laughed, now fully in the conversation, convincing me they were all half-listening the whole time.

"I stood up for you," Jordan shoved my shoulder lightly. "When it came to Danny being an ass... and so did Haley."

Danny agreed, "Haley used to chew me out any time we fought."

I was grateful we could all joke around and keep things light, even Danny, who I knew was more uncomfortable with my relationship with Drew than anyone. We were like those incestuous groups of friends on soap operas—you know the ones who have all fooled around with each other, but still stay best friends. Well, I guess we're not that bad—just me. I would probably be the villain who was trying to turn over a new leaf twenty years later.

By the time Sunday came around, I was actually excited for Mother's Day. I dressed Ben in a cute little bow tie and khaki pants. I wore a coral blouse, making sure to leave Drew's pendant displayed across my chest. We went to Tavern on the Green for brunch. Danny brought his mother, Haley and me flowers.

Haley and I didn't speak through brunch, but we weren't exactly ignoring each other either.

"Uncle Drew's game starts in two hours," Aylin said, checking her phone.

"You guys are welcome to come back to our place to watch the game," Jordan said.

Ben was on my lap making faces at Haley. She was sticking her tongue out at him and he was smiling.

"Can I hold him?" Haley asked.

"Of course," I nodded, standing up and walking Ben around to her.

She took him in her arms before surprising me with a hug.

"I'm sorry," she said softly. "I'm happy for you and Drew."

I looked at her face as we pulled away. Part of me wonders if she and Jordan were just trying to keep the peace, or if they really were okay with Drew and me. I figured time would clear away any skepticism they had. Aylin, on the other hand, couldn't be happier. She already had Drew and me getting married and having kids.

I could tell it was a bit much for everyone to take in—including myself. One day, though, I wondered if I could actually marry again and have another child. Would I be ready for that? Would Drew be ready?

EPILOGUE

"Surprise!!!"

Drew jumped back in shock as the room shouted at him. It was Fourth of July weekend, three weeks before Drew's twenty-ninth birthday. The rooftop of my apartment was done up in twinkling lights with a deejay and a small stage. There was a bartender and caterer as well.

Drew turned to me first.

"I can't believe you..." he laughed before kissing me.

He left my side for a good forty minutes as he greeted all fifty of his guests, twenty of them being his teammates. Danny offered to spend the day with Ben rather than make it awkward by coming to the party. He and Drew haven't had much contact with one another. They were civil, but not brotherly like they used to be. I felt guilty for that.

As for Drew's parents, well, I made every effort to reach out to Coryn, who didn't return my call until last night. She said she was going out of town with her new fiancée. The woman was going on her fourth marriage! As for Chuck Ashton, he had some business convention across the country, but I was relieved he wasn't coming to the party. We didn't exactly get along. Chuck didn't like me, mostly because he never liked Danny, but also because I was a successful business woman. He was a bit of a sexist ass. Part of me wonders if Chuck didn't want to come to the party because I was throwing it.

The deejay began playing dance music. Drew and about five other Yankees took over the dance floor with some choreography they must have practiced on the road. They sure were a sight as they did ridiculous pelvic thrusts to some new hip-hop song that was overplayed. The guests were all cheering them on. Afterwards, Drew took turns dancing with Haley, Aylin and Tasha.

I was perfectly fine with just watching and mingling with guests to avoid embarrassing myself on the dance floor. I wanted to spend as much time with Drew as possible, though, since he would be gone for another full week in a couple of days.

It wasn't long before Drew sought me out and pulled me onto the dance floor. It wasn't that I hated dancing. I just felt like I wasn't good at it. Drew says it doesn't matter if I can't dance;

all I have to do is shake my ass and no one would notice anything else.

He spun me around before pulling me close; his hands low on my back, practically on my butt as we swayed, even though the music was still somewhat fast-paced.

"Thank you for this," he smiled, kissing me.

"You're welcome. There's one more surprise," I said, seeing Matt peek his head into the party.

He gave me a thumbs up before getting the deejay's attention. The music cut off. A moment later, the music started again. An introduction to a pop song came on. It was "I'm Home" by Sound Wave, which was released to radio last week.

"It's our song," Drew smiled.

Just then, Sound Wave stepped onto the roof singing the song. Drew began to whistle and cheer as I laughed at him.

"I got your favorite boy band for you," I said, wrapping my arms around him.

He laughed and danced with me to the song. Aylin pulled Jordan onto the dance floor and I had to laugh. Jordan was not happy he was dancing at all, especially not to a Sound Wave song.

After the performance, we only had a few minutes until the Macy's fireworks display began. We had a perfect view on the rooftop. Drew pulled me over to the only secluded spot.

"You really outdid yourself," he smiled, kissing me.

"I just wanted to do something special," I shrugged.

"Cami," he swallowed. "I've been meaning to ask you something..."

Just then, the first firework went off causing us both to jump. I laughed and held onto him as we watched the sky.

"You can ask me anything," I said putting my head down on his shoulder, but wondering why he seemed nervous.

It hit me then. Was Drew going to propose? Part of me loved the thought, but a bigger part of me screamed no; it was too soon. I haven't even been divorced for four months! Drew and I haven't dated much longer than that. We hadn't even discussed marriage yet, or kids, or anything like that.

"Will you move in with me?"

I pulled away to look up at him. His eyes glanced down at me. He was smirking, like he knew what I was thinking.

"Camilla?"

I narrowed my eyes and shook my head.

"No, Andy."

I reached up and touched the top cartilage of his ear. He wigged out and I laughed. I had finally found his sensitive spot. It always amused me to see a muscular guy like Drew squirm away like that.

He laughed, "Can't you just give me an answer and stop being difficult?"

I smiled, "Would you expect anything less?"

"No. So Cami," he emphasized my name. "Will you be my roomie?"

"Yes!" I squealed, hugging him.

We kissed as another firework went off.

"Where's the rock?" Cisco asked, putting his arms around us.

Drew and I both laughed at him.

"No ring, buddy. Just changing addresses," Drew said.

The rest of the party was crazy, fun and exhausting. It seemed Drew and I kept trying to get back to each other, but someone else would want to butt in to talk. I couldn't really gage Jordan and Haley's reaction to Drew and I moving in together. As much as they seemed to support our relationship, I think they still worried it was all going to end in disaster—like Danny and I did.

Could I blame them? No. Did it hurt? Yes. Time would only tell. Time would prove them right or wrong. I prayed to my mother every night that everyone's negative thoughts about Drew and me would be wrong. I know I worry myself about our future—just from my own history, but with each day that goes by, the further I fall in love with Drew. My faith is slowly restoring itself and my heart is becoming whole for the first time.

Around two-am, the last of the guests finally left. The deejay and bartender left as well. Drew poured two glasses of champagne. We toasted to us before kissing.

"You're going to have to propose to me," Drew smirked, his nose rubbing against mine.

"What?" I laughed.

"You tell me when you're ready," he said. "I'll wait."

Drew's hang-up was proposing and getting turned down. I could understand. No one likes rejection. When Katie turned Drew's proposal down, I'm sure it not only hurt his heart, but his pride.

I smiled at Drew, "You won't have to wait too long I don't think."

Drew looked at me with those big, puppy dog eyes. He didn't say it much since he didn't want to pressure me, but I knew he wanted to get married and have a family. He even mentions retiring from baseball early so he could settle down.

I kissed him softly before whispering in his ear.

"Take me home, Drew."

He smiled before picking me up over his shoulder. I yelped and tried to hold my dress down as he brought me back into my apartment building—excuse me, our apartment building.

For more information on Sandy Lo & her projects:

Check out other titles in the "Dream Catchers Series" by Sandy Lo on Amazon!

Dream Catchers – Book 1
Breaking The Moon – Book 2
Expressions – Book 3
Take Me Home – Book 4
The Reunion – Book 5
Spotlight – Book 6
Fanning The Fame – Book 7

And look out for these stand-alone novels also available on Amazon!

Lost In You

The Watch Dog

Indigo Waters

Decaf for the Dead

Acknowledgments

Thanks to Melissa Marini for editing. To my family and friends for all your love and support throughout my writing career. Thank you to my mother and my big brother, Sebie for their love of the Yankees. I consider myself a fan, but mostly because of the warm memories that stem from my mom and brother watching games.

To the fans of this series – this is for you. "Dream Catchers" holds a special place in my heart and I'm glad so many readers out there feel the same. Let's continue to spread the word!

Sneak Peek

THE REUNION

Dream Catchers Series – Book 5

Prologue

I lie awake, holding the small black velvet box. My boyfriend, Drew, was passed out next to me. It wasn't often he got drunk, but tonight it seemed everyone at Carney's Pub wanted to buy Drew a shot for his winning homerun. No, Drew doesn't play baseball for some bar league. He's Andrew Ashton, #12 and co-captain of the New York Yankees, my favorite baseball team since birth.

As for me, I'm not sure how I got so lucky to have his heart for over three years now. Drew brings out the best in me. He argues that fact repeatedly, though. Everyone knows me, Cami Woods, as a hard-ass bitch, who is a savvy entertainment mogul with a cold heart. Or at least they knew me as that.

Things kind of changed when my marriage to Danny DeSano, drummer for the chart-topping band Tortured, ended miserably, and I gave birth to our son, Benvenuto. That year was the best and worst for me. I fell into a deep depression that had me re-evaluating my life.

Out of nowhere, Drew Ashton swept me off my feet. What I thought was purely a physical thing with the kid, after all, he is eight years younger than me, wound up being love. Real love—not just the stuff I pretended to feel for my ex-husband.

Fast forward a few years, and here I am, the eve of my fortieth birthday trying to muster up courage to propose to the love of my life. I meant to do it at dinner, but one drink led to another, and before I knew it, we barely made it to our penthouse apartment on the Upper East Side to have sex.

Drew has made it clear to me from the beginning that if I wanted to get married, I would have to propose to him. He had proposed to his college girlfriend, Katie—his first, and only love before me. She turned him down and it crushed him. I really can't help but to hate that girl for hurting my baby that much, even though I understood her not being able to handle his career. Some girls just can't deal with all the traveling and crazy schedules, or the fame.

As for me, I would be a hypocrite if I didn't support his high profile career. These days, my name is in the press just as much as his. Not only am I his girlfriend, but my relationship and divorce with Danny was big news a few years ago, and I am the most known music manager in the industry. I am constantly signing waivers to be involved in various reality shows—whether to be a guest judge on music competitions or to have one of our artist meetings filmed.

Drew and I deal with each other's careers just fine. We get how important it is; how our careers gave us confidence, purpose, drive and passion that we just did not have growing up. On top of Drew "getting it," I knew he'd make a great stepfather to my little Ben. The kid already idolizes Drew. So, why am I wide-awake pondering the decision to marry him? Fear. Drew's hang-up is the proposal; mine is the actual marriage. Danny and I were married for so long and we're lucky we didn't kill each other. I know Drew and I have a totally different dynamic, but still. Marriage can change everything. Why ruin a great thing?

Still, nothing would make me happier than becoming Drew's wife. Would that make him happy, though? He would love nothing more than to have a child with me. We've been trying for months. Between my age and difficulty conceiving in the past, I didn't have to wait to hear it from the doctor to know it would be difficult, especially without fertility drugs. I decided I wouldn't put Drew through the side effects of those drugs. I heard horror stories of how women acted, and I didn't want to become a raging bitch, especially not to Drew. He still has hope though. I admire his confidence and positivity, but if we get married and can't get pregnant, will he wind up hating me?

"What's that?"

I jumped and nearly threw the ring box at the ceiling. I looked over and Drew chuckled.

"What is it?" he asked again, as I slipped my hands under the blanket, trying to casually find the ring box.

"Nothing," I glanced at him quickly.

"Nothing, huh?" he fumbled around under the blanket.

"Drew!" I yelled, trying to restrain his hands, and I felt the box slip further down the bed.

"Do you have a sex toy or something down there?" he asked, lifting the blanket, trying to peek in the dim lighting.

I laughed hysterically, "What?"

"Seriously," he stared at me.

I turned on my side and rested my head on my arm.

"Why would I need a sex toy, first of all? And if I did like that sort of thing, why would I keep it from you?"

"Maybe I just don't do it for you anymore," he smirked, tracing a finger down my cleavage.

"Um, did it seem like you didn't do it for me earlier?" I asked, scooting closer to him, feeling the ring box ricochet off my knee.

Drew smiled and leaned in closer to me. As I got lost in his kiss, I forgot all about the ring box. When we pulled apart, he held it up to me.

"What's in here that you need to hide from me?"

"Drew," I sighed, ripping the box from his hand.

"What? Did some guy give you jewelry? Should I be jealous?" he asked, not looking the least bit worried.

I'm glad he trusted me so much. It made me smile. I knew what I had to do, but more importantly, what I wanted to do. I turned on the light and sat up in the bed. Drew did the same.

"Everything okay?" he asked. "I wasn't really worried, but now you're scaring me."

I leaned over and pecked his lips.

"I love you, Drew, and I want to be with you forever, but I need to know how you'll feel if we can't have kids."

Drew's big brown eyes crinkled at the thought.

"It'll happen for us. I know it," he smiled, taking my hand.

"But if it doesn't?"

"Cami, did the doctor say something?"

"Just what she's been saying. At my age, and with my complications, it's unlikely. It was a miracle I had Ben."

Drew sighed, "Right. It was also a miracle Haley and Jordan had Aylin, remember?"

Haley and her husband Jordan are my best friends. Jordan is also Drew's older brother. Again, I admired his optimism.

"We'll keep trying," I said.

After all, trying was the easy part that didn't change anything about our dynamic other than holding out hope for something that just wouldn't happen.

"But I just... if you won't want to be with me, I'll understand..."

"Shut up," Drew groaned. "You're talking crazy. If we can't have a baby, we'll adopt or something."

I nodded, and looked down at the ring box before handing it to him.

"Open it," I smiled, tucking my hair behind my ears, and cuddling closer to him.

"It's for me?"

"Yes."

"But it's your birthday," he said, squeezing my thigh, and glancing at the time. It was 12:09 a.m. "Happy Birthday officially, baby," he kissed my cheek.

I smiled at him, "Just open it."

Drew opened the box. He looked down at the platinum band in astonishment. I got up on my knees and he looked over at me as I leaned over him.

"Will you marry me?"

His face broke out into a huge grin and he laughed.

"Hell yes!" He grabbed my face and pulled me into a kiss, causing me to fall into his chest.

He rolled me onto my back.

"Thank you," he whispered, kissing my neck. "I thought you'd never ask."

"Me neither," I laughed.

"We have to get you a ring, too," he said, rolling my nightshirt up to my navel as he began sucking on my stomach.

"I don't need a ring," I said.

"Right," he chuckled, sending goose bumps across my skin.

"Well, there is this one ring I saw when I went to pick up this one..." I laughed, setting the ring box aside.

"It's yours," he said, moving lower on my body.

I realized I could probably get him to agree to anything at that point as he loved on my body. I can't believe I'm getting married again!

THE REUNION (Dream Catchers Book 5) is available on Amazon!